F
Azzopard   Azzopardi, Trezza.

Remember me.

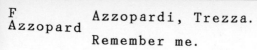

F
Azzopard   Azzopardi,
                Trezza.

Remember me.

DATE	BORROWER'S NAME	

Seneca Falls Library
47 Cayuga Street
Seneca Falls, NY 13148

BAKER & TAYLOR

remember me

Also by Trezza Azzopardi

the hiding place

trezza azzopardi

remember me

GROVE PRESS
New York

First published in 2004 by Picador,
an imprint of Pan Macmillan Ltd., London, England

Printed in the United States of America

FIRST AMERICAN EDITION

Library of Congress Cataloging-in-Publication Data

Azzopardi, Trezza.
Remember me / Trezza Azzopardi
p. cm.
"First published in 2004 in the UK by Macmillan Company"—T.p. verso.
ISBN 0-8021-1767-8
1. World War, 1939–1945—England—Fiction. 2. Reminiscing in old age—Fiction. 3. Problem families—Fiction. 4. Homeless women—Fiction. 5. Aged women—Fiction. 6. England—Fiction. 7. Theft—Fiction. I. Title.

PR6051.Z96R46 2004
823'.92—dc22   2003060944

Grove Press
841 Broadway
New York, NY 10003

04 05 06 07 08   10 9 8 7 6 5 4 3 2 1

Fic.

In memory of

Francis Xavier Azzopardi
and
Mark Derbyshire

Acknowledgements

Many thanks to Derek Johns, Linda Shaughnessy and Anjali Pratap at A.P. Watt; Ursula Doyle, Candice Voysey and everyone at Picador; and Elisabeth Schmitz and everyone at Grove Atlantic.

For advice on everything from blue rinses to rare birds, but also for their friendship: George Szirtes, Clarissa Upchurch, Benedict Keane, Clair Myhill, Graham Etherington, Andrew Smith, Marion Catlin, Penny Williams, Karen Fisk (Shovelhead), John Kemp, David Hill.

For their love and support, and for sharing their memories and anecdotes, thanks to my mother, Pamelia Azzopardi, and to Carmen and Edward Rees. Most of all, thanks to Stephen Foster, for all that and just about everything else.

Note

Although Winnie is a fictional character set in a fictional Norwich, she was inspired by Nora Bridle, a resident of the streets of Cardiff. I am indebted to everyone who took the trouble to write to me with their memories of Nora.

I'm not infirm, you know: I am my grandfather's age. That's not so old. And the girl didn't frighten me; she just took me by surprise. I don't know how long I lay there. I only heard her, first. The door at the front of the house was stiff; you had to put all your weight on it, come winter, just to shift it an inch. It groaned if anyone came in. The girl made it groan. It was quiet for a bit, then there was a soft sound, footsteps, someone on the stairs. She came up careful over the broken treads. I wasn't afraid: there was nothing to steal. There was nothing anyone would want. Mine wasn't a house with a TV set or a video player, there was no computer, no jewellery in boxes, no money. All it had was empty rooms, and me. And it wasn't even my house. None of this mattered to her. She was looking for something else entirely, but I didn't know it then; I only heard her as she came.

I'd settled for the night in the corner of what used to be the front bedroom, tucked myself in next to the alcove where it was warmer. The girl stopped at the doorway, then went over to the fireplace, holding her hands out for a minute in front of the heat. I thought maybe she hadn't seen me; unless you were looking, I'd be easy to miss. I watched her slip across to the far end of the room. On the wall, her shadow was giant. From the corner, she studied me. The fire died down and I kept still. I wasn't afraid, then; she could please herself, is what I thought. She's only a girl, and not the first I'd seen on the streets. She did nothing for a while, just stood there. The wind was butting at the glass, but she didn't shift. She was black in the darkness, and when she finally moved, it was a creeping thing she did: slowly, slowly, feeling her way over to where I lay. I thought she wouldn't take any notice of me. I was wrong. I closed my eyes and kept still, like a mouse in the shadow of a cat.

The next thing I knew, her hands were on my face. I couldn't look; I was playing dead, and she was so quick, running her fingers over my head, under my chin, along my neck.

And just as quick, she was away, jumping the treads at the bottom of the stairs, shrieking like a firework as she landed. I could feel my heart, like a bird, trapped in its cage, banging at my ribs. She wasn't out. She was in the hall. She was moving through the back of the house. A shunt of sash, a blast of air: she was gone.

I stayed quite still. I think I was in shock. The day came up and showed me an empty room, a dead fire, a blue morning. All that I had left was the plastic bag with the face on it. I kept it in my inside pocket, next to my heart. She didn't get that.

It's only another loss; it's not as if I've been harmed. I'd like to say she didn't touch a hair on my head, but that would be a lie.

everything

I'll take my time. It won't do to miss things out. I'm sure I'd never seen her before: names won't stay with me, but a face is my prisoner for life. I'd been living in the house for a good while. To be straight, I was living in just the upstairs room. It wasn't always empty either; people came and went. I didn't mind them and they didn't mind me, and sometimes we knew each other. It used to be a shop, on a parade that was full of shops: Arlott's the butcher, a bakery with its bicycle outside, a post office run by two old women who looked like twins; and this one on the end, which was a fancy cobbler's. It had a sign painted in gold across the window: Hewitt's Shoe Repairs and Fittings, with Bespoke picked out in smaller lettering underneath. The front was already boarded up when I came back, but the words were still there in the glass; you could see them, etched backwards, from the inside. I knew what it said anyway: I had visited this place when I was a girl. Hewitt led me into the back room, for a fitting, he said. Called it the Personal Touch. He had Devices, Methods, cunning hands.

The only window that wasn't boarded up was the upstairs bedroom at the front, which is why I liked it. At night, you could look out at the blackness, see the stars. All the other sleepers stayed downstairs. They were just lads, really, lads with nowhere else to go. Lads afraid of ghosts. They said they could hear Hewitt bumping about, and one of them told me he saw him on the top landing, holding an iron bar above his head. Describe him then, I said, and the lad puffed himself out big and made a roar. Well, that wasn't Hewitt; he was small, with a face like a ventriloquist's dummy and a voice to fit, as if he'd got a tiny man trapped in his throat. So perhaps the lads were just trying to scare me off. They couldn't know, could they, that Hewitt's ghost wouldn't frighten me one bit; it wouldn't hurt me to think of his restless spirit. But I don't like to think of Hewitt at all, if I'm true − not of him, or his time. I used to call it Before, like BC but without the Christ. Then I stopped calling it anything, and the past didn't trouble me. This is the only time there is, I used to tell myself: there never was a Before. I'd got to thinking it was a fact. That was how I managed.

It's not as if I was a derelict. I knew what I wasn't, even if I didn't know what I used to be. And I can remember things if I'm pushed. The Sisters from the House had found me a place. Let me out the side door and put me on my way. Run by nuns, they said, as if I hadn't had enough of them already. I might have gone there, but I knew what they would want; they would want to cleanse me. Start with my soul, I'd say, but they wanted me clean from the outside in, pulling at my clothes like a clutch of thieves. They said I was an Object. An Object who had fleas. They said cleanliness is next to godliness. Well, I know that's a lie. I wasn't having that, lying nuns and thieving to boot. And it was me who was supposed to be the thief, me the liar.

When the Sisters decided I could obey the rules, they let me go. I took my case and walked. And when I found Hewitt's place again, I stayed. They'd laugh at me now, the nuns; now that I've lost everything to a sly girl in the dark.

The day she came was ordinary. Sometimes there's an event, like a snow, or a funfair, or Christmas lights going on in the city, and it reminds you how the year rolls over.

But mostly there's no edge, just tumbling days, which is how I like it. I have a routine which is rarely spoiled; it stops me having to think. I go down to the open market in the morning to fetch boxes. I like the colours on the fruit and veg stalls, and the men there never change. The stalls are on one side, and a row of shops on the other with girls' dresses – bits of rag more like – on dummies in the windows. They wear smug, eyeless smiles, expensive clothes; some of them are bald, some naked. They've nearly all got bare feet. I stay on the stalls side.

They call it The Walk, this street, and it *is* like a place to promenade, with the castle on the mound, and the market with its awnings, and the two grey churches crouched like dogs on either side. At the back of the market is the city hall, which I've been to often enough, and round the back of that is the police station. I've been there too, if I'm true.

No, there was nothing exceptional to the day, unless you count the pumpkins. All the stalls were orange with them, piled up on each other, glowing like a monstrous hatch. They were for cutting into faces. Some of the stallholders had made their own lanterns and hung them over the displays, grinning and twirling in the wind. The thought of them at night-time, lit up and jeering, was horrible to me. I was lucky with the firewood. There were lots of crates, on account of all the pumpkins. I found some broken bits, and the boy on the flower stall gave me a bin liner to carry them in.

There was a panicky sort of wind about, swirling everything up from the gutter and blowing dirt in your face. Eyes full of grit; with my case and the bin liner, I was preoccupied with weather, the fret on the air. I wasn't stopping; not stopping even to thank the boy on the flower stall, not stopping for anything. I was wearing my silver coat. Precisely, if I'm true, I was wearing my silver coat with the plastic bag in the inside pocket, and the shoes I'd got from the Salvation Army the week before. I had my case with me. I always took my case. It was all so ordinary, but these things seem important now: the pumpkins grinning, me carrying the sack, wheeling my case along, not stopping, wearing my silver. As if to alter just one thing would have brought about a different end.

I forgot myself in all that, worrying about the wind and would it bring rain, and would my hair get wet. That was my worry: would my hair get wet. I feared the rain, when it came. I had a routine; getting soaked through was not part of it.

I planned to make a fire when I got back, straight away, to dry things out. Not drying things makes them smell. I do not smell. I do not want things that smell.

~

When I settled in Hewitt's, there was plenty to tear, lots of things to burn. He'd left the storeroom piled with boxes full of unclaimed shoes, and row upon row of insoles sliding on each other like dead fish. Under the counter at the front of the shop he kept thick wedges of tissue paper, leather-bound books of accounts. There was the open cabinet near the door, the kind that people have in their houses to show off their china and glass. Hewitt's cabinet was full of carved wooden feet – lasts in an assortment of sizes. Each had its own brass plate with a name etched on it. They looked like museum pieces now.

Everything was torn and burnt, in the end. The boxes went first, then the counter, then the shelves, and then the cabinet itself. At night I'd hear the lads downstairs, smashing and cracking and breaking the wood into pieces small enough to fit in the hearth. Sometimes one of them would call me down. Robin, he said his name was. He was the only one that didn't have a dog.

I'm wary of commitment, that's my trouble, he'd say, which would make the rest of them laugh. He was a nice boy, too thin though, always near the fire, always toasting something. The others would joke about my boyfriend the ghost, but I'd put up with it, and Robin would give them a look, or change the subject. They weren't to know, were they, and I was thankful for the warmth. How could they understand the twists a life could have? They were so young. And so sure of themselves. They could talk all night; gossip and dreams and wishful thinking – what they'd do if they won the lottery. Robin would always say it would never change him, and one of the others would laugh and say, yeah, sell your granny for a fiver, you would.

Now I have to think about it, I consider another thing: I liked to watch it all being ripped to bits, the lads tearing out the pages from the ledgers, balling the paper up in their hands and throwing it in the grate, or twizzling a long strip in their fingers and using it to light their cigarettes. The account sheets looked like a musical score, with its lines and notations; the owing and debt carefully registered in old brown ink. It was satisfying to see Hewitt's neat little figures go up the chimney, watch the flames lick around his writing, see him burn in hell. But I never let on. I never let on how much I enjoyed it, not even to myself.

When the ledgers were gone, only the lasts were left. No one liked to destroy something that looked so human, but after a while, they went too. Cold alters your thinking: they were only made of wood. We'd sit and watch them go black and blacker, then burst into flames, like the foot of a mythical god. I kept one back, just for me. It was divine to hold, small and perfectly smooth. It had a name cut into the brass plate. I put it in my case, for safe keeping.

~

The wind was bringing in winter. The boy on the flower stall complained about it, stamping his feet like a horse in a paddock. He was breathing out smoke, or frozen air. He mentioned the wind. The market boys always went on about it, blowing from the east; straight off the Steppes, they'd say. That's why I bedded down in the alcove that night; the wind was banging at the front window, coming down the chimney in gulps.

~

Once Hewitt's fixtures were burnt, there was nothing left. By then, I was mostly on my own. That was summer just gone; people who hadn't already moved on were finding other places to go. I don't know where they went. Robin told me of the refuge on Bethel Street being reopened, and a new hostel down near Riverside. He had a plan, he said, some halfway scheme.

Halfway's better than no way, he said, Might as well give it a try.

I didn't have a plan. Not a thought to go anywhere else. No one invited me when they went, and that suited me well. I think I thought I was immune. Precisely, if I'm true, I didn't think at all; it was my routine, to not think about anything, just to go on. The nights drew in.

~

I took the sack and my case upstairs, and made my way down to the back of the house. It had been nailed up from the outside with sheet metal, but one of the lads had pulled the board off the window, so you could get into the house from the back, if you had a mind to. I didn't see the point, when there was a front door to use. They liked it though, this through-way, and it didn't bother me. I had to climb through the window to get into the yard. There's a shed in the corner where Hewitt used to store coal. It was all gone, the coal, I knew it would be, but I found some slack and loose pieces, cupped the dust in my hands and went back upstairs. It needed three trips, climbing in and out the window like Buster Keaton. I'm not infirm. I am my grandfather's age. I left a trail of shimmer all through the hall and up to the top, like a great snail. Making the fire took most of the light out of the day. By the time it was properly going, the sky outside was black.

Apart from my bedding, the room was empty. I spread my coat out in front of the fire. Flames turned the silver to gold. My case with everything in it was at my side. My plastic bag was in my pocket. My hair, of course, was on my head, drying nicely. Everything was normal.

I might have looked out of the window then; I might have seen her. But I was preoccupied with the small things: staying dry, keeping warm, keeping to my routine. A step further back into the day, and I can almost believe that I would have passed the girl on the street. Perhaps I even looked at her. I would have wondered, wouldn't I, what she was up to here, on The Parade, where no one goes shopping and no children play. I am not unobservant. Perhaps she didn't come until late. Or she might have been waiting for it to get dark, waiting for her chance.

But I didn't look back into the day; not this or any other. I never looked back and I never looked on, and if I told myself anything, if a memory came creeping into my head, or if I found myself out of a dream where I was a girl again and my life was flapping out in front of me like a flag, I'd say, That wasn't your life, now, that belonged to someone else. That was just before.

My plan was just to go on as I was going on, each day the same until the end. I will consider it, now I'm forced: there *was* no plan. I kept out of the way. I was nothing much.

~

She took it all. I can picture her watching my face, kneeling down at my side. Her fingers were cold. She must have been looking for jewellery; why else put her hands on me? She could have just lifted my case, and left. She didn't *have* to touch me. The girl put her fingers on me, the girl took everything I own. Now there's some accounting to do. Her hair was red as rust: Telltale. I used to have red hair, when I was a girl.

part one: before

one

I've got to go and live with my grandfather. I don't know him, and my father won't be coming with me, but there's nothing to be done. It's been decided.

Needs must, Pats, my father says. It's a mystery to me. He doesn't explain the words, and I'm not allowed to question. I'm going to live with an old man that I don't know and my father can't abide. He used to call him That Old Devil, but now that needs must, my father doesn't call him anything at all. I've never met the devil, but I've seen his face.

Under the stairs in the pantry there was a carton which I wasn't allowed to touch, sitting alongside other things that weren't touchable, like the Vim and my father's shoe polish. The carton had got lye inside, which is poison. There was a picture of the devil on the outside, to prove it. He had a red face, red hair, pointed teeth, and a tail going up in a loop, sharp as a serving fork. He didn't look at all like my grandfather. My mother kept a photograph of *him* in a silver frame on the table next to her bottle of Wincarnis. I wasn't allowed to touch that either. The picture was in black and white. When my mother did her hair, or sometimes when she slept, I would sit on the stool by her bed and stare at him, and think about the devil inside. I reasoned that his face *could* be red in real life, and he wasn't smiling, so he could easily have pointed teeth. In the photograph, he looked uncomfortable. That

13

would be the tail, doing that: he'd be sitting on it. In his little round eyeglasses, I could see someone else standing a long way off. Two someone elses, one in each eye, holding a bright thing in the air above their heads. I imagined this was a cross of fire to ward off my grandfather, sitting there having his photograph taken. I wanted to compare him with the devil on the box of lye, put the pictures side by side, see if they made a pair, but I couldn't get them together in the same room if they were not to be touched. I tried to memorize them instead: the devil was easy, his wide grin and his hair so red; but my grandfather – he just looked like any old man, any plain old man in the world. And then one day I saw for myself how not like the devil he was.

We lived near the lanes, in Bath House Yard. We'd always been there, so I knew all the faces round about: next door to us was a tiny woman called Mrs Moon, with no husband and four children all alike; and in the corner lived two brothers with a bulldog that bit your legs when you ran past. Across the yard was the knife-grinder. He did the rounds on his bike. When he came home, he'd leave it in the yard outside his window. There were cloths tied to the back, and a basket full of tools on the front. The dog never messed with him. He preferred the butcher, who lived in the rooms on top of us. I didn't know the butcher's name, and hardly saw him in the daytime, but I heard him, moving above my head in the morning, singing when he came home at night. Sometimes I looked out of my window to watch him staggering up the steps; he'd be hanging on to the railing like a man at sea, with the bulldog snipping at his boots, waiting for him to slip. It was easy to slip on the steps; the whole yard-end was leaning one way, as if any minute it would run off through the gutter and down into the city. My father said it was because of the quarrying underneath. We lived on lime, he said. My mother said it was the ghosts that made things tilt. If anything happened in our house, she blamed it on the ghosts.

They made everything slant. Our front door turned out onto a path of cobbles made of flint. They looked like pigs' knuckles laid out flat. Except they didn't stay flat, they sloped, and when it rained, the water came in under the door. My father put up a low wall around our door to stop the water. Everyone in the yard admired it, but no one wanted one of their own.

My grandfather came to see us just after I'd started at school. According to my father, it was because I didn't go often enough. In truth, I hardly went at all. My father came to collect me at the end of the first week, and found me sitting at the back of the room at a little table, just me on my own. While all the rest of the children were doing the alphabet, I was sticking felt animals on a board.

Call that learning? he asked the teacher, who could only say that the idea of learning was beyond some of us and it was nothing to be ashamed of.

She'll not be shoved in a corner, my father said, To be forgotten.

After that, I didn't go any more.

My grandfather paid a visit to Talk Some Sense into us. My father wasn't worried, he said the Moon children never got any bother, did they, and anyway, he wanted me at home. It wasn't as if I missed going to school. I liked to play in the yard. I'd join in Ring-a-Roses with Josie and Pip Moon, but if the bulldog was out and about, I'd sit on the butcher's steps with my legs tucked underneath me. The day it all changed, I was doing just that.

A grey man came and stood at the wall. He had a hat in one hand and a piece of paper in the other. From where I was sitting, I could see the bald bit on the top of his head. He didn't knock on the door, and he didn't say anything, he just looked up at me. He reminded me of someone I knew.

You must be Lillian, he said, after a bit. He sounded friendly, but I couldn't answer back. My father has told me

I must not speak to strangers, and I wasn't sure whether he counted. So I just looked at him. After a minute, he tried again.

You *are* Lillian, aren't you?

It's a trick question, I thought. Then I thought, Maybe I am a Lillian? And ran down to ask my father. I'm always getting stuck with my name, but Lillian at that moment sounded important, and the way he said it, the grey-faced man, made it more familiar than my other name, which my father always calls me by. It's Patsy, my other name. My father thought it was important too. When I told him what the man said, he ran like a rat from the bedroom where my mother was kept, straight through the living room, jumping the wall out the front. I'd never seen him run like that, pushing me aside as if he was fleeing the devil, not rushing to greet him. When I followed, he shouted.

You stay there! Don't move!

I stayed right where he pointed, on the doorstep, and watched as the two of them had words. The piece of paper was exchanged. My father turned without looking back and grabbed me by the hand. He had a fierce grip. He was squeezing my fingers in one hand and the piece of paper in the other. He slammed the door on the man, unfurled the paper in front of the fire and burnt it straight away.

Who was that man? I asked, watching the paper curling blue.

That was your grandad,

was all he said. Then he went in to my mother.

It was the first time I'd seen my grandfather in colour. He *did* look like the photograph. I wanted to ask him why he called me by the wrong name and why my father thinks he is the devil.

After a bit, I went into my mother's room. She was lying on her side, with my father sitting on the stool next to the bed. They stopped talking and looked at me. The shutters were closed. I went to the window and opened them a crack to see out. The man who was my grandfather was still there, waiting, his hands hanging open at his sides. I thought he might wave, but if he saw me he didn't show it. He was staring straight at the door, eyeing it just like the bulldog eyes me. I wanted to compare him to his picture. I glanced over to where my mother kept it, but the frame had been turned face down on the table.

Come away from there, Pats, said my father.

But he's still there!

Come away now, he said.

My mother gave a slow blink. She didn't talk much, but she didn't need to; her blinking said it all. It said she wasn't going to get up and let him in, and I really shouldn't ask questions at a time like this, or stand near the window like that, for everyone in the yard to see our business.

Why did he call me Lillian? I asked. No one spoke. I asked again.

My mother's eyes were shut now. My father took a breath,

I'll tell you in a bit. Go and put the kettle on for your mam.

I did as I was told. But I knew if I looked out of the window I would see the man again, standing still and waiting like a dog.

~

Soon after that, the photograph of my grandfather disappeared entirely, and the frame was put on the sideboard with the glass cracked and nothing behind it but white. And then one morning, the frame was gone too. It was the time of the ghosts. It was the time, my father decided, that I should learn history.

two

It's May 1930: a war has begun. Two men are standing in the shadow of a church inside which I'm about to be christened. Here is my mother's father, thin-lipped under his furious moustache, and standing a foot away, black hair slicked and shining, is my father. He would rather stand somewhere else to argue; the wind is so low and bitter, even the headstones look as if they're ducking out of the way. But there's hardly any room, what with the graves and my pram and the bells. Eight colossal bells are lined up on the edge of the path, their dark skirts tilted to the sky. They are hulled and empty, apart from the largest one at the far end, which houses a small boy enjoying a cigarette. His legs, stretched out from the lip of the bell, are the only bits of him that are visible.

It's a fine spring day, despite the cold. I am wrapped in a shawl and covered with blankets to keep me warm. Underneath the layers, I'm wearing a white christening robe. My mother wore it when she was christened, and her father before her. In between times, it has been folded up in paper and stored in a trunk in my grandfather's house. It has been handed down. I'm wearing a bonnet too, which has not been handed down: it's new as mint. It's a sap, according to my father, a sap to my grandfather. This bonnet covers my hair completely.

The men don't enter the church, they close in among the bells, as if in hiding from the world. This is a private conflict.

Lillian! says my grandfather, It's been decided.

It's Patricia, says my father, We agreed on Patricia!

I agreed to nothing.

Both men stand firm; they would like to fight, hands round each other's necks, rolling over on the stubbled grass like a pair of urchins. But they are aware of the boy, his feet dabbling the path as they whisper at each other, and the two men keep their hands to themselves, pulling on their own suits, fingering their cuffs. My father aims a kick at the nearest bell, half hoping it would let out a peal, some sound to break the silence. The bells look helpless lying down like this; unarmed, naked.

He first saw them last spring, up in the belfry. He was one of the gang of men who climbed St Giles tower, and came quickly back to earth again, their hands stinging with fear, legs like water. My father tried to grip the wooden guide rail as he tumbled down and the whole piece came away, thin as splints. The beams had rotted to dust, but it wasn't this that made the men afraid. They had been standing in a careful circle around the nest of bells. It was just a slight tremor to begin with, so that my father thought the foreman behind him was having a joke, jockeying the slats they stood on; and then a deep rumble which turned everything to jelly: the sky outside, the frantic bats, the bells swaying in the grit air. All to jelly. The bells didn't seem so harmless then. A month later, people were still talking about the earthquake that shook the city. Another month, and the work to fix the beams was lost: the bells needed to come down, and it was not a job for a carpenter. My father had met my mother by then.

A year on, and he's staring at the bells once more, his hands are sweating, his legs are water.

You've no right, he says, through his teeth.

No more have you, my grandfather says.

She's my daughter, says my father, I have every right.

My grandfather does not reply to this. He closes the discussion,

Anyway. It's been decided.

They are back to the beginning, which to my father seems like no beginning at all, just a curve in the circle. He would let the matter drop; he is my father, after all: he can call me whatever he likes. But this is not his church, and not his parish, and the priest is not his priest. Watton was my father's home. Once a week, knotted at the neck, he went to his own church. It had no crumbling tower, no beacon, and just one solitary bell with a desolate clang. When he left for the city, he thought that he had finally escaped the churches and priests and cold stone mornings. And apart from his wedding and the recce of the bell-tower, he hasn't stepped inside St Giles once. But it wouldn't matter if he was regular in his attendance, it wouldn't matter if he was devout, the priest would not favour him. My father is an incomer, after all. The priest is perfectly civil; he gives all the appearance of benevolence, and a thin smile of welcome. But my father isn't fooled; he knows how things can slip away and splinter, even if they *look* solid, even if you hold on tight.

My father and grandfather are too busy arguing over a name to notice that someone is missing: my mother is nowhere to be seen. It's not as if she hasn't prepared for the day: she has a long satin dress, a new hat, a pair of handmade silk slippers in cornflower blue, worn just the once, on her wedding day. They're all laid out and ready, but my mother is slow to get up and slow to get dressed; she makes my father impatient. He stalks about the room, then up and down outside the bedroom door until she bleats at him to go. She'll meet him at the church; she promises, emphatically, that she'll be there. My father leaves her; he has to attend to me, after all. I am the reason for everything. The arrangements are all to give me a name; the priest has been summoned to give me a name; my mother has to get out of her bed to witness me being given a name; the two men standing outside the church are arguing about my name. It has passed from simmering disagreement to bellowing rage.

Lillian! shouts my mother's father.

Patricia! goes my father.

Lillian Patricia Lillian Patricia. The boy in the bell listens, dabbles his feet, flicks the dog-end of his smoke onto the path. He'd go for Patricia, but they won't ask him for an opinion, nor anyone else. No one will come to save the day, to offer a compromise, to make a show of peace, despite the sending of the lace-edged invitation cards. The acquaintances will stay away. This family is tight as a fist. I can't say I'd rather be one thing or the other: I would tell my father, if I could, that in the end it will make no difference to me what I am to be called, because my fate, which no one knows yet – even if they can dress me and christen me and take me from my mother – is that I won't stay with a name at all. This war will be for nothing.

~ ~ ~

I present the facts, all the same; names are to be Learned; they are to be Remembered. My grandfather's name is Albert Price. My father re-christened him That Old Devil. My mother is called Lillian; she was a Price first and then a Richards. My father also has a name: he's Richard Richards, so, clearly (according to my grandfather), from that sort of idiot family he cannot be trusted to name a turnip, let alone his first child. The bells lying in the churchyard have names too: Baxter, Brend, Brasyer; their makers have inscribed themselves on their creations. This is all my father wants to do. The boy in the bell is not nameless: he is called Joseph Dodd.

The girl who stole from me is not nameless: someone will know what she calls herself.

~ ~ ~

The boy traces the name cut in the curved inner of the bell; he knows the feel of it well enough, but not what it says. If he had a blade, he would scrape his own initials on the iron. But Joseph has nothing in his pockets; he has smoked the cigarette he stole from the vestry and now he's bored with waiting; he would like a coin to buy his breakfast. When the men and the baby go inside the church, Joseph takes his place, hand open ready, at the door.

Above the rows of empty pews, the saints in the window shine like jewels; the angels vault the ceiling, a bell is sounded from a recess. Watched by my father and grandfather, the priest moves towards the font like a man in mud. My father longs for the sound of footsteps behind him. He's willing my mother to come. He turns around once, twice, sees only the square door of daylight and the outline of the boy framed within it, hopping like a goblin from one foot to the other. If she were to come now, she could change it; she could tell the priest there's been a mistake.

~

Where is my mother? She's waiting. She lies straight as a poker underneath the bedclothes, and stares at the clock on the dresser. She's waiting for the hands to move up to ten. When the hands reach ten, she tells herself, she will get up and get dressed and go. There will still be time. She fixes on St Giles with its ceiling of angels, the rainbow window of saints, the wisteria hanging in beaded clusters over the walls. But then the noise of the bells begins, ringing people to mass. She will not hear the eight bells of St Giles, but she listens to the rest. The sound is layered, cacophonous: tolling and pleating in her head; there are six churches within a mile of Bath House Yard. It's a bright sound on a bright morning, but not to my mother. She listens to what they're saying, a language of tongue on metal only she can understand. The sounds are different but the meaning is the same: Lillian, Lillian, Lillian, rolling over each other, calling louder and darker and longer, until her angels are cracked and crumbling and the saints are shredded glass. Lillian, Lillian, Lillian. She thinks they're calling her name: they're calling mine. I am Lillian Patricia Richards. But not forever.

three

And she never came?

My father shakes his head. He echoes me,

She never came.

We're in the kitchen, with the back door open, because my father is making a soup. Mrs Moon has given him a remedy for a calming broth, to help my mother get well. She's been worse since my grandfather came and stood at the wall; since I've started going to school again. She tries to tell me what's wrong, but it doesn't make sense.

It's a thing inside, is all she will say.

I try to get her to point to it but the thing keeps moving. It's never in the same place twice.

Oh, here, she says, passing her fingers over her eyes. Another time, she'll put a hand on her chest, or tap her throat just where the dent is.

Is it the ghosts? I ask, because I know they're responsible for everything.

Yes, that's right, she'll say, Silly ghosts, eh? Never giving me a minute's peace.

My father doesn't tell Mrs Moon about the ghosts. He tells her it's the meddling that makes my mother so ill.

That meddling Old Devil, my father says, Doesn't know when to leave well alone. He wants to make sure *she* goes to school, to sit in the dunce's corner and learn nothing!

He points at me like I'm a culprit in the meddling. Mrs Moon makes a sympathetic face and comes back with a recipe. She says it's for my mother's Disposition.

My father's good at things like tea and toast and potted beef on bread, but he doesn't know how to make soup; he has burnt two pans already. The back door is open to let out the smoke: he doesn't want my mother to smell things going wrong. He hands me one of the burnt pans and a scrunch of newspaper.

See if you can get that off for us, Pats – he says, turning again and looking hard at Mrs Moon's writing – I shall have to . . . Keep Stirring, he reads.

He stops immediately, scoops up a mound of leaves and dashes them into the pan. A cloud blooms up. I'm thinking this through, her not coming to my christening.

Da-ad?

Yes.

Dad, *why* didn't she come?

My father prods at the leaves with a spoon, his head parting the steam as he stares into the pan. He's sorry he told me now.

It wasn't anything to do with you, Pats. It wasn't your fault or anything.

It comes out before I can stop myself:

Maybe the ghosts wouldn't let her.

I picture them in their white nightgowns, blocking the door; my mother standing there in her satin dress and blue slippers, trying to swerve past them like you do in British Bulldogs. Or if they knew she was heading for the church, they might be chattering at her, grabbing her with their bony fingers, asking her to send a message, asking for a prayer to be said. You never know what a ghost might want from you.

My father stops stirring. He doesn't believe in the ghosts. He rests the pan on the draining board and takes a bunch of hyssop from a paper wrap. He sits down next to me on the step.

Budge up, he goes, moving me over. The hyssop smells of fields. Some of the heads have tiny blue flowers, which he drops into my lap.

Y'know, Pats, they're not real, the ghosts.

But Mam says they don't give her a minute's peace.

He finds this funny. He does a quick laugh, then stops. Sucks air through his teeth.

Your mam suffers with her nerves, he says, And the ghosts – well, she was just trying to explain what it feels like, that's all. Like they live in her head. But she'll be right as rain with a bit of rest, you wait and see. So don't you go worrying about the ghosts, Pats, they're only on the inside.

~

My father is telling lies: the ghosts are real. He admitted it, in a way; he said they live inside her. I know how that feels: I've got a bird inside me; it flaps if things start to go wrong. When I'm at school, for instance, and the teacher asks me something I don't understand and the other children laugh. I'll be sitting there in the back of the class, at the table in the corner, all the other children scratching their heads in front of me, and the bird will start to flutter. I bet that's when the ghosts seize their chance: I'm looking at the felt animals trailing two by two into their felt ark, at the picture books with Jesus doing his miracles and St Brendan standing on an island which was really a whale, probably the same one that had Jonah in its belly, and all the time, the ghosts are at home, pinning my mother to the mattress with their bony fingers.

They were always gone by the time I got back. My mother lay on her bed like Snow White in her glass box: skin the colour of pond ice, wide eyes, long black hair. She wore it twisted in a plait, wound round her head and clipped up with a silver comb which shone its teeth when she moved. Her hair was her glory, she said. That was before the ghosts came to live in her.

Going to the school put me out of their way. I tried to stop it. I thought by memorizing how she looked, I could keep her just as she was. But I was distracted by other pictures: the Virgin looking startled in her pale blue frock, Moses floating down the river with his pink fist raised to the sky, Jesus standing on a mountain, handing out bread.

At first, she teased me. She said I'd forget my own name if ever I could remember it, so how could I do my schoolwork and *still* be minded to look after her?

Could Jesus help? I asked, thinking of a miracle. She smiled.

Maybe, she said, If you promise to say your prayers every night, like a good girl.

I avoided cracks in the pavement, I crossed my fingers and touched wood, and at night, I prayed. Despite everything, the ghosts took their fill. Each day a little more of my mother was stolen. In no time at all, her eyes went hard as jet; her hair, brittle as spun sugar.

Once or twice in the day she would get up from her bed and make her way to the closet at the end of the scullery, her bare feet inching along the flags. Watching the journey back again, I could feel the time it took: balancing with her arms held out on either side, walking her tightrope between this world and the next.

~

I try not to mention the ghosts. My father doesn't like it. It's not his fault if he can't see them. I'm learning to believe in some things, but not others. If I close my eyes I can picture the lists on either side of my slate: God and his mysterious ways on one side, the ghosts and meddling devils on the other. My father believes in home remedies, and rest, and time. He's full of ideas. Today, he's putting his faith in hyssop, stripping off the woody bits, scraping at the edges with his nails.

Don't know what your mum'll make of this, Pats, he says,

holding up a stem and sniffing at it. He pulls a face and holds it out to me, What do you think?

I don't tell him that I think my mother won't be allowed to drink it, that the ghosts won't even let it touch her tongue.

I think it smells lovely, is what I tell him.

~ ~ ~

I am my grandfather's age. I'm not infirm. I have outlived my mother and my father, which is just as it should be. No one wants to live longer than their child.

~ ~ ~

The breaking started that night. My mother never got to taste her calming broth because the ghosts snatched it from her and threw it at the wall. I knew they would. I didn't actually see them myself, so when I asked her which one of them did it, she pointed to a space behind my head. I looked at it for a bit; there was just a spreading stain down the wall where the liquid had run. When my father saw it, he gave me a funny look.

Her aim used to be so good, he said.

~

It's over a month since my grandfather stood at the door and went away again. My father is preparing me for the Worst, as he calls it.

If the Worst comes to the Worst, he says, when he's explaining what will happen. According to him, the Worst will be that my mother will go into the hospital and I'll have to go to my grandfather. My father doesn't understand that there are more terrible things. We can't begin to know what the worst will be for her. But for me, it's leaving her alone; forgetting her. I know if I go away, the ghosts will eat her up, piece by piece. I try not to mention them, but I can't help myself. I nag him all the time.

Why will I have to go?

Y is a letter, you ought to know better, he says.

But why?

I'm not a disobedient child: I say my prayers, I try to remember things, I try to be useful.

Who'll look after Mam? I argue, And who will help you clear up? I have to stay!

He looks at me and then down at his shirt, so I think he might cry. It's not that I'm no good at tidying, it's just that so much has been broken, and so much stolen. It began in a small way with the broth. Next was a vase my mother kept on her dressing table. I went in to see her before bed, and my father was down on one knee, wrapping something in paper. The flowers were in a neat bundle on the lino, just next to his foot. He looked like he was genuflecting. When he saw me, he held the paper close to his chest and put his finger to his lips: my mother was asleep.

The draught got it, Pats, he whispered, Silly, eh?

Shortly after, things began to vanish: our porcelain lady on the mantelpiece, the two gold-edged dinner plates from the top shelf of the dresser, my mother's handmade slippers, and my coronation beaker with George and Elizabeth smiling on the front. I was given it last May. I thought it was a picture of my mother and father until one of the moonface children told me it was the new king and queen. So it wasn't such a loss.

By the time the mirror got broken, my father had run out of things to blame. It had been smashed in the middle, the slivers jutting from the frame like icicles. The loose pieces squeaked as they came free, but some of the splinters were lodged fast. You could see yourself in pieces. My father didn't mention any draughts that time. He just looked straight into the place his reflection would have been and said,

Your mother never did like that picture.

Then he laughed.

We didn't have much to start with: we ended up with

nothing. I'd wake up in the morning, or come in from playing in the yard, and something else would be gone. My mother didn't seem to notice: she was too busy getting thinner, lying in her bed with her eyes shut tight against the ghosts. She didn't care about anything else; keeping the ghosts out, that was her occupation. She used to tell me about her slippers, how she got them made specially for her wedding day, getting her feet measured, and how the man said they were remarkable feet, the tiniest feet he ever saw.

It's better that they're gone, she said, when I told her about the slippers, Your father never liked them.

I thought that when the ghosts took all they could, they'd leave us alone. I even considered helping them out, hiding a few things round the back of the yard so they wouldn't find them. But by then, there was nothing left to hide. All broken or smashed or stolen. The ghosts had taken everything; the only other thing they wanted was my mother.

nothing

It was nothing. I kept telling myself it was nothing. I told myself other things as I went, looking at my feet, not looking up. If I didn't see anyone else, they wouldn't see me. I kept telling myself it was an easy walk, early enough, not many people would be on the street. The morning was bright spark clear. The trees on the Avenues dripped gold. That sort of morning, it could make you cry.

I kept telling myself that it didn't hurt, my face, and there wouldn't be so much damage. But my head felt tight.

I thought it might look bad. Your skin isn't so robust when you're older: it's like parchment, it tears more easily. I was trying to find something to cover my head when it happened. I had nothing, you see, the girl had left me nothing at all. I must look a fright, is what I thought, so I went downstairs into the back of the house to see if there was something – anything, an old bedsheet or a bit of cloth – to cover my head. It's not vanity. The morning came up sharp as ice after all that wind and storm, and I didn't want to be seen out like that in daylight. If I'm true, with my head bare I felt stripped. There was nothing downstairs that might be useful. Nothing in the cupboards or on the floor. The window was wide open, just as she'd left it, so I climbed out to see what I could find in the yard. The house at the back is broken into flats. It's called vulnerable housing. I've got that wrong. It's for the

Vulnerably Housed. It means they're not safe. I've been offered it before now. The Sisters said it was like a shelter, but there was something about the name of it: vulnerable, vulture, revulsion. I got confused; the idea of going there – I couldn't entertain it.

As it turned out, I ended up in the next street. I wasn't to know. I wonder now whether her saying the name of the place suggested it to me; put the thought in my head. Everyone puts a thought in my head. I've barely got room for one of my own. But at least I was living there by choice, under my own steam; at least I wasn't a Case.

The couple in the bottom flat had got themselves a dog. At first I didn't see it. The fence runs along the end of the yard; it's not high, you can look over the top into their garden, and I was just doing that, looking over it, that's all.

If I'm true, I was looking to see if I could find something; even truer, if I could steal something from their washing line to cover my head. I'm not proud of that. The dog leapt up from behind the fence and bit me on the face. I didn't see it, it was so quick, and it was just one bite – a snap, really – then someone swearing on the other side. It stung, but I think that was the shock. There was no water on, so I couldn't even wash it under the tap. My cheek went hot and cold. It felt blown out when I touched it, like the pricked skin of a sausage. When I looked down, I could see it pinking up a sunrise in my eyeline. I just went straight out of the house. I wouldn't be going back this time, is what I told myself. I was naked on my head, and my face was puffed out and split like those pumpkins on the market, but I wasn't going back to that house. I began thinking that the lads that were staying last summer had a point and the place *was* haunted. Old Hewitt, lying in wait, ready to bite.

Your head feels fine, I said, as if saying the opposite would make it true. Only I didn't say it out loud. I don't speak out any more, not ever, unless it's to the boys on the market, or if somebody should ask me something direct. Then I keep my answers short, and to the point. I have lost the art of conversation. I have buried it. But if I was going to say anything, I'd say what a time of it I've had: last night and then this morning. Nothing happens for years on end and then – bingo! – everything happens at once. Like buses. Wait for ever, then along come three.

There was the pain, and the shock, and an old, familiar feeling in my chest: something fluttering to get out. I had to keep telling myself that it wasn't real, not like there was a bird in there, in my cage; it was just anxiety. Somebody once tried to convince me that pain was only an opinion. Walking into the city at dawn, looking down at my feet and trying not to think about the cold cutting into my face, I was of the opinion that I felt quite a lot of pain.

I kept telling myself the same thing, because there was no one else to tell me.

It would all be all right. It was nothing.

43

four

Go gently now, gently!

My mother put a hand up and pressed it flat against her head. Her nails were ragged from biting. Like a cat examining its catch for signs of life, she would scrutinize her fingers, now and then selecting one to gnaw. Fragments of blue fluff from her bedjacket were caught in the snags.

I sat behind her, my legs bent. Every time I brushed, her neck jerked back. It was pliant as a reed. I was trying to be gentle, but her hair was a mess of knots, fuzzy in places from where it rubbed against the pillow. I tried not to pull the strands; pulling made it come away like candy floss.

I'd better do it, she said. She sat up on the pillows, hanging her head to one side, easing out the tangles with her fingers. She wound it up on top and secured it with her comb. When she finished, she turned round and patted the edge of the bed.

Come here, then, she said, And let me see.
She tilted my face up to hers, and stared into me. Her eyes narrowed.

Who is the fairest of them all?
My mother had started doing it after the ghosts smashed the mirror, so I already knew what to say.

You are, my Queen.
A smile breaking at the corners of her mouth.

No, she'd say, *You* are.

Staring deep into my eyes. Trying not to smile.

No, Queen. *You* are!

On and on, until one of us laughed and broke the spell. Sometimes I did this on purpose; I didn't like the way she stared, as if she really could see someone else inside my face.

We lived in her room, on Caley's chocolate and stories: the one where a girl grows her hair and a Prince climbs up it, where an ugly cobbler with a funny name steals a baby from a Princess, where a wicked Queen poisons a young girl because she's jealous of her beauty. My mother was just like Snow White. Most of the time, she didn't care what she looked like, she only wanted to lie down and sleep. Until suddenly, the ghosts went quiet. And just as suddenly, my mother woke up.

There was going to be a fair at Chapelfield on midsummer's night, with boat-swings and sideshows, and a cinder circle where people would have a dancing contest. My father had promised to take me. Mrs Moon was very excited when he told her. She said she could leave her Bonnie to look after the kids, and then she could come too.

I haven't been dancing for years, she said, twirling in the yard for everyone to see, Not since Edward.

Mrs Moon had doll's eyes, round and shiny. Whenever she spoke of Mr Moon, she'd blink very deliberately, the tears dropping down her cheeks like drips from a tap. My mother didn't see her performance, but she heard it. The idea of staying at home while Mrs Moon went in her place did not appeal; she decided that she must come with us. My mother announced that she wanted to be in the world again; she would like to dance too. My father was pulling on his work clothes when she said it. He stopped, the vest halfway down his body. His ribs were blue with bruises. He'd only been working with the drayman for a week, and hadn't got the hang of catching the barrels. He gave my mother a strange look.

Dance? You? he said.

Us, she said, Just like before.

Holding her arms up high above her head.

Like that? he said, pointing at her nightgown, her bare feet.

I can put my lovely slippers on, she said, forgetting they were gone, My wedding shoes.

My father shot me a warning look.

Haven't worn those slippers since I don't know when, she said, swinging her body over the side of the bed, Now, where have I left them?

He pulled her upright, put his face very close to hers.

They're gone, remember? he said, Medicine doesn't buy itself.

Then I'll dance barefoot, she said, turning away, See if I care!

~

She plagued him with it for days, chewing on her nails, worrying about how best to do her hair, asking me if I knew what Mrs Moon would be wearing. My father never said No, but he never said Yes. He just said Wait and See. And told me I must watch her.

He must have known. By the time midsummer's day came, she'd forgotten all about the fair, Mrs Moon stealing her husband, the idea of dancing in her blue silk slippers. The ghosts were her only interest: seeing them, and getting them away. They were fat as pumpkins, she said, she could see them floating above her head, their round faces grinning.

There, that one up there, get it, Pats. Get it down!

And I would chase a shadow from the wall, just to please my mother. An hour or two might pass, and then she'd start up again.

Are you blind? Over there! she'd say, as I fretted the ceiling with the broom, That one!

She said the windows needed cleaning,

To frighten the buggers away, let God's light in,
and the floorboards under the bed had to be swept, because
they were clever and small, they could hide themselves in the
rolls of dust. But she couldn't do a thing herself.

I'm weak as a kitten, she'd moan, clinging to the furniture
as she crept around the room. So I cleaned for her while she
sat in her bed, waving the spiders out of her face. On the
Friday, the day of the fair, she closed like an eye.

Now I'm ready, she said.
But she just lay there on her bed, her skin snow-white and
sweating in the heat. My father said we could go anyway,
even if she didn't want to come. But I had to promise to stay
with her until he got back from work.

Keep her company, Pats, he said, Just in case.
It was as if he didn't trust me.

I don't need to promise, I said.

Promise me now, he said, crouching down so his face was
close to mine, Promise you won't leave her.
I nodded, but said nothing.

I want to hear you say it, Pats. Cross your heart and hope
to die.
I licked my fingers and made a sign of the cross on my throat.

Cross my heart and hope to die, I said.

~

Snow White lies in her glass case. She won't show them she's
awake. She knows that if she did, she would not be allowed
to stay, to watch the clear sky overhead, or the trees, their
branches stirring in the breeze. She is not aware of the ivy,
creeping like a thief over the surface of her tomb, its suckers
seeking purchase on the glass: her protectors have cleared a
broad circle through which to observe her. Each day, between
the slits of her eyes, she detects their forlorn expressions
staring down at her. She remains completely still. Sometimes
rain falls; thick drops that spatter inches above her face. She
cannot taste them, though her tongue longs for it. Snow

White watches as the splashes soften to trembling blobs. They are bell-shaped mirrors on the valley, they hold a rainbow, a curve of fern, the halo of a sunset. When the drops dry, they leave stains that only she can see. Sometimes a leaf falls, a bird dangles a worm, a snail spends the day, its silver belly quivering a trail of mist across her face. She lies intact.

Snow White chooses to remain asleep. The thought of waking is abhorrent. Here she is entombed, undisturbed. At night, when all the faces go away, she has the privilege of the moon. In her head, under winking stars, she dances.

~

I'm quiet as a mouse. My mother lays flat on the bed. She doesn't want any chocolate and she won't do stories; all she needs, my father says, is peace. Her palms are turned up towards the ceiling, white as lilies. Her nightgown is open at the neck, the ties hang loose and tremble as she sips the air. The dip in her throat is a well of sweat. The room gets hotter with every breath.

I want to help, but all I can do is look. Look and count. I sit on the edge of her bed and count the slats on the shutters, then the strips of light across the ceiling, from broad to narrow and back again. I count the spikes of mirror stuck in the frame.

Her eyes flick open.

What's that, she says.

I think she's seeing the ghosts again, and go to fetch the broom. She stops me, blinking quickly, turning her head to one side.

That noise.

We're both listening.

There, she says.

I can't hear it. I think it must be the ghosts, bending over the bed, whispering in her ear; making demands.

Shall I do your hair, Mam? I say, to distract her from them. Maybe if I sit close they'll clear off for a while.

Her brushes are kept in the top drawer of the dresser. They are backed with mother-of-pearl. But they're gone. Only a chipped bone comb with a hair hanging from it like a line of spit. Where the brushes used to be there are more lumps of hair, twisted together into a nest.

Her head is heavy in my lap. I don't mention the brushes. I comb carefully, watching the bone teeth as they scrape a path through the strands. Her eyes are two slits.

Not now, she says, raising a hand, Leave me be.

A smell comes off her skin, like pear drops. Sweet, and stale underneath. It makes me feel hollow.

Shall I open the window, Mam? Let some air in?

There it is again, she says.

I get up on the stool near the shutters. The noise is inside them. It starts at the bottom and works its way to the top, then silence, until it comes again, up and up, a fizzing noise. I open the shutters a crack, using my fingertips to ease them apart. Just a tiny sliver of light coming in. She won't mind that. A wasp is trapped between the wood and the glass. It zigzags all the way up, drops onto the sill and spins round on its back. It jumps up and starts again. In the yard I can see the Moon children, playing a game. Eddie Moon has a scarf tied over his eyes. He's staggering like the wasp, his hands clutching at the space in front of him. The others pull at his clothes, run round him in rings. The smell of pear drops is stifling. I can't find the wasp, but I hear it, spurring. I push the window open and the air comes new; the cries of the Moon children carry on the breeze, daylight hangs broad as a bedsheet over the yard. Inside my mother's room, the blackness swims before my eyes.

~

At first, Snow White thinks it is a shroud. She finds it difficult to move. Her arms are numb, her head is heavy on her neck. She practises moving, starting with her mouth, stretching it wide. Her lips crack: she tastes blood. She opens her eyes.

They are filmy, there is no focus, just a trail of sparkle from the snail on glass, which isn't a sparkle at all; it's a bar of light. There are many bars of light above her. They must have moved her from the wood, moved her into a horrible place, a shed or a workman's hut; she can't make out where she is. There is a noise of humming, a slow familiar drone. Wasps, and no glass case to keep them out. They will feed off her; they can smell the slice of apple, lodged in her throat. She must turn her head. It takes a long time; it's full of stones. She sees a small child sitting beside her. The child has her hand open and is counting on the fingers. Snow White sees the numbers mouthed, but hears only wasps. The child speaks, but Snow White is unaccustomed to the sound of voices. The child is asking, the child is fetching. She lifts Snow White's head onto her lap. Now she is staring up at the child, at a hoop of orange light around her face, as if the child is on fire. The child is pulling something, dragging it across Snow White's head. The pain is fierce and burning.

~

Why don't you –
my mother from her bed, her words strung out like the pennants on a kite
    – Go and play?
Outside, the Moon children shriek. A cheer goes up. Eddie has caught his big sister Bonnie. Inside, the sound of my mother's voice, breaking open.
    Go on. Go. Let me be.
    I can't, I say, I've promised Dad.
    Out there, she says, Go. Let me be.

~

I go and play with the Moon children. We leave the bulldog tied to the water pipe, and we leave my mother, sleeping on her bed. Outside, the air moves with me. I run into it. We play Tag, racing through the lanes and down to the park, Bonnie chasing Eddie through the gap in the hedge at the back of Chapelfield, yelling at him to slow down, let up, so at first all I hear is noise: Bonnie's shouts, Josie and Pip calling after her, the grind of a machine, and above it, floating in and out like a wheeze, a bright metallic music. And then I see.

I've never seen such a thing. There must be fifty of them. A hundred. Their manes are silver and yellow and gold and black, their saddles are knobbled with jewels that glitter in the light. Streaming towards us and away; sucking the air from our bones, blowing it straight back in.

The gallopers!

Eddie stands stock still, his arms raised up in the air as if to be lifted. Above us, the horses fly.

~

On the pillow beside Snow White's head is a comb. She recognizes the smell of it: a smell of death. She remembers the face of the deer, a curious blinking eye, and the beige underside of its tongue, licking away a fold of snow. An arrow of light breaking the sky above her, and the deer sighing, slanting to the ground. She knows the smell of death. Snow White raises herself from her bed. The child has gone now; there is no pain.

Where is my mirror, she says.

~

Sorry, mister, says Bonnie, not sounding sorry at all, We've got no money.

Bonnie tries to negotiate with the man. If he lets us ride the gallopers, we'll tell everyone we meet, we'll come back tonight with all our friends, we'll come back and pay for the free ride he doesn't want to give us now. The man looks unimpressed. He wears a vest like my father's, but has hairy arms, and a thick black belt holding up his trousers. He reminds me of the giant in *Jack and the Beanstalk*. The horses stand frozen in a leap, teeth bared as if to bite him. The man wraps his hand round the twisted pole that is speared through Bonnie's mare.

As soon as it had slowed enough, we jumped on the platform and claimed one each. Now the man wants money from us.

She don't go until I stoke her up, he says, pointing his thumb over his shoulder, So you lot can suit yourselves.

We are happy just to sit, racing each other on the spot and geeing with our invisible reins. Eddie has climbed up to sit with me, his two fat legs hanging over the side. He's hot and sticky, he wriggles against my lap. I want to push him off, but then Bonnie leans over from her galloper and grins.

He's side-saddling, she says, Ent he posh!

The other horses are all taken. People are waiting to go, shouting at each other over the polished manes and then shouting at the man to get a move on. He tries to look stern, but then he sees Eddie, his fingers white from gripping the pole, and he relents.

One go, he says, That's all. One go round and then you're off.

I nod at him.

That's a promise 'n' all, he says, pulling one of Eddie's legs over so he straddles the horse. I think he wants *me* to promise. I lick my finger, ready.

Cross my heart and hope to die, I say.

Hold him tight, now, he says, pointing at Eddie.

The music wheezes to life, and then we turn. We turn, and then we fly.

~

Who is the fairest?

My mother gets up. She looks at the room, at her sweated bed. It might as well be her coffin. She looks for the mirror. There is the back board of the frame in dull brown wood, and the frame itself with the gilt flaking off. Inside it, a jagged oblong of silver shards show where her reflection should be. A stool near the window, where the child likes to sit. The child's name comes to her so easily, she thinks she must know it. Lillian Price. But it doesn't sound right. Lillian Price is her own name. And the child is not like her, not in any way. Hair as red as rust, eyes pale and round and staring like an idiot. Feeble-minded, they said she was. Lillian the mother sits on the stool and ponders Lillian the daughter, and Lillian's father, and her own father. She stares into a slit of mirror. Her hair needs cutting. She straightens out the knots with the fingers. The strands come away in her hands.

~

By the time I remember my first promise, the day is gone, the yard half in shadow. The bulldog has been taken in, and the knife-grinder's bicycle is back against the wall. I'm weightless with flying, with flying and sitting on the edge of the platform, feeling the gallopers kick their legs above us, and the thick oil swell of the engine below, juddering our bones. We watched until the sun went down behind them, and the man watched us.

From my mother's window comes a light: sharp, like a sunburst through a cloud. It's swaying. I can see my father in his work vest, holding a candle up high. He must have come home early to take us to the fair. I'm standing in the yard and thinking about the best thing I've ever seen, and will he be angry with me for breaking my promise to him, and will we go back again to the fair. I'm not really looking, but then something happens in the window that is new to me. My father is holding my mother by the waist; they're dancing. The flame jumps as they move across the floor. She bends like willow in his arms. He catches her up, she bends again, he holds her to him. I have never seen them dance.

~

Cobwebs stop the bleeding, Richard remembers this from his childhood. He was running fast, climbing the railings that bordered the orchard where if he and his friends could have tasted the fruit they would have found it bitter. But then the man was coming towards them and they fled, the point of the railing catching him in the soft part of the thigh, right at the top, so he had to keep it pinched together all the way home. His mother raised her arm above her head, as if absently swatting a fly, and pulled down a cobweb from the porch. She wound it tight around his leg; said there was no need for a doctor to fix it.

Cobwebs would stop the bleeding, but there are no cobwebs. There is not even a speck of dust.

~

My father staggers as she slips, their shadows curtsy off the walls, come back to meet them. His free arm holds the candle high above his head; the wax spattering like stars. I watch my mother and father from the yard, then watch them closer, edging my way to the door. They are dancing on pure light, breaking the glass into smaller and smaller shards. He wears his heavy boots; her feet are bare. The floor is full of pieces of sky. I see the heels of her feet as he tries to lift her, I see my mother peeling from him like a shadow. I see the black around her, a river staining the floor. I see the ghosts, oozing.

My father turns. He looks through me, his hand coming down on top of the flame, red, redder, black. And then I see nothing at all.

bargain

All my own teeth, as they say in the papers. I don't read the newspapers, they're full of lies, but I like the Classifieds in the freesheet: Bargain Buys, For The Home, Lonely Hearts. The men always say Own hair/teeth if they're over forty. And 5 foot 8, which you know is going to be a lie. No one over seventy ever puts an advert in the paper. You've given up by then. Well, I have. Not many of us can boast all our own teeth. Pensioner, arthritic hip, deaf in one ear. You might as well ask the undertaker to come round and measure you up. I prefer the For The Home section. It's different with furniture; the older it is, the more value it has. When I'm trying not to think, I picture a place of my own. I furnish it in my head. It passes the time. Bargain!!! Antique cabinet £145. It's a bit dear, but I wouldn't mind that. Set of four dining chairs, teak-effect, £80 ono. A lot of money just for something to sit on. And who would want Jays. Stuffed. Two. In cabinet. Very nice condition. £90. Who would want two stuffed jays? They look best alive, staggering over the grass like drunks on a night out, not dead in a glass case.

The wedding section comes at the end, in between Videos and Weightlifting. Champagne Flutes. Engraved bride and groom. New. £10. And the dresses, you almost want to buy them out of pity: Wedding Dress. Size 16. Pearl trim.

Veil and tiara. Unused. Cost £700 will accept £200. It makes you wonder.

I passed the time. I read the freesheet. I waited. Me and the fluttering thing in my chest and the pain that was more like a shock, like being struck by lightning. A sharp streak of light. That's how I imagined it. Waiting for time to move. Paradise would open at nine o'clock. I always got my clothes from Paradise. It's a boutique in Swan Lane. It's got a good name; the girls who work there are just like angels. Sometimes if they saw me going by they'd shout to me and take me through the back to have a rummage. They called them Freebies.

We've got some Freebies for you, they'd say, bustling me in, all smiles. I'd never just go in by myself, that would be brazen, but if they call me off the street – well, it would be rude to refuse. I didn't have to buy from a newspaper, not my shoes, not my clothes. I've got standards, and besides, you don't know who's died in them.

I'm lying, if I'm true: mostly I got my clothes from the Salvation Army Centre. And you can bet your life someone *has* died in them. Needs must, as my father would say. My silver coat came from there. I didn't have to pay – you don't, as a rule: the Sally Army will give you things, clothes and blankets, and if you've got a place, they'll supply the furnishings. It's terrible stuff. The shop's fit to bust with dressing tables and mattresses, coffee tables perched on top of each other, radiograms and grey spin-dryers smelling of nappies. Mirrors on everything, sucking the life from your skin. None of your antique cabinets or stuffed jays. I only went in because I saw the coat in the window. Before I knew it, the assistant was turning me round in front of a vanity unit, saying,

Doesn't that fit nicely, dear?

She had a patronizing tone; not like the angels in the boutique. I can't tell you if it really *did* fit nicely, because I wouldn't look. Never trust a mirror: full of lies, just like the papers.

But the coat was warm, and beautifully shiny. It felt like it had no memories in it; it felt space age.

I thought about putting my own advert in the paper, or maybe tying a notice to the lamp-posts in the city centre, like they do with a lost cat, only this would be more of a personal ad:

Wanted. Thief. Formerly red-head, now dark. Has stolen—

Well, has stolen everything. I could've given a full description. That white face and that horrible hair hanging like a caul over her eyes. She haunts me. Her fingers haunt me. I could've given a description, all right; I could've done all sorts.

But I didn't know *what* to do, if I'm true. I could talk to myself all day, tell myself it would be fine and not to worry and you'll get sorted out. But I couldn't even begin to think straight, let alone tell anyone. And who cares about an old woman and a few bits of tat? No one, that's who, no one in the world.

five

RULES
is written in thick black ink. There are Rules, then a wavy
line, followed by *Things I Must Remember*.

It's all down on a sheet of paper and pinned to the back
of my door. The list is to make it easy for me in my new life,
my grandfather says. I'm supposed to look at it every day. He
calls it an Aide-memoire, as if *that* makes it any easier.

Rules are – 1: Do Not Run On The Stairs, but On The
Stairs has been crossed out and Anywhere In The House put
in its place after I gave Mr Stadnik a shock one morning
coming through the passage. I was chasing Billy the dog, and
Mr Stadnik came out just as I was passing his room: his tea
tray went sky-high. Mr Stadnik is the lodger. He works shifts.
The next rule is Do Not Chase Billy. It was such a novelty,
having a dog that I ran after instead of the other way round,
but it's a Rule now so I mustn't do it. Rule 3 says Shoes. At
All Times, but Rule 4 is a puzzle: it says NO jewellery. It's a
mystery to me because I don't have any jewellery, not a thing.
I think my grandfather is confusing me with someone else.

Things I Must Remember has my new name on it, Lillian
Price, and my age, and my new address: 9 Chapelfield. Water
The Plants, which is my main job in the house, comes next,
along with Say My Prayers. Saying my prayers won't be easy,
but at least there's nothing in the rules about making a promise.

I live with my grandfather now. This is my new life. Needs Must decided it, my father said. My grandfather's very different from him. He's blunt. That's what he says when he's going to tell me something bad.

To be blunt, Lillian, he says, It will not do, you're eight years of age and you haven't learnt a single thing. Now. I'll show you just this once.

And then he shows me something I'm bound to forget.

On the very first day of my new life, it's tying my laces. My grandfather is persistent; he tries to make me 'get it' one more time, and one more time becomes another one more time. He lifts me up onto the breakfast table, muttering about how could I get to be my age and not know how to do such basic things. Mr Stadnik sits low in the armchair, skulking, with Billy underneath it, poking his head out from between Mr Stadnik's legs. They both watch. My hands on either side of my skirt are studded with breakfast crumbs.

Right over left, right one under, pull tight, loop on the right, left one curled, left loop through. Come on now, Lillian, you do the other one.

My grandfather isn't like my father in another way: he isn't very patient. Whenever I got things wrong, my father would make a joke of it. When I get things wrong with my grandfather, he sniffs like a sergeant major, opens the back door and goes for a walk down the garden.

I'm sitting on the table with one boot done. I'm at a loss. My grandfather has gone down the garden. Mr Stadnik watches him go, then stretches his face like Mack Sennett and gives me a wink.

Do like me, he says. He bends down and eases his boot off. He isn't wearing any socks, and the tops of his toes are black. His bootlaces stay exactly where they are. Then he catches the flap of the tongue, holds the boot in the air, and slips his foot back in.

There! he says, Done! Why would you want to do a thing every day, when you only need to do it once?

He gets out of his chair and ties my laces again, loose enough to slip my foot in and out, and then he knots the ends.

We live near Chapelfield, opposite the park, with the chocolate factory on the other side. The smell of it carries on the air all day, you can taste it just by breathing. My grandfather doesn't care for the smell, or the factory, or even the park, which is full of Ruffians, he says, and Types; but he's very proud of his house.

It's a proper home, Lillian, not like that slum you used to live in.

He says 'slum' so it sounds like an animal, a snail dragging its broken shell, and I see him in the garden, stamping on them, or throwing them over the wall onto the tracks below where the trains will flatten them into gobs of glue. The wall runs all the way along the garden; if you pull yourself up, or stand on the bucket, you can see the footbridge over the railway line with people passing along it. I've seen a boy standing there: he was hanging half over, balanced like a plank, spitting down onto the top of a passing train. That was before it was forbidden for me to grip the wall with my fingers and haul myself up.

Just look at your boots, Lillian, all scraped. They don't grow on trees, you know!

And then when my grandfather saw me standing on the bucket, that was forbidden too, on account of buckets not being for standing on but for mopping, which only Mr Stadnik is allowed to do because of his agile hands.

I learn slowly. I learn that Rules are not just things written on my door, they are everywhere. Rules and forbidden things go together, but can be opposite too, like the holy ghost and the devil. Some are spoken rules, like not climbing walls and not standing on buckets and not rescuing the snails; some of them have to be written down; and some are silent, like not asking about what happened to my mother, and not mentioning the ghosts.

You can tell my grandfather has never had a visitation from the ghosts just by looking in the parlour. It's full of things. Two china boys wearing turbans stand guard on either side of the fireplace. One of them is holding a basket and the other one has his hands pressed together, as if he's praying for Father Christmas to come. They're nearly as tall as me. Above it is a picture of a beautiful lady floating in the water, her long red hair covered in flowers. Then there's a corner cupboard going up to the ceiling, full of plates we never eat off; a grandfather clock with a glass door, and a flat brown cabinet with a row of medals and a letter in brown ink.

At night we sit round the fire in the living room. My grandfather might read to us, or have a conversation with Mr Stadnik. I've got my own chair, made entirely of wood. There's a name carved across the headrest: it says Lillian, which is my name now. But the chair's quite old and the lettering is worn, as if someone has passed a hand over it and over it, wearing it down. It wasn't very comfortable. I didn't complain, but one evening Mr Stadnik said, Try this for size, and spun a cushion through the air for me to sit on. Mr Stadnik knows things without being told about them. One morning when he came back from his shift, he looked at me over the breakfast table. He placed his finger under one eye, then the other, then pointed it at my face.

They can't harm you, you know, he said, The dead are the dead. Only the living can harm you. So sleep tonight. He knew even without me saying how I feared the ghosts. But Mr Stadnik wasn't right about everything. They can harm you. He didn't know what they did to my mother.

~ ~ ~

I'm not allowed to see her. My father shuts the door to my mother's room. He puts the candle on the sideboard, fetches a match from his pocket and relights the flame. He moves me to the window, pressing down on my shoulders to make me sit. His hands are cracked with wax. He takes his good shirt off the back of the chair and rips it down the middle. His cracked hands are shaking. He rips it again, lengthways, tearing at the cotton with his teeth, and goes back into my mother's room. He leaves a trail of broken threads across the floor. I could tidy them up before my mother gets to see them, but I've been told to sit. I can't even do that properly. My legs are jumping up and down, it's as if they don't belong. They remind me of the wasp on the sill. I wonder if it's still there, banging its head against the glass.

When my father comes back, he's out of breath. He smells of iron and sweat.

Patricia. Listen to me. I want you to stay right here.

He doesn't make me promise. My legs are jittering, my mother is lying next door, spilling ghosts.

What about Mam, I say, but he's running from me now, out through the door and leaping the front wall.

Stay there! he shouts, and is gone.

I sit at the window and watch. The yard is blue in the moonlight. A dim light cuts a square on the cobbles. I'm in it. I bend forward and back, watching my shadow follow on the flints. There's a light falling out, and I'm inside it: I'm the shadow. I picture my mother, bending like a hairpin as my father tried to hold her. The two of them like puppets, putting on their show in the window. Only not dancing.

Bonnie Moon runs into the yard, followed by my father, followed by Mrs Moon, flapping her hands. He sends her straight back in.

Is the doctor being fetched? I ask. It was normal for Bonnie to be sent for the doctor when my mother felt unwell. I would like normal things to happen again. My father doesn't speak. He goes into the scullery and comes back with a bottle. He takes a drink from it, budging me along the sill, staring beyond me into the yard. He holds the bottle an inch from his lips. When I turn to look, our shadows have melted together: a two-headed monster fills the cut of light.

Your grandfather's on his way, he says, nodding at the window.

My knees start jumping again. He puts out his hand to still them; it is scrubbed clean. He smells different now, of night air and carbolic. He takes another sip from the bottle,

This weather's got to break.

As if he has summoned them, a few specks of rain fall on the glass. The moon hides itself behind a bank of cloud. We stay in the window and watch the change, from soft drops to thick, drumming splotches, the sky going acid yellow, the smell of dust rising. We wait for my grandfather to come.

~ ~ ~

We don't have shutters, Lillian, we have curtains. What do we have?

Curtains, I say. So can I?

It was a slip of the tongue, that's all. I had asked my grandfather if I could go and open the shutters — meaning the curtains — in the parlour. It's Saturday, and my father is coming to visit me; I want to sit at the window and watch for him. I want him to see Gloria. Mr Stadnik made her out of one of his gloves. He's put buttons on for her eyes, one just higher than the other so she looks like she's staring at someone just over my shoulder, or having a think. Her hair's atrocious: stringy, the colour of an old blanket. He was wearing Gloria when I first saw her, terrifying Billy. He was shouting,

Put your Dukes up! C'mon, fight like a man!

Billy was twitching out little barks from under the couch, licking his chops and barking again.

All rightee, fight like a dog!

When he saw me, Mr Stadnik smiled. He got up off his knees and saluted me.

What would you like to call her? he said, waggling the glove.

I couldn't think of anything except what she was.

Glove, I said, and he seemed happy enough with that, but then I offered 'Patsy', because I knew 'Glove' didn't sound like a girl's name. Mr Stadnik went quiet for a second. He held the glove to his ear, pulled a face, finally nodded his head.

She says her name is Gloria. What do you think?

I nodded too.

Gloria is born! he said.

Mr Stadnik said she had come to protect me. She would keep the ghosts away, watch me while I slept. She was my very own. I wanted me and Gloria to wave at my father when he came.

My grandfather says my father won't be here until the afternoon, so I have to help him in the garden. He is obsessed with things that grow. There's a glasshouse thick with tomato plants, neat rows of vegetables tied up on sticks, and at the far end of the garden he has fenced off a perfect square. It's full of flowers. They're tied on sticks too. All along the wall, my grandfather has hung a line of broken mirror pieces, twinkling like diamonds in the sunlight. A huge one hangs from the roof of the glasshouse. He says they're to keep the birds off, although Mr Stadnik secretly feeds them in the mornings, so it doesn't always work. In between the jitter and shunt of the trains below, my grandfather enlists me in a duty.

Here, take this twine for me, Lillian, and watch where you're putting your feet. The twine is rough, dark brown, coiled upon itself. I hold it close in my hand, feeling the spring of it in my grip. He leads me a cautious path, past the glasshouse and the rockery to the fenced-off perfect square. The heads of a hundred flowers are drooping on their necks: white and pink and creamy orange and velvet brown. They have all got their own names: Roses, Dahlias, Chrysanthemums. I must learn which is which; I must learn to tell the difference between things by their names.

They should be straight, he says, lifting the head of a chocolate dahlia, So we'll give them a bit of help.

We have to wrap the twine around their stems. I don't want to do it; their necks are so skinny and their heads so heavy and full I'm afraid I might choke them. The first one I touch falls to bits; the petals go everywhere. My grandfather takes no notice.

A young thing has to grow straight and tall, he says, wrapping a caught neck to a stake, You don't want to grow up all crooked, do you?

I don't want his flowers to droop, but the question has nothing to do with me. Except, it feels like it *does* have something to do with me, and I'm being forced to agree with him. He takes the twine from between my fingers and shows me how to wrap it, going round near the head, careful and silent.

No prizes this year, he says, That storm nearly did for them,

and then he gives me a quick look, as if he's said something wrong; as if he has rules he must obey too, and he's just broken one. He's right about the dahlias; they're almost gone. From the house they look perfect, but up close they are weary and bedraggled; the weight of the rain must have been too much to bear. We go along the rows, putting their heads to rights with bits of twine. I'm careful where I put my feet.

My grandfather's so pleased with my progress, he's smiling. He's funny when he does it, as if his teeth are causing him pain. He says can he trust me to do the bulbs. I don't know what they're for, the bulbs, but all I have to do is watch him and copy. I want him to trust me, but I'm not going to promise.

Watch me now, Lillian, he says.

He takes a bulb and puts it in the centre of a pot, pressing it down with his finger. It's the same jabbing action he uses when filling his pipe. The finger on his right hand is yellow. When I ask him why, he says it's the tamping that does it. I tamp the bulbs all morning; he says I do a grand job.

~

There's no wall outside my grandfather's house; he's got a gate. It hangs a bit to one side and the hinge needs oiling; on the path is a long scar from where it's been opened and shut again. You can hear if someone's trying to come in: the gate bangs against the post when it's pushed. I'm waiting in the parlour for my father to come. I'm allowed, because I've done so well in the garden. I must sit quietly and not touch anything. I'm used to that; that's one rule I can remember. I've got Gloria for company, and the two boys in their turbans, and the clock plays a bong every so often to let you know how much time is going past. I'm waiting for my father to come. I'll hear the gate, and then I'll wave.

The first night of my new life, in my new room in my grandfather's house, I couldn't sleep for the gate and the noise it made. I kept seeing my mother on the floor, the black spill around her, and the horses galloping, the lights of the carousel turning, the flame my father held, dancing then spinning down to my mother on the floor. I wanted the doctor to make her well again. He came with my grandfather, and they looked like brothers; they were both wearing round glasses and they carried cases. The doctor's case was small and brown; my grandfather had a green one with a label stuck on the front. It said Lillian Price. I didn't know it was going to be mine. I was still Patsy then. No one looked at me but I felt in the way, as if I was a hole they had to step round and not fall into. They went in different directions. The doctor disappeared into my mother's room, and my grandfather went into my room at the back. My father sat out the front on the wall. The bottle was in his pocket by then. He took swigs from it, and when he wasn't doing that he was smoking a cigarette. I wanted to be next to him, so I got as close as I could, sidling along the edge of the wall until we were nearly side by side. He smoked one cigarette after the other, lighting a new one off the old one, flicking the stub away into the yard, watching it spin in the swirl. The rain was blowing in gusts, soaking his head and vest. I thought he must be angry with me.

You have to go away for a bit, Pats, he said. Then he said something else which was taken by the rain, something about my grandfather, and Don't worry, twice, Don't worry, Patsy, promise me you won't worry. Promise me.

Cross my heart and hope to die.

~

I *tried* not to worry but the gate kept me awake, swinging open and shut in the wind: bang, nothing, bang, nothing, bang, nothing; so in the end the silence had its own sound too, and it was a huge heart I heard, beating through the dark. In the morning, my grandfather brought me tea. He opened the curtains and stood at the window, chatting about the weather and his flowers and what needed doing in the garden as if he always did this, as if it was an ordinary day, and I had always lived here.

six

My father won't come into the house when he visits; he leans his elbows on the gate, swinging it and staring at the crescent scrape in the path, while my grandfather helps me into my coat and beret. When I'm ready to go, I have my father in front of me and my grandfather at my back. They look but they don't speak. Around my neck I wear a doorkey on a long piece of string, which my grandfather has given me in case he's in the garden and won't be able to hear me knock, and his silver watch so I'll know the time. The watch is heavy and cold, then warm, against my chest. I'm ticking like a bomb. My father looks smart in his blue suit. He leaves it hanging in Fisher's window all week and fetches it out on weekends, just to visit me. I'm not allowed to mention the watch; my grandfather says my father would hock that too, given the chance. I don't know how to tell the time, anyway. I just wear it to please him. I don't even have to use the key because my grandfather's always there when I come back, waiting behind the curtain in the parlour.

You never know what might happen, my grandfather says. But nothing ever does happen. So the key I don't use and the time I can't tell stay on the string around my neck. I come home, I knock and I wait, while my grandfather makes sure my father is far enough down the path, then it's my grandfather in front of me, and my father at my back. This is the pattern of Saturdays.

My father tells lies all the time. He told my grandfather that we go to visit my mother's grave. I think we almost did go there once, but then he changed his mind and took me to the pictures instead. We always leave the same way – over the bridge and towards St Giles – so even though my father doesn't say so, my grandfather thinks we're heading for the churchyard. He cuts flowers from his garden for me to put on the grave.

That one there, he says, pointing to one bloom or another, That one's a beauty. Not the dahlias, Lillian, they're just about finished, they are.

On the draining board in the scullery, he slices their stems with a quick strike of his knife, wraps them tenderly in newspaper. He breathes through his mouth as he does it, short, anxious sips of air, as if inhaling the scent of the flowers would use it all up.

My father takes me up the steps at the end of Chapelfield and along the bridge. It's the same bridge I saw on my first day in the garden, when I stood on the bucket and watched the boy balancing his body over the tracks below. I'm looking at things from the other side. That first time we crossed it, my father and me, I got a strange feeling, a cold water rush on my skin. I saw what the boy would have seen: the railway lines streaking off past the mill, and the crooked terrace with my grandfather's house tilting a bit at the end; the dark tangle of elderberries hanging in clusters over the wall at the far side of the garden, and the garden itself, neat as a stitch, with the mirror pieces twirling in the wind. Something was wrong with the picture. Then I saw, exactly, what the boy would have seen. In front of the glasshouse, I spotted her. She was very still, her red hair fuzzed like a halo in the sunshine. She was watching.

I felt her fingertips gripping the sooty wall, and her eyes, staring at the bridge. I felt the cold of the bucket seeping up through the soles of her boots. I caught my father's sleeve to tell him, but he was looking at another thing, a trail of steam in the distance, a dense cloud eating up the sky, and in the corner of my eye I saw his hand, coming up to point it out. But he wasn't pointing; he was taking the flowers from me, unfurling the paper wrap and opening it, shaking it out like a dishcloth over the edge of the bridge. The heads twirled down onto the tracks and were lost in the smoke of the train as it passed beneath us. When we reached the end of the bridge, I looked back into the garden; the girl was gone too, only the garden and the wall, and the twirling mirrors catching bits of sky. I could have told my father about her, but with the flowers spiralling down so fast and the smoke coming up like a cough and the shuddering bridge making the light jump black and white – with all that – I couldn't speak. One of the ghosts had followed me. I didn't want my father to know I could see her.

~

On our days out, we go to the picture house. It's The Ranch for cowboys, and the new Regent for everything else. My father likes to see films where the girls dance in patterns. He looks hard for one that reminds him of my mother, and then he points her out to me. He won't go to the churchyard, but he tries to find her everywhere else. I can never follow the story, because he'll keep nudging me and saying,

There she is, Pats, the spit of your mam. The absolute spit. She'll be wearing a sequinned evening dress or a bathing costume, or a fancy head-dress with feathers sticking out of the top. When there's a close-up, she'll show her perfect teeth, and my father will smile back at her. It's like they're having a conversation: the girl's big head nodding down at us from the screen and my father staring back with the side of his face lit up, his eyes glowing in the dark like oysters. The girl never looks anything like my mother, really, but I have to watch out for her all the same. I want to know what it is that he's seeing and I'm not.

Sometimes, if we've been to a picture more than twice, my father promises me a boat trip on the lake. We'll walk along the riverside, right up to the bend where the heath sits on one corner and The Flag on the other, and my father will wipe his forehead and say,

I'm parched, Patsy. Shall we wet our whistles, first?

I'm not allowed inside The Flag, so we slip through the gate and into the yard at the back. I have to sit on the wall under a tree and wait, while he goes round again into the front like an ordinary customer. He comes out through a side door, holding a drink in each hand, and says, Ta-ra! as if he's a magician who's just sawed someone in half. My father has black ale with a froth on it, and I have ginger beer, which he says isn't a beer at all. He always gets it for me, even though I don't much care for the taste, and he puts it down on the wall and always says the same thing:

Just like your mam. She loved her ginger beer!

He wants me not to forget. But it would be easier if we both remembered the same person. He always brings a thing of hers, a ribbon or a handkerchief edged with lace, and tells me the history of it. The ribbon could be anyone's, and the handkerchief has a smell I don't recognize, and the wrong initials embroidered in the corner. I didn't like it at first, not because of the initials, but because of him. Sometimes, my father thinks I'm dim. He pretended to find it behind my ear, but I knew it wasn't really there. He'd magicked it. I didn't think it was funny.

Don't you want it, Pats? he said, looking hurt. He scrunched it up in his fist, blew on it, and the handkerchief was gone. I wanted it back immediately. It wasn't the thing, but the gone-ness of it, the feeling of something lost in thin air, something missing. It set off the fluttering inside me. But my father doesn't bring me things just so that he can take them away again, and in a few seconds it had reappeared in his other hand, unfurling like a leaf. I must learn the correct expressions: happy face, surprised face; pure joy, wonder.

Today, my father has a heart-shaped locket in his hand. He clicks the fastener to open it.

See here, he says, Come on, have a look,
holding the cleft heart up for inspection. Inside are two locks of hair, coiled up on either side: one black, the other shining red. We sit in the yard of The Flag, me with my ginger beer and him with the locket, balanced on his palm.

I try to tell myself it's just a story, made up, like one of Mr Stadnik's stories, or like the parables. If only my father didn't want me to believe it was true.

~ ~ ~

The first time he saw her, she was framed in the archway leading to the rear of the shop. She had the back door open and was standing on the step, shaking out one cloth after another. My father could only see her silhouette, the wide-shouldered uniform with its nipped waist, the skirt bellowing to her ankles, and all around her the air, glittering with dust. She reminded him of a figure in a snowscene. When she sneezed, bending back into the room, he caught the whiteness of her hands, the sharp edge of her jawline, and the spool of hair pinned up on her head; she sneezed again, so hard he thought it might come undone. He hoped it would; there was something about the hairpin which was familiar to him, and faintly unpleasant. My father was sitting on a long wooden bench which ran the length of the shoe shop, from door to wall. The room was hectic with customers; he would have to wait his turn. He heard his name called once, or maybe someone else's, repeated twice – Richard, Richard – and cast a guilty look around. It was another man, standing in the corner, who nodded and took his position in line.

Richard had not started out with the intention of buying

shoes; he was on his way to St Giles church to look at the belfry. No one had been back up the tower since the earth tremor, but it was his job to deliver the firm's estimate. Evidence of the death-watch beetle had been found in the bell frame, and a replacement would be costly. It wasn't the thought of breaking the news that upset him, it was the memory of the place: a smell of bats, thick in the air; the floor tilting away under his feet so the sky outside went sideways; the feel of the splinters slicing into his palms as first he slid along the stair rail, then flew, then fell, to the bottom. And now there was the death-watch beetle. Richard had never seen one, but he'd heard it was a menace. He imagined one single insect: huge, earthquake-sized, black as pitch. It would have pincers sharp enough to cut through a man's arm. The slightest movement of its heavy body would make the tower shake and the bells fall. His legs went to liquid whenever he thought of having to go into the church, having to sit in the vestry and drink tea while the thing manoeuvred its clicking body somewhere in the space above his head. Richard had been putting it off all week, and today, when he was braced to do it, he found himself instead amongst the lines of men, standing in rough queues or sitting and staring at their socks.

The opening of the shoe shop on The Parade was an event. It had been advertised in the newspaper and on handbills given out in the street. The man sitting next to Richard had rolled his up into a tube, which he put to his mouth now and then and blew like a trumpet. There was a feeling of excitement, a circus atmosphere, which didn't fit well with Richard's dread of going – or not going – to the church. He studied his handbill. It was written in thick black ink with a variety of lettering styles covering the entire space, and at the bottom, an illustration of two single shoes, one style for men and one for women. The back of the handbill was as inky as the front. It heralded a new machine from America, called the Amazing Fluoroscope. A diagram showed what looked to him like a Peepshow box. It was a Device, he read, for Precisely Measuring the foot using the Latest Technical Advances. This, and the promise of credit, had drawn a Saturday-morning crowd. Richard only caught sight of the actual machine in glimpses, when the crowd parted just enough to let another customer try it out. Each man was invited to place his bare foot inside the box and view the resulting measurement through a square of glass. There was laughter among them as the next man up removed his socks, and much nose-holding and wafting of handbills. And then a hush would come down while they waited for the shriek of surprise. The proprietor, aware of his female staff, asked the men to refrain from cursing.

My father soon grew bored with the gasps of wonder and delight. He didn't particularly want to put his foot in the machine. He didn't want to see the bones of his toes, glowing through the skin like embers in a fire, but nor did he want to leave and make his way to the church. The girl in the back of the shop had caught his attention, and he was content to sit and watch her while she shook out the dusters and arranged them in a pile at her feet, and sneezed her sideways sneeze.

What are you looking at?

The girl was moving through the archway now, the heap of dusters folded on her arm. She didn't stop for an answer, sweeping past him so he had to pull his feet up or risk an injury. She stepped over them, holding the edge of her skirt just high enough for him to glimpse her thick black boot. He looked up into her face: a sheen of sweat breaking on her forehead and the stray hairs clinging to her neck. And his eyes followed her as she bent behind the counter and crammed the dusters into a drawer. The clip at the back of her head was a thick black oval of jet, glittering in its twist of hair. She drew her hands down her skirt and folded them in front of her, a waiting pose, as she had been taught on her first day, her face serene and open.

~ ~ ~

It put me off a bit, Pats, I can tell you, he says, Seeing it crouching there like a dirty great beetle. But not the hair. Beautiful hair, she had. Everyone said so. See how lovely it was?

The locket is still perched on his hand.

Whose is that one? I ask, pointing at the coil of red.

This, he says, Is yours. Cut it from your head, when you were very small.

It looks like a thread of copper. I want to ask him what it means, cutting the hair and keeping it inside a heart, in the dark, but his eyes are moving over the top of my head. There's nothing to see, unless he's looking at the flowers. I'm sitting under the tree; it has a few close blooms in dying pink. When the breeze gets up, the petals shower down, crisp and brown and soft off-white. I have to sweep them from my lap. I could be buried beneath the petals for a hundred years, waiting for a Prince to come and brush them away. I don't know the name of it. If my grandfather was here I could ask him, he would have it straight off, he'd have it in Latin. But he doesn't know we go to The Flag, and I'm not allowed to say. My father takes no notice of the tree, or me. He won't find a story about my mother in its leaves. But the piece of metal in his hand – the heart which is supposed to remind him of her and the glory of her hair – that's important. He will want me to have it. I don't see her in it at all: I see a dead black strand in the shape of a question mark. If I look very hard, I see a single hair hanging from a comb, a coiled-up nest, a broken mirror.

~ ~ ~

Richard passed the shoe shop on the following Monday. At first, he didn't understand why he went out of his way, and blamed it on the church and the job he had to do. It had become a real aversion for him; each time he set off, he found himself walking anywhere but up St Giles towards the church.

The tower could be seen for a good distance around the city, so he also needed to avoid the streets and alleyways that might lead him to a view of it. He thought this was his reason for returning to The Parade, just to walk along without a worry, but when he got there he rushed by with his collar up and his cap low over his eyes, feeling oddly exposed. On Tuesday he found himself passing down The Parade again, and by the end of the week, he had grown nonchalant: lots of people walked this way, why shouldn't he? On Friday morning he stopped and looked in the window of the shoe shop. He couldn't see anything for his dry mouth and the choking sensation of his pulse, thumping in his throat. He couldn't get beyond the lettering etched across the window and his own dark reflection staring back. He couldn't see her.

But she saw him, and Sarah, the other shopgirl, saw him too. A thin-faced, worried young man, his Adam's apple bobbing up and down his neck.

He's back, she called, Lillian, it's lover boy!

Lillian went to the door and opened it fast. Later, she would say she was going to have it out with him, ask him what he thought he was up to. Later, they would joke about this almost-meeting. But Richard was too quick for her. Hearing the door bell clang, he ducked down a side passage, moved fast, not stopping until he got to the top of Cow Hill, where he saw the thing he had been so carefully avoiding: St Giles church, with the snake of wisteria winding its way along the wall and the chiselled flint of the tower behind, full of memories of the earthquake and now infested with the death-watch beetle. But not a bell in sight.

Joseph came to his rescue, although Richard didn't know him then, and wouldn't recognize him, a year on, as the little boy who hopped like a goblin outside the church door. It was a fancy of Father Peter's that a goat should be used to keep the grass short around the graves, and that a boy should be employed to tend the goat. The two came together, although

Joseph would say, if he was ever asked, that the goat preferred the flowers left in the tubs, and had a spiteful kick, and was a cloven beast who had no place in God's garden. It was Joseph himself who kept the gravestones neat, using the shears Father Peter had given him, and then pulling the grass out by the handful when the shears rusted. Joseph was employed for as long as the goat was employed, and made himself useful by tying up the animal on a very short rope and tending the grounds himself. In between times, he scaled the tower, or stood at the door on wedding days and christenings, and collected some coins for his trouble.

Joseph sees the man, sweating, out of breath, staring in wonderment at the naked square of light in the tower where the bells should be.

Farrar's in Thetford have come an' take 'em down, says Joseph, Father Peter say they won't be hung again till next spring.

He holds out his hand, judging that this piece of information deserves payment, and Richard freely obliges. His relief is visible. It won't be necessary to go back up into the tower, and he needn't bother with the vestry and the tea and the careful estimate furling in his inside pocket; his firm specializes in carpentry, they won't be given the contract. He feels so light, he could float up to the sky.

~ ~ ~

My father stares into his beer, dabs quickly at the foam with his free hand, lifts it to his face and scrutinizes it: on the tip of his finger, a blackfly kicks its legs.

I didn't expect it, he says, frowning at the insect.

He holds his finger up in the air to show it to me, like Jesus giving a sermon.

I was let go a fortnight later. If there's no work, there's no work. So I went to London, and bought the lady something special.

He smiles at his other hand with the locket on it, open like a butterfly. He has two insects now, one with sharp jaws and the other drowning in beer. He wipes the real one along the edge of his trousers and extends the heart locket to me. He calls them keepsakes.

You can have it if you like, Pats, he says, She would've wanted you to have it. She kept all these nice things just for you.

My father says he went all the way to London to buy this piece of jewellery for my mother. Or he won it at a fairground in Yarmouth while she was having her photograph taken with a monkey in a hat. Or he found it in the aisle of the Regent Picture House after they saw *Stars over Broadway*, and offered it in lieu of a wedding ring. I've heard all these stories before. There's no reason to disbelieve him, but I do. He brings her back every time, sees her in everything, but he won't put a foot in the churchyard, where she lies under a weight of earth. He won't know her that way.

I don't say a word. I want him to tell me again, to tell me all the other versions, the ones where he can believe how it might have been. I've yet to learn that memories aren't real, that nothing except the thing itself is real, not an image of a pencil-thin woman lying flat on the bed, not the smell of sunlight baking a room, or the shape a life makes when it spills across the floor. But a handkerchief, a ribbon, a heart-shaped locket speckled with rust; these are objects, artefacts, proof of life. I balance his memories, all the same, storing them on top of mine, carefully leaning one against the other like a stack of playing cards. I am building a tower without bells. Later I will bring them down, in an earthquake of my own.

paradise

I thought I was known; I thought I was a face. But the angel
gave me a right look. She couldn't see who I was. Maybe she
didn't recognize me through the plate glass, and I have to say,
I *was* altered.

I wouldn't just go in, I'd never go in unless they asked me
to; that would be brazen. I bided my time. The shop didn't
open up before nine, and it was only ten to by the city hall
clock. Not that you could trust it. Clocks and mirrors: liars
both, but it was all I had to go on. I stood near the window
and waited. They'd put a new display up, a white Christmas
theme: the dummies were wearing thick fur coats and fancy
hats. Snowflakes twirling on string, and more silver string in
the corners with cupids hanging off them, blowing trumpets
and playing lutes. It was only just November. The year rolls
round more quickly in the shops. I thought I'd just stand there
until they noticed me. There was no one else on the street,
apart from that lad who sells magazines. I've seen him often
enough down the Centre, playing pool with Robin. I've heard
him singing as well,

Can I interest you, can I te-empt you, to *A Big Ishooo, A
Big Ishooo!*
At first you think it's funny, but it gets on your nerves in no
time. He sings all day. I should think there are complaints.
It was too early for a song, thank God, so he just leaned in a

doorway, smoking and waiting for the city to wake up. He was giving me a funny stare. We were both too early on the street. I kept my distance. I turned the other way. The bite on my face was itching now, making everything look different, large and then small. I knew it was just a trick of the swelling, not my mind doing it. The left eye was a bit closed, that was all, and fuzzy on the inside. I must've looked a fright. The wind made the cut sting cold, it made my eyes water. Still too soon for Paradise, but there was nowhere else.

The girl unlocking the door wasn't one I knew, but she opened it and let me inside. There's a lovely smell in clothes shops: the girls' perfume and spray polish and fabric, and something faint underneath, like machine oil. It's all neat at the start, with everything in its place. She'd been vacuuming the carpet. The flex ran over the floor and behind the counter. They hadn't put the music on yet, so it was quiet. Not that cavernous silence you get in a church, but the lovely soft quiet that you find in an airing cupboard or under thick bedclothes. That's what my angel was doing – putting the music on – bending down behind the counter. I could only see her hand at first, gripping a bunch of keys on a chain. The hand looked like it was off a dummy. That's what I thought, with my vision going in and out, that it was going to be put back on one of the dummies in the window. I got a shock when the rest of her came up from under the counter, and the music came on loud. She had a shock too, seeing me, and then she did a little bounce on the spot, back down, and turned the music off again.

Mind this till, Debs, she said to the other girl. Debs's face was white coming deep pink up her neck. I'd seen that colouring before: it said something was going on, like a fire alarm or a shoplifter getting caught.

I'll need those keys, Carol, she said.

I thought she was going to throw me out. You lose all sense of what it's like, being touched. But Carol turned on her heel and pushed the door to, then came towards me. Her voice was calm,

Looks like you need a doctor. C'mon, she said, walking down to the back of the shop, My car's out the back.

I wasn't going to any hospital. The door said PULL. I always get it the wrong way round; it wouldn't budge. Carol stepped up and stopped me.

All right, all right – giving her friend at the counter a look – Let's see if we can sort you out.

She led me into a cubicle and sat me on a stool. There was a white chiffon scarf hanging off a hook and a box of tissues on a little ledge. Someone must have left them behind.

I'm just going to get something to clean you up, she said, very carefully, with a voice soft as milk. She pulled the curtain across, like a nurse going off to fetch a doctor. I thought maybe she *was* going to get a doctor, and I panicked until I saw the rails of blouses through the crack in the curtain. It was still a clothes shop after all. I had to keep reminding myself. Carol was going to clean me up, but Carol had left me there alone in the changing room with a hook and a mirror, where you can leave your old skin hanging on the wall and look at yourself in a new one. They don't call them changing rooms for nothing. I wouldn't look in the big mirror, but there were two narrow ones in the corners, and I couldn't help but see the reflection in strips: a bit of shoulder, a sliver of neck. I tried to think about something else.

Whatever happened to you! she said, cheery voice this time. She'd brought back a bowl of pink water and began to wipe the side of my face with it, wrinkling her nose and coughing now and then into her fist. She did my eye first, very carefully, with a nest of cotton-wool balls bunched in her hand. She dropped each one into the waste bin behind me. It was TCP I could smell.

That's not bad, she said, It's just a scratch, really. Not *too* bad. She put her hand on my head, tilting it first one way and then the other.

How long have you . . . um, how long has it been like this? How?

Your hair. Your head.

My eyes began to sting. I had to wipe them. I bent over to get one of the left-behind tissues. A blue one came out, an orange one next. I wanted to keep pulling, see how many colours would come. I wanted to be sure I wasn't seeing things. The trick my father did, a handkerchief swallowed in one fist, opening like a bloom in the other – I had to be sure that here was real, that Carol was real and that I was too: real, and in a clothes shop called Paradise having my head stroked by a lovely scented girl who wasn't going to rob me.

Carol didn't ask again about my head, just frowned a bit, turning me this way and that with her fingers on my jaw. Cool hands, rings on them.

Okay, she said, Be brave.

She started pulling the clips out, slowly and gently, dropping them into the bowl. I couldn't see what they were with my head back, but I knew. It felt like having stitches removed.

They keep the thing on, I said, trying to help, Underneath, you wear a thing, see? To keep your hair down. To hide it.

I watched her face. I couldn't tell if she understood me; there was a word missing and I couldn't find it. I knew it was called something. The head-something? The word had left me. Her eyes were brown as buttons, shiny like Mrs Moon's. So I told her. I told her lots of things, but all backwards, because my words were clotting up. I told her that I thought her eyes were like buttons, and wasn't that appropriate what with her working in a dress shop, but I said *living* in a dress shop by mistake and then I wanted to take all the words back and start again. Except I'd forgotten the word for round things, stitched on the shirt.

Isn't that funny, I said.

She gave me a long look. I told her I was robbed by a girl, bitten by an animal. It was hard to talk. I was out of practice of putting things in the normal order; my mind knew what the normal order was, but my mouth didn't. I wanted to explain about the mirror and how just when you think there's one of you, there's suddenly two and how can the number of human beings get multiplied just by looking? I could've said, Why would anyone steal my stuff, what would a girl want with an old woman's case? But the words refused to come.

She stole my hair, I said, which wasn't strictly the truth. It wasn't my hair, it was a wig, cut from a Russian virgin's head. It was black and thick and long and shiny and it belonged to Miss Foy and then it belonged to me. So it *was* my hair, twice removed, and then removed again by a thief in the night. Three times removed. *I* felt stolen.

I couldn't tell her all that, so I told her about staying at Hewitt's on The Parade and how I'd been robbed all those years ago when I forgot my promise and my father couldn't hold my mother, and about the two jays in the newspaper I'd found on the bench next to the police station which I'd used to cover my head on the way. That bit must have made sense to her, because she said,

You've been to the police, then?

I would have said, No, not on your life, but she was stroking my head very gently, as if I were a child. I wanted to tell. I could have told her everything, about my mother, my grandfather, Mr Stadnik and my Aunty Ena, about my father. My handsome father, conjuror, Houdini in his sack, twisting away in front of the whole world. Pretending a thing was both magic and real at the same time. Making things disappear, making them come back. But not my mother.

I could see Carol looking at my head. She'd removed the pieces that were stuck; she must have been admiring my hair underneath.

Aren't I just the princess? I asked, Aren't I just?
She stood back from her work.

Now that's an improvement, she said, Much better.

seven

Yes! Yes! A great improvement!

Mr Stadnik is holding his arm out in front of him, palm flat against the air. He looks like the traffic policeman on the corner of St Stephen's. I don't know whether to believe him. Perhaps he's trying to be kind. I can't help thinking that if my father had had his way, I wouldn't have gone to school in the first place, and then none of this would have happened.

My new school is called Little Ketts. Big Ketts is round the corner, and next to it is the asylum, called Bethel Street House. There's only one room to the school, with a bit of yard at the front where we have Playtime. Sometimes we can see the men in Bethel Street garden, leaning on the fence, sharing a cigarette. They all wear the same clothes, all brown. There's a wall down the middle, with women on the other side. There are girls in there, ash-faced and glum, wandering about the rose bushes. When I ask my grandfather why the girls are in there, he says they've fallen on bad times, and that I should be grateful, having people who care for me.

Miss Balson is our teacher. She likes a cigarette too, and wears a similar costume to the women in the asylum: baggy brown cardigan, olive-green pinafore, green stockings, wrinkled at the ankles. She looks like a newt shedding its skin. There's a handbell on her desk, which she clangs when it's time for us to go into the yard and play. She enjoys the ringing. She puts her fingers round the handle and grips it slowly, her eyes going up like sparks.

Guess what time it is, girls? she says, and we're supposed to shout Playtime! as if we've been waiting for playtime all our lives. Miss Balson sends us outside whenever she wants to have a smoke; she clangs the bell about five times a day.

On the first playtime, the other girls stood in a semi-circle, round-eyed, silent, looking at me. The tallest one broke away from the rest and came up close. She put her jaw so far out I could see the birthmark under her chin.

We want to know, she said – swivelling her head left then right to include the others – Why you're wearing that hat.

It's not a hat, I said, It's a beret.

I pronounced it the way my grandfather did when he put it on my head – 'berrett'. I'd never seen one before. He tucked all my hair up inside it, every single strand. My neck felt exposed in the air. He said I was to wear my beret all the time, and that he'd spoken to Miss Balson and she agreed it would be a good thing. All the other girls wore plaits. They were so alike, you couldn't slide a straw between them, except for the tall one with the birthmark and the jaw looking like it was made for a punch.

Well, Clever, we want to know why you're wearing that . . . *berrett*, she said.

I didn't know why, except that my grandfather told me I must. It wasn't a written rule, it was a spoken one. He often tells me to do things I don't understand.

You've got Telltale hair, Lillian, he said, So we'll put it away and then there won't be any tales to tell, will there?

I knew I couldn't say that to the girl, so I kept quiet. But she wouldn't let up.

What're you hiding under there? she asked, stepping round me.

Nothing.

Let's see nothing then, she said, catching the beret at the back of my head and whipping it off.

Pikey hair! she said, clapping, and straight away the other girls took it up.

Pikey pikey pikey!

Until Miss Balson saved me, clanging us in for Scripture. But her second cigarette break brought more of the same. It was Birthmark again.

We can skip prials, she said, Bet you can't.

I didn't know whether I could or not. I didn't know what sort of thing prials could be, and I'd never had a skipping rope, because my father said the whooshing noise would give my mother a fright. The Moon children had one, but it was mostly used for tying up the bulldog in the yard.

I don't think I can, I said, not liking the sound of it.

I preferred other games, ones where you ran and got chased, but this hoop of girls wanted to do tight things, complicated manoeuvres; steps and rhymes and spiteful jabs. Birthmark was their leader; they called her Alice. While she organized the games and made up the rules, I sat on my own. I had no one to talk to except Gloria, who came everywhere with me, in my pocket. Until Alice noticed.

What's her name? she asked, creeping along the fence.

Gloria, I said.

That's a stupid name. I've got a doll too. Her name's Charlotte. That's a proper name. And she's got real hair.

She inched closer, pretending not to be interested, looking back at the other girls to see if they were watching.

I know, we'll do a swap, she demanded, holding out her hand, You have Charlotte and I'll have her.

I shook my head. Even if it meant being Alice's friend, even if Charlotte had real hair, I wouldn't swap Gloria for the world: she kept the ghosts away, she watched over me while I slept. She was Mr Stadnik's gift.

I'll bring Charlotte in tomorrow, Alice said, wheedling, You can have her, I promise. She's pretty.
She was stroking Gloria now, tickling her with the tip of her finger,
Go on, go on.
And suddenly,
Give!
Snatching her away, laughing, waving Gloria on her hand,
Bye Bye, Dirty Pikey, I'm going to a new home with my new mummy!
She ignored me after that. When I asked for Gloria back, she said I was a dirty Pikey liar, she said there was no Gloria and that I made the whole thing up. And when Miss Balson questioned her, Alice stood up and lied to the whole room, her voice clear and calm, her eyes wide with innocence. Gloria was gone forever.

Things got worse without Gloria to help me. The girls were free with their name-calling, poking me and then sniffing their fingers with a disgusted face, or pretending to be friendly and then turning their backs and smirking at each other when I tried to join in. Alice had invented a new game: Adam and Eve and Pinch Lil, she called it. I never did get to the bottom of it. I never learned not to trust them. By the end of the week, my arms were sprinkled with neat blue bruises.

My grandfather inspected them, holding me by the elbow and turning my wrist under the lamp. He said it was always going to be difficult, what with me being so different, but I had to learn to mix in. That night, he showed the bruises to Mr Stadnik.

Look at this, Henry, he said, Spiteful little buggers!

It's that beret, Mr Stadnik said, It sets her apart. And I know how it feels, to be set apart.
He winked at me.

It isn't always necessary.
My grandfather said nothing to this, unfolding his newspaper

and pretending to read it. I thought they might have one of their discussions, which started off with them calling each other Henry and Albert, and ended in a slamming door. But this time they just sat facing each other, both of them breathing heavily through their noses. Without warning, Mr Stadnik sprang from his seat and bent his head down close to mine.

A fine head of hair, don't you think?
It smelt of goose fat, but apart from that, it seemed normal. I said I thought it was very nice.

Us two, he said, waggling his finger at my grandfather and then at himself, We could be the exact same age!
I didn't know what to say to that.

But look how young I am.
My grandfather snorted. But he pushed his glasses further up his nose and held them in place with a yellow fingertip. He frowned at Mr Stadnik's head.

Is it some sort of dye you use there, Henry?
I would call it Enhancement, he said, his lips spreading tight over his teeth.

Now, Henry, it's all right for you, but our Lillian's so fair-skinned. I don't want her looking foreign.
Mr Stadnik made no reply, but he raised an eyebrow. He put a hand on top of my head.

Black is not the only colour, he said.
And turned to me with one of his winks.

A princess may be many colours. You, Princess, may be anything you like!

~

Mr Stadnik has dressed up for the occasion in a long white butcher's apron, fed crossways round the back and tied with a bow at the front. Sleeves rolled up to the elbows. He wears a leather cuff on his left arm, secured with a lace. I've never seen this before, but as I've never seen Mr Stadnik's brown, hairy arms before, I think it's all part of the costume. My grandfather has not dressed up; he's spent the last hour boiling something on the stove in the scullery, now and then butting his head into the doorway to ask Mr Stadnik for advice. The windows are steamed white; the whole house reeks of jam.

When Mr Stadnik says it's ready, we follow him into the yard where he's taken the tin bath from its hook. He pours some water in, produces a slim white bottle out of his apron pocket, and adds a thimbleful, swishing it round with a wooden spoon.

Secret ingredient, he whispers, pushing the stopper back. I kneel on the mat in front of the bath and stare into the water. Sunlight glints back at me; and through it I see the girl again, floating below me like a ghost under water. I shut my eyes tight. There's a smell of heat and steam, and the school outhouse in the morning. It's bleach. My grandfather stands on the doorstep with a bowl of something mashed, having second thoughts.

What about this, Henry, he says, holding up a dripping spoon, It looks . . . very *blue*.

It's perfect, says Mr Stadnik, Trust me.
I hover over the bath as my grandfather pours jug after jug of water over my head. The girl is drowned beneath it. As it gets wet, the colour of my hair goes from gold to rust, trailing in my eyes like smelter.

Eyes shut! Keep still! shouts Mr Stadnik, retreating. He's standing well back, as if I'm a firework about to go off. The last thing I see before I close my eyes, through the steam and the water and the running red, is Mr Stadnik's boots: he's already halfway up the path.

My grandfather starts in with the mash, pasting it on my head, then rubbing it with his fingers and making noises of disgust.

Keep still now, it will burn! Mr Stadnik yells. He's confusing me with Billy the dog: when he gets wet, he shakes off the water in a frenzy. I will do as I'm told, and keep still. Mr Stadnik is giving the orders. He's so pleased with himself, he can't help shouting, even though I'm not far away.

You must leave it set, he says. He comes back down the path, and, bending over the edge of the bath, says it again. His face is black against the sun.

It will feel quite hot, and in a few minutes, we will rinse you. Do you understand?
I try nodding, but my head is as heavy as the world. It makes him shout again.

Keep still, I say! And you – to my grandfather – Wash your hands!

~

There is no mirror in my room any more. For the first week, I put up with it being there. I didn't tell a soul, but even at night, even though it was dark, I felt her inside it, sitting in the frame, waiting for me to come and look. Watching me sleep. In the morning, when I'd forgotten about her, there she was again, staring straight at me. I'd try to take her by surprise, edging into the corner of the glass, peeping round it with my eyes half shut, hoping to find her looking the other way, or gone entirely. But she was always there, too quick for me: the girl I saw from the bridge, the girl with the orange hair. Looking at me with her empty eyes.

My grandfather seemed very pleased when I said I would rather the mirror was put somewhere else. He said, yes, they were full of sorrow.

But there *is* a mirror, hanging over the fireplace in the livingroom. It's too high up for the girl to watch me in. Not unless she climbed on a stool, which is Against The Rules. Mr Stadnik fetches it down off its hook. I don't want to see.

Look, he says, Look, how – transformed!
I open one eye. The girl with the orange halo is gone; there's just me. My hair all blonde and shiny like Binkie Stuart's. Hair white as snow. Mr Stadnik dances round the room like he's on elastic. He claps his hands with joy.

Who is the fairest? he cries.

eight

A single sound will betray me: the click of a bone in my foot, the shush of my fingertips on the wall as I feel my way downstairs; breathing alone will do it. This house is my enemy. I am my enemy.

Billy the dog lies flat as a cut-out in front of Mr Stadnik's door. He doesn't raise his head, but I see his open eye, liquid in the moonlight. He thuds his tail once, twice, as I pass. I go careful and blind, my tongue stuck in my mouth, holding my breath. I have to make sure.

The living room is washed with a pale blue shine; everything looks unreal in this light, like in the films. My grandfather's high-back chair, Mr Stadnik's armchair with the spring poking out, my own wooden one with the cushion on it and the name carved in the back. They look as if they're waiting for the three bears to come and try them for size. The fire is out. Above it is the mirror, dead as the fire. I have to make sure. I have to climb up and look in and make sure. I take the chair, slide it, drag it, rucking the mat in front of the hearth, scraping the flagstones into a screech. It's too late now to stop myself. Not edging up into the glass. Not going sideways like a thief, stealing in from the corner of the frame. I will face her, straight on, wide-eyed, as wide as my eyes will go, wider and wider to let in the light from the darkness, wider and wider so that I can be sure. I have to be sure she wasn't just hiding, trying to trick me. But I can't see a single thing. It's black as a hole. No one looks back at me, there is no one on the inside. I get as close as I can, trying to see through the mirror, to see through it and beyond it, beyond the glass sheet, and the silver, through the wooden back of the frame and the rose wallpaper and the chimney and out through the brick and into the night. Trailing specks of mortar, black ash, dust, flying in the darkness to seek her out, find the girl, show her that I am me.

~

Mr Stadnik called it my nocturnal adventure. He said the fright could've killed him, seeing me standing up there in front of the mirror, all alone in the dark. Just like a ghost, he said. He had to lift me off the chair and carry me back to my room. He made me get back under the covers. The cold of the sheets set me shivering. He didn't say anything for a while, just sat on the end of my bed and looked at me, in that way he had, a bit like Gloria the Glove, head cocked to the left so one eye appeared higher than the other; as if he'd swallowed a fishbone and was waiting for it to go down.

My soul is young, he said, But this – resting his hand flat over his heart – Is a poor weak thing. Broken many times. It fears a fright.

And then he was silent again, dawn-lit, like Valentino in a pose. Except he was more like Wee Willie Winkie, with his long white nightgown and the net covering his hair. He wasn't wearing the leather cuff. At last, just when I thought he might be angry, he smiled.

You were like the Statue of Liberty, he said, Like so – raising his arm above his head – Stiff like a stick! So I carry you, thus:

And showed me how he caught me under his arm, marching up and down the narrowness of my room like a clockwork soldier. When he reached the door, he clicked his feet together and turned on his heel to face me. Under his nightgown were his boots. But it wasn't that I was noticing: it was his arm. When he held it up to show me how I was, I saw the marks, two short fat streaks of white, raised up along his wrist. From the leather cuff, I thought.

No more sleepwalks, he said, Or we must tie your leg to the bed. Like a prisoner.

He let out a little laugh. I wanted to tell him how free I felt. I wanted to take him back downstairs and show him there was no one in the mirror, that we'd got rid of her at last. But my grandfather's waking cough halted us both. Mr Stadnik bowed at the door and saluted me.

Like the Statue of Liberty, I said, raising my arm.

Yes. Very good, he said, But no more walking about. Sleep must be completed lying down.

Mr Stadnik, why do you wear it if it rubs so much? I pointed at where the cuff would be. He gave a quick look at his wrist, a slow one back at me. He folded like a leaf.

A heart can be broken in many places, he said, shutting the door.

~ ~ ~

What you doing?

A long grey shape pulls itself away from the shadow of the bridge and comes towards me.

This is my bridge, the boy says.

He bends over the railing, lets out a long swinging spit, wipes his mouth along the edge of his sleeve. As if to prove his boast, he vaults onto the ledge, arms out, placing one boot carefully in front of the other, as if he's treading air. He walks a dead straight line towards me. I know him now. He's the one that see-saws like a plank. He's the one I wasn't allowed to stand on the bucket and look at when I was in my grandfather's garden. He's Against The Rules.

I'm just looking, I say, not telling him who it is I'm looking for.

He's tall close up, an older boy. Not in my school. Twelve.
Thirteen, even. Not even going to school maybe.

You must pay a toll if you want to cross.

Standing on one foot, the boy holds out his hand. He's all
balances.

I don't want to cross, I say, I'm just looking.

He follows my gaze down into the back garden where I saw
the girl. I'm looking for a halo of hair.

Can't see nothing, he says.

She's gone, that's why.

Saying it will make it real. The boy studies the space for a
while. Then he smiles, as if he's thinking something funny.
Bronze-coloured eyes, wet-coloured, flint-coloured.

I know 'er, he says, She look like you, 'bor! Only ginger.
She your sister?

I couldn't tell him she was a ghost, or what Mr Stadnik did
to make her go away.

She's gone, I tell you. There's just me now.

~

The boy's name is Joseph Dodd. His eyes are bronze and his
hair is rust and there's a birthmark under his chin. Just like
his sister Alice. He lets me cross the bridge, he even walks
with me, although there's nowhere I particularly want to go.
My father always says Never look a gift horse in the mouth,
and this boy I'm walking with has let me pass over the bridge
for free. I can't refuse. I only wanted to stand there and make
sure, and now I'm going somewhere. I'm crossing the bridge,
which I'm not supposed to do unless it's with my father, when
we pretend to go to the cemetery. He hasn't been to visit me
for ten whole Saturdays. I don't know what's on at the Regent.
I don't know where he is. When my father does come back,
he might not even recognize me.

Do you go to the films? I ask the boy.

He looks at me quickly and away again, like a bird sensing
movement, sticking his chin out just like Alice.

I *can* go, he says, almost as if I was picking a fight, If I mind to, I can go.

It wasn't what I meant. I wanted to ask him if he liked the musicals. We could've sang a tune. We walked a bit further, Joseph hitching up his trousers every few steps, so that if I didn't look straight ahead or up at his face, I had to see the state of his boots. Scuffed and laceless, one tongue flapping and the other ripped completely away.

I get in sometimes, see the cowboys, he says at last.

That's at The Ranch, I say, I've only been once. My father won't take me again.

I don't tell Joseph it's because I don't like the arrows, the whooshing of them as they travel across the screen, their sharp tips puncturing the sky, a tree trunk, a cowboy's arm. I tell him what my father always said; that *he* didn't like the shooting and everyone going bangbang in the seats behind us.

He won't be joining up then, says the boy, If he can't abide a bit of noise.

I think of joining up words. My father taught me to read from his American songsheets. Joining up meant only that to me, but the way Joseph said it, I knew it wasn't about reading.

What's joining up?

Joseph stops dead. He looks into the far distance, like Errol Flynn in *Captain Blood*.

Joining up for the fighting, he says, We're going to a war. I knew what that was. My father had told me about the first one, when he fought my grandfather over a name. Now there was going to be another. Perhaps that's why my father had stopped coming. There'd be guns going off. Screaming. Joseph was staring at me now.

That don't mean you. Not you, 'bor! You're a girl and too young. Me as well, never mind if I'm tall enough. That include your dad, though, even if he don't much like a bang.

He was shouting this last bit, because by then I was running. I had to get home and stop the fighting. I could feel the before times shooting past me like arrows: the ghosts and the red girl in the mirror; my father's eyes lighting up in the cinema dark as he searched out my mother; a locket open like a butterfly in his hand; my grandfather's own hand, his fingers grabbing the skinny neck of a wilting dahlia that mustn't be crooked. I go fast, back along the bridge into Chapelfield and through the gate and up to the door and fumbling for the key dragging its weight around my neck and swinging the door bang against the wall. But there were no bodies. No fighting. Inside, everything was peaceful.

nine

It's a Saturday but I'm wearing my Sunday best. My grand-father polished my boots first thing, muttering to himself as his ridged yellow fingernails pinched at the knots Mr Stadnik tied in them, muttering to himself as he spat, then rubbed, then spat at the leather. Now they're on my feet, gleaming and straight out in front of me on the boards of the wagon. I hardly dare let them touch the floor for all the muck and bits of straw on it. My dress is stiff at the collar and tight under the arms and on my head I'm wearing an unfamiliar brown hat. It smells of must, and I don't want it on because there's no need to hide my telltale hair any more, but my grandfather issued me with some new rules before we set off: I must look my best and must not fidget. I must always be a good girl.

Mr Stadnik has got me tight. The wagon is full of children and us. We're going to the country. Billy the dog is coming too. He barks as more children load up behind us, so much that they won't get on; the girls clutch each other's arms, their petticoats flirting in the breeze. It makes Billy worse, all the fuss. I've half a mind to tell them, but everyone's offering advice and some of the mothers are saying he shouldn't be allowed up there. I think they mean the dog and not Mr Stadnik, but then a lady steps forward and pokes him on the arm.

You. What d'you think you're up to?

Mr Stadnik says nothing, just grabs hold of Billy, hoiking him by the string and squashing him beneath the plank that we're using as a seat. He still won't stop barking. Mr Stadnik clamps him round the muzzle, holding it fast, while the others climb up.

Coward, says a voice from the crowd.

Spy, shouts another.

Mr Stadnik still says nothing. A blob of spit lands on his cuff. He doesn't look to see where it came from. He takes his handkerchief from his pocket and wipes it away. I look for my grandfather to help, but he isn't coming with us. He's standing on the corner where the mothers and fathers have gathered, ready to wave us off. He's easy to pick out: he's the one with the white hair. It occurs to me that I don't know how old my grandfather is. I think he must be at least a hundred, with hair like that. But he's not infirm. He told us we were all going, but this morning he changed his mind. He says he has to stay home and look after everything. He'll be all on his own, but it doesn't bother him one bit.

Why would I want to go to the middle of nowhere just to stare at a load of cabbages, he said, When I've got the garden to think of?

Think of the child instead, said Mr Stadnik, meaning me. But he wouldn't shift for anything.

Besides, he said, I might be needed.

That made Mr Stadnik laugh. A row followed. They did it in private; only the door slamming at the end of the hall told me it was happening.

Mr Stadnik doesn't think *he'll* be needed, because here he is, saying nothing, with me and our suitcases, mine with my name on it, and his battered and brown with peeling stickers all over. We've got Billy the dog on a string, a parcel of sandwiches my grandfather gave us to eat on the way, and another one shaped like a box for Aunty Ena, who we're going to stay with until It's all over. We're loaded up where the sheep should be and we're setting off to the country. I'm excited by the wagon, despite the crowd and the spitting and the sight of my grandfather's white hair. I've never ridden in a motor before. I look at the other children for faces I know, but there's no one. Just as we're full to burst, up runs Alice Dodd, yelling. She hasn't got a suitcase or anything. She wears a print dress just like mine with thick black stockings, and a hat stuck flat on her head. Under the brim, her eyes are as pink as a pig's. She doesn't give me a second glance, even when I call to her. Mr Stadnik puts his hand on my arm.

Leave her be, now, he says, There is a time for words and a time for silence. This is the time for silence.

Billy the dog uncurls his purple tongue and snuffles up the sheep droppings on the floor of the wagon. I'm waiting for Alice's brother to jump on next, but no one else comes and we must be ready now because the driver shouts for us to mind out and pushes the gate up and bolts it. Everyone in the wagon is waving, and on the street, the mothers and fathers are waving back. But not *my* father, who never comes. My grandfather raises his hand to the air, as if he's testing the wind. His face is black in shadow and his hair glows silver on top where the sun shines through it. But my father never comes. We're pulling away from the market square, slowly so the wavers can wave, handkerchiefs flittering, mothers crying, the smoke of the engine billowing behind us, passing the cinema on the left where the girls dance in patterns, and round the corner, waving, past The Flag where there were stories and ginger beer, and further on, past Fisher's the pawn-broker, and still my father never comes. It's there I see it, quick, but no mistake. Hanging limp in the window, no body to fill it, is my father's suit. Pulling away from our past life like an arrow, like gunshot, I wave goodbye to his suit as we pass.

protection

It's called a skullcap. I remembered it too late, half a mile from Paradise and on my way into the city. The skullcap is the thing that's used to keep the real hair down so that the wig-hair can sit nicely on the head. When you first put it on, it itches you, mad as maggots. It takes a while before you get used to it. First it feels mad, and you can't help but slide your finger up between the rubber and the hair, going for a good scratch. It's like nail biting, or a nervous cough. Once you start, you don't know you're doing it. You can't stop.

You'll get an infection, said Jean Foy, slapping at my fingers. Leave it be, now, she said, You must get used to it. At night, after we had washed and knelt and prayed, Jean Foy wrapped my hands in bandages, bending the fingers over into a fist and winding the gauze over the knuckles, neat and closed and tight. To stop me scratching; to allow me to become the person I should be, in order to suit her. In order to suit her and Bernard Foy, my saviour and saint. Not Jean Foy now, not Bernard Foy yet. First, there's Aunty Ena surrounded by her sky.

Eventually, you stop feeling the itch. Then the other thing feels strange: the *not* wearing the hairpiece, as if you've got too much space around your head, or the air's too light. I never liked the sensation; if I'm true, I enjoyed the weight of hair on me. It made me feel nearer to the ground; a way to stop myself from floating off into space.

There's a new method nowadays I expect, but back then, before my time, that was how you wore your hairpiece: comb the real hair flat, grease it down if necessary; ease on the cap and hold it in place with two long pins, one behind each ear. Pull on the hairpiece, more pins to secure it. What Carol in Paradise was seeing was just the skullcap. I hadn't taken it off since I don't know when. It was glued, nearly. She made a good job of removing it. At least it didn't smell.

ten

Cabbages as far as the eye can see: my grandfather was nearly right about that. Aunty Ena's house is set bang in the middle of two long fields. It's called Stow Farm, but it doesn't look like the farms in the films: there aren't any animals on it, and from the back approach there's nothing but ridges of caked earth, row upon rutted row of dusty tracks, slivering into the distance. The only things growing are the stinging nettles, clumped up in gangs round the edge of the fence that borders the house. At the front, where other people might have a garden, Aunty Ena has a field full of cabbages, rotting where they sit. At the far end, a scarecrow tilts in the wind. The sky's very big here; it's almost all the view there is. That, and the fields full of stinking brown.

We arrived in the dark. Waiting at a turn in the road was Aunty Ena. She was holding a lantern on a stick, like Florence Nightingale come to greet the wounded. With the light at her shoulder, her face glowed like a ghoul. Me and Mr Stadnik were the only ones left on the wagon. The driver asked Aunty Ena if maybe he could stay the night before setting back.

There is a Public House in Stradsett that will Meet your Needs, she said, very sharp and sounding a lot like my grandfather. I expected from her tone there would be more rules to follow. I was wrong.

I got a proper look at her when we got inside. Tall, thin,

with hands like paddles. There was just her in the house, the scent of recent polish and, underneath, lingering and stale, the smell of dead cabbage on the air.

She showed us our rooms. Mr Stadnik's was a dark square with a skylight over a narrow iron bed. There was a wardrobe with a sprig of rosemary on the middle shelf, and a washstand with a jug and bowl, empty apart from a dead spider. Mr Stadnik peered up into the skylight and smiled.

How charming! he said, I shall see the stars shooting!

I immediately wanted this room. Mine was only a few steps along the corridor, but it had an ordinary window and an ordinary bed. No stars shooting.

Ah, but here now, said Mr Stadnik, calling me over to the window, Here, you can view the whole world.

That was true enough. The whole world as far as it went, right to the edge of the horizon; the whole world of mud-track yard and long brown field and the sky hanging like dirty washing.

Aunty Ena's tour was brief, a hand flung out to this room or that, and so quick that all I could get was a glimpse of half-light, the bare reflection of a window on a wall.

There's nothing in them, not a thing. Everything is sold. She put a hand to her throat, as if she'd said something rude. Mr Stadnik made a little cooing noise.

Times are difficult, he whispered.

Yes they are – her voice went high – Especially out here. People like Albert don't realize. It's harder out here. There's nothing, you see, nothing and no one. And he sends the child! Mr Stadnik just rested his hand on my head and kept it there.

He has sent me too, he said at last, To help you. I would be glad to do it.

The tour ended in the kitchen. Everything was set out in a heap on the table, cups with broken handles and saucers piled up on each other, a silver toast rack with no toast in it and a pitcher half-full with dusty water and a small can of jam with a tarnished spoon stood up in its crusted centre.

You'll see I don't have visitors, she said, her hands splashing at the space in front of her, So you won't mind helping yourselves. But he – she said, pointing at Billy the dog – Must fend for himself in the barn. No food for animals here.

She left us alone. Whatever Aunty Ena had received in the parcel from my grandfather, which we decided must be food, she wasn't sharing with us. Mr Stadnik set about opening the cupboards. Each one smelled worse than the last, as if the cabbages had invaded every gap with their own ruinous scent.

No food for people here also, he said, lifting the lid off the empty bread barrel. He found some crackers in a wrap of paper on the dresser, took the rime off the jam with a knife, sniffed it then held it out for me to do the same. We ate the crackers dry, straight from the paper, Mr Stadnik chewing slowly and making a face every time he swallowed.

Very good, he said, when we'd finished, Tomorrow, we buy food, and after tomorrow, we make it.
He spread out the crinkled wrap, blowing off the crumbs and pressing it flat with the palm of his hand, and began to make a list.

In the morning, we walked the mile to the village, down the track we rode up the night before. The sky was pearl, heavy as a shroud. The birds weren't singing, there was no wind. Only the sound, growing fainter as we walked, of a piano being played.

~ ~ ~

Ena leans forward, rising off the piano stool in order to watch them go. They are both too short, increasingly so, she thinks, craning her long neck to follow their path into the village. He is older than she imagined, fifty at least; he wears ridiculous clothes. But his eyes are full of light. He's from somewhere else; he speaks like a hero in a romance. She imagines where somewhere else might be, and how a hero in a romance might speak, even if he's far too short to be a proper hero. The child is peculiar. Ena sings the word. That hair, that white hair, like a starlet. Like a child star. The child star and the romantic hero are holding hands as they negotiate the wide ditch at the bottom of the track that separates Ena's land from everywhere else in the world.

~ ~ ~

The shop has no name above it, nothing in the window but a sheen of white steam. The only reason we know it's a shop is because the man that's been trudging in front of us along the lane turns abruptly into the doorway and we hear the bell. Mr Stadnik holds his finger in the air and smiles at me. He often does this when he makes a discovery.

Inside, there's a counter with a grey cat spread along it, and a woman behind the cat with her hands folded under her pinny. She's talking to the man. She looks at us, but doesn't say hello. At the back of the shop, behind a second counter, another woman in small round glasses is weighing a pile of parcels. She writes on the corner of each one before putting it aside.

Look like 'er gonna spit, Doris, the man says, nodding at the darkening sky outside.

'Bout time 'n'all, she says.

We wait our turn in the darking gloom. It gets so dim in the shop, the cat on the counter goes invisible, nearly, except for its burning eyes. The woman with the parcels has to squint to write on them. The rain falls in a rush against the glass.

Stay steady till it pass, Doris says. The man sits down on a stool next to the counter, running his hand over his face and grinning now at Mr Stadnik.

You take a turn, 'bor, he says, Ise on a promise!

Doris makes no move. It's the other woman who serves us.

She stops her parcel writing, and comes to inspect Mr Stadnik, so close she's practically standing on his toes. She looks him up and down. Her eyes behind her glasses are as big as the cat's.

Can we help you? she says, in a voice that says she can't. Mr Stadnik would take off his hat if he hadn't forgotten it. He bows his head a little instead, smiles at the woman, and produces our list from the pocket of his overcoat.

~

It doesn't blow over. It rains. It rains for the whole day, and then on into the night. It rains the next day and the next day and the next. The dust on the land is picked up by the wind, coating the windows with a film of grit, finding its way into my hair, crunching like salt between my teeth.

Outside, the sky is over everything. Inside, Aunty Ena plays the piano. She hums under her breath. At first, thinking I need to be entertained, she finds things to occupy me.

You ought to *do* something, she says, with a kind of bright terror in her voice, You must do *something*!
She brings me items to polish – blackened pots, a dented brass plate with a milk maid stamped into it, two tarnished spoons, a fistful of knives with ivory handles.

Be careful with those, she says, dropping them with a clash onto the table, We don't want an accident, do we?
Holding the knives with the edge of a duster, I spread the vinegar paste along the blades. I do it with my fingers. It's not the sharp edge making me shudder, it's the feel of bone. I won't touch the handles.

When everything is gleaming, there's nothing left to do but sit. Aunty Ena says she isn't much of a talker, but I don't mind that, because neither was my mother. But my mother never sang the way Aunty Ena does; *that* would've sent the Moons flying to the doctor.

~ ~ ~

Late autumn sun in Chapelfield comes like spring. My grandfather feels it on his head when he's tending the garden, on
his neck as he bends to pull up the weeds encroaching on the
path. He senses the last warmth of it; rain is aching through
his bones. For a while now, the trains on the tracks below
have been more frequent, carry a heavier vibration, as if
they have changed their nature. The rumbling alongside the
garden wall is like a premonition. My grandfather avoids
the wall entirely after a while. He tends to his garden. He
doesn't look up at the sky.

~ ~ ~

Even though it never stops raining, Mr Stadnik sets to work
in the field. He doesn't mind the wet; he doesn't mind that
the earth is sodden and that every morning, whatever had
been dug the day before is turned into a pool of quag. He's
digging a channel, he says, for drainage. Aunty Ena says it
looks more like a moat. Often Mr Stadnik unearths things
buried in the sod: a gnarled beet wearing a smile, a blackened
coin, a small knit of bones. He has a way of dealing with his
finds: the beet is lobbed into a sack, the coin he spits on,
rubbing it with the bulb of his thumb before slipping it into
his pocket. But he is careful with the bones: he makes a tidy
pile on his handkerchief, spread out flat at the edge of the
ditch. I can't think what Mr Stadnik will do with them;
perhaps he's saving the bones for Billy the dog. I know he
hates the feel of them too; I've seen him, pulling the edges
of the bundle together, careful not to touch, his breath short
and heavy and his face like stone.

Billy stays in the barn. He catches rats, I suppose, although
all I ever see him do is bounce backwards and forwards on a
long chain tied to the door. He makes it look like elastic,
running the pure length of it, jerking so hard at the end that,
for a moment, he's flying. His bark is constant, hollow yaps
that sound like someone way off in the distance banging a

piece of iron. But there is no one way off in the distance; there is only distance. Mr Stadnik says you can see your neighbour coming to visit you before he decides to set out. Pleased with this joke, he repeats it to Aunty Ena. She doesn't laugh: she goes very clipped.

Our neighbour is Mrs Myhill, she says, And her daughter, Agnes. You will have met them at the shop. They do not visit.

Aunty Ena spread her arms wide, as if the gesture would explain.

You see, Mr Stadnik, I am an incomer. And you – lifting her hands together now to a point – Will be even less likely to receive visitors. You are a foreigner. You'll find that life is very quiet in the country.

I lie in bed at night, and between the hooting bird and the keening wind, I think about the countryside being quiet. It's not true. Noise fills my sleep: Billy's chain becomes the knocking bones of skeletons as they rise from the fen; the rain is a shower of silver coins; the barking is the scarecrow standing in the far field, knocking his pipe out against the fence. His head is bent to one side and his hair is luminous against the sky. He wears my grandfather's face.

In the rare silence, the moments midway through the chain unravelling and the barking, my mother visits me, smiling, her hair piled up on her head and her bare feet soundless on the dusty track. She's happy to see me, she says, she tells me she is resting, now. She doesn't ask about my father. He never comes back. He stays hanging in Fisher's window, waving like a puppet. There is nothing I can remember to bring him close: no voice, no words. Despite all the stories, he is a shape without a noise. Then the din of the countryside starts up, and they are all lost again inside it.

~

Mr Stadnik is convinced he can make things grow. When the ditch is finished and the digging done, he plants himself at the end of a row and, bending and unbending, prods seed after seed into the soil.

Be good and strong, he tells each one. From far off, it sounds like he's singing. He works without a shirt, and despite the cloud hanging on his shoulder, his skin goes dark as the cuff on his wrist. Aunty Ena leaves off from her piano and takes to looking out of the window. She looks out of the window every day for a week, craning her neck like a giraffe nuzzling a branch. There's nothing to see, except Mr Stadnik getting smaller and smaller as he disappears into the sky, then bigger and bigger as he comes back. Occasionally, she calls me to her side and remarks on his progress.

I've told him, she says, But does he listen? Nothing can grow there. Black land, they call it. Dead land.
The watching softens Aunty Ena. Even though it's dull most days, her eyes are full of light.

Look how far he's got, Lillian, she'll say, He's whizzing through that land!
I don't think he is. To me, having been called to look only a few minutes before, he's inching up the furrow like a worm. But Aunty Ena is content. Sitting in front of the fire, I keep an eye on the hands of the clock, edging the hours into dark. I listen to the slow tick, to the wind, to the squeak of Aunty Ena's sleeve on the window as she wipes her breath from the glass.

~ ~ ~

Chapelfield, and my grandfather moves from kitchen window to hearth and back again. Sometimes he looks at his clock on the mantelpiece. One day, he realizes that what the time is doesn't matter. He lets the clock wind itself down. There is rain on his garden, and snow, and in later days, a sharp, clean sun. Things grow. He lets them grow. Sometimes, when the noises start again above his head, he sits on the upturned bucket behind the cellar door, and remembers me.

~ ~ ~

One Sunday before church, Aunty Ena swaps her black fitted long-sleeved dress for the same in maroon. She wears a white blouse underneath it, with a small round brooch pinned to the collar.

Opal, she says to me, with a crooked smile, Supposed to be unlucky! But superstition is for heathens, Lillian. What is it for?

Heathens, I say, not knowing what one might be.

She turns to Mr Stadnik,

Are you a heathen, Mr Stadnik?

A man prays when he cannot act, he says, sounding like someone else.

Mr Stadnik has never been invited to church with us, even though he walks us to the lane, bowing low as we jump the ditch. If he had a cloak, he says, he would throw it down. It's plain he's keen to go. I would tell him that he's not missing anything. The church is big and rocky on the outside, and inside it's hollow and cold. The vicar speaks the words, Aunty Ena fishes about for the book with the tiny writing in it, everyone starts up singing, and I pretend I am Jonah in the whale.

Today will be different. Aunty Ena tells Mr Stadnik to put on his suit and accompany us. Mr Stadnik doesn't have a suit. He has a jacket with shiny elbows and a stiff shirt with frayed wings, which I think won't do for Aunty Ena. But when he presents himself, standing at the turn of the stairs with his hair slicked flat across his head, smelling of goose fat and rosewater, she blushes and puts her chin on her chest.

How Exotic, she says into her brooch, May I introduce you as Henry?

Mr Stadnik does one of his little bows. He smiles up at her, a show of yellow teeth.

And you may call me Enid, she says.

They walk either side of me, up the lane to the ditch, Mr Stadnik holding my left hand, and Aunty Ena – Enid! –

holding my right. Their hands tight and sweaty, squeezing me between them. There's a break in the air, a smell of matches, a noise like a storm overhead. A point of light runs through me, out of Aunty Ena, up one arm and across my chest and down the other arm and into Mr Stadnik. It grates through my veins like the sound of Billy flying on his chain. My hair rises of its own accord off my scalp. I can feel it lifting.

Oh look! says Aunty Ena, pointing into the distance, A shooting star. Quickly, we must make a wish!
We watch the star fall, which is not a star at all; it's a shard of grey metal with a streak of light attached.

No, Mr Stadnik says, Not a shooting star. What should we do?
A suck of air, a pocket opening in the sky, and then a roar. Aunty Ena starts to run, dragging me with her, and I drag Mr Stadnik. Both of them running now, jerking me off the ground, nothing beneath my feet, my stomach in my throat, all of us running away. It's like riding the gallopers at the fair. They don't stop: I'm strung out between them like a kite and as they run, they laugh, lifting me and swinging me, laughing so hard it's frightening now. Before the corner of the church-yard they stop still and listen. I can hear a wheeze like a bellows in Mr Stadnik's throat. He leans on a headstone while Aunty Ena composes herself. Mr Stadnik repeats his question.

What should we do?

We should pray for them, Aunty Ena says.
Mr Stadnik wipes his forehead with the tips of his fingers.

But we'll tell someone? he says, Someone can help them?

No. It will draw attention to— she corrects herself – Where none is wanted. We didn't really see it, did we? If we were looking the other way, we might not have seen it. And they may be safe, after all. We might cause a fuss over nothing. I want Mr Stadnik to challenge her, but he turns away from the thin line of smoke in the distance, turns and nods, as if this is the right thing to do. Mr Stadnik said people pray when they cannot act; and I'd like to believe that Mr Stadnik is always right.

~

We didn't see a shooting star. According to Aunty Ena, we didn't see anything. But whatever it was or wasn't, I would like to see it again. I would like to make a wish.

By the time we get to the church, Aunty Ena and Mr Stadnik are silent, ashamed in their looks. They stand apart and pretend they are strangers. Instead of praying, instead of pretending to be Jonah, I close my eyes and wish anyway.

eleven

Perched like a crow in a treetop, Joseph Dodd watches. From the tower of Trinity Church, he has a clear view of the surrounding flatland, the great sweep of Middle Drain cutting through it like a slake. On fine days he can see the old windmill on the lip of the horizon, and another church, floating on a distant field. More often the air is mist, drifting like liquid in front of his eyes, so he can only see what lies immediately below. Much of the land here is busy with work: women in overalls with high-pitched voices. There is nothing remarkable in this for him, nothing he would need to keep secret. Nothing that might *betray* his secret. His interest lies in the two fields either side of Stow Farm. This is it, a forbidden interest from a forbidden vantage point.

Joseph sits on the ledge, dangling his legs and smoking. His right arm is bound up in a sling. If people ask him how it happened, he lowers his head. Father Peter sent him here to mend, and because his sister Alice was sent here too. He has yet to find her among the fen and flat, but Joseph has found someone else.

At first, he only saw the man down there, coming and going along the track, digging a trench which filled overnight into swamp. Joseph recognized his gait, the small, hunchedness of him, but couldn't remember where from. He watched the man, and the dog in the yard, leaping backwards and forwards as if plagued by a hornet. There was a stiff old woman who sometimes came to the door and called at the man; he had seen her in the village too, bending her way up to the church in the field. And then he saw the girl. He knew her straight away. Hair like glass: the girl on the bridge at Chapelfield, who said she had a red-haired sister, waving from the wall in the garden down below.

He watches as at last the three figures negotiate the ditch at the edge of the farm. Now the man will bend from the waist, flourishing an arm, and make his way back up towards the house. Now he will stop and look over his shoulder, like a reluctant dog. Now the man will stand and wait as the two walk away, down past the shop, left up the lane, and out of sight to the church. But this time the man doesn't stop, doesn't bow, doesn't stand scuffing his boots in the dirt. He walks with them, holding the hand of the girl with the hair, walking with them all the way. Joseph has no time to consider this development; a flash of white light in the corner of his eye, a sharp metal wail, distracts him. Above their heads – Look out! – Joseph cries, still not used to the way the perspective is flattened, the plane turning on its nose, cutting the day in two, dying. Joseph stares open mouthed as it sinks into the fen.

He would like to run down and tell the vicar what he's seen. But he isn't allowed up the tower; he would no longer be able to sit with the birds and the bird's eye view, watch the girl as she makes her way to church. Joseph decides to say nothing. He knows how the fen will suck any weight into itself, remembers the cow in the bog, no trace of it by the time the farmer arrived. The plane's cockpit is under now; in a few hours, even the tail will be invisible. Joseph decides it's already too late.

~ ~ ~

Aunty Ena's wish came true. Mr Stadnik's boots with the knotted laces now sit side by side outside her bedroom door;

unpolished and caked in mud, with the socks stuffed into them. I wished for my hair to always be white, a cake on my birthday, and that I would be allowed to go to school in the village. I wished for Billy the dog to come back in out of the weather.

That one didn't work. He stays outside, grating his chain through the night, while my grandfather the scarecrow stands alone in the far field, bending his white head under the weight of rain. I lie in my bed, listening to the usual noises of the night, and to the new ones: the laughs and sighs and muffled ohs from the room over my head. They sound like falling stars. I wished again that night, because I'd forgotten just about everyone. I wished them all back: my father, my grandfather, my mother. I wanted her to get out of her bed on the other side of wherever she's gone and see what kind of a house Aunty Ena keeps, ghosts or no ghosts. I wished for the men in the plane to be safe and not buried in the fen. I wished them all back.

When nothing happened, I consulted Mr Stadnik. I found him at the end of the field, whistling to himself and scraping the earth with a pitchfork.

How long does it take for a wish to come true? I asked. He gave me a guilty look.

That would depend on whatever the wish might be, he said.
He examined the end of the fork very carefully, pulled a stone out from between the tines and bowled it in front of him. I couldn't tell him what my wishes were, so I said nothing.

Sometimes, he said, It is better to be grateful for small things.

I wished for Billy to come back indoors, I said, That's not such a big thing.
Mr Stadnik smiled.

Ah! he said, But what does Billy wish for?

~

I think this is the pattern of days and nights; I think it means forever. Mr Stadnik works in the fields during the day and sleeps above my head in Aunty Ena's room at night. On Sundays, we all go to church, like a normal family; they swing me over the puddles and ditches, and let out their guilty laughter, and sit silently on either side of me in Aunty Ena's pew. Except no one speaks to us, and the women move very deliberately out of the way as we pass, their eyes sharing a joke with each other. Their bullying is refined and cool, but they are still bullies. Aunty Ena shows that she's above it, holding her head high and wearing a haughty expression.

They were always against me, she tells Mr Stadnik, And now they're jealous. They just want what I've got. Well, it's none of their business!

Mr Stadnik doesn't think so.

Jealousy. It's a powerful weapon in the hands of an enemy, he says, watching the sky. At Stow Farm, this is all we ever do: looking out of the window at the rain and mist, speaking of the weather, which does nothing but hang, thick as a bag, over everything. I think this is the pattern.

The newness, when it comes, is unexpected: I wake up, and the sky has moved. It's moved about three miles up in the air.

At last, says Aunty Ena, bashing at the windows with her fist in an attempt to force them open.

That's torn it up, says Mr Stadnik, pulling on his boots and stuffing his socks in his trouser pockets, Now everyone will want to know your business. You see if I'm wrong.

It's the cleanest deepest light, it shows me the green of Aunty Ena's eyes, the black under Mr Stadnik's, the pinkish stains around Billy's mouth, the house in its shroud of dust.

Outside, this new light gives me a windmill where there was only mist, a long road where there was water, the sail of a wherry, gliding through a field. I can't think why Mr Stadnik is so cross; it's such a beautiful, clear world. When I ask him, he holds his finger under his nose.

What? I say, not getting a clue, What is that?

The corn, he says, although we have no corn, It makes me cry. It will all be ruined.

Mr Stadnik is right about nearly everything. The clear light brings a visit from the vicar. The clear light shows that he lives only a field away, but Mr Stadnik says he wouldn't trouble to visit in poor weather, on account of maybe falling in the fen. He is banished to the scullery when the vicar comes; sitting on the pantry steps, ranting under his breath about fair-weather friends and muddy skirts and women's hands, while I am brought out for inspection. The vicar catches me by the shoulder, turning me round on the spot, staring intently at my head. He doesn't mention Mr Stadnik, and he speaks in code to Aunty Ena. He says I am impression-able, unschooled; I will soon be a young woman. That she must set a good example. He's sure that she would understand his meaning.

I see now what Mr Stadnik feared. The clear light shows him that there is nowhere to hide; it shows me too that wishes don't come true. No one comes back; not my grandfather, or my father, or my mother, or the men in the plane. And my hair at the roots has begun to fill with red: slow, like blood, seeping out from beneath my scalp; all our secrets will be revealed.

twelve

Mr Stadnik left me in the middle of the night. He didn't tell me he was going. It was one of the new things, like the sun that was too bright, and his polished boots, and him putting his socks in his pockets. New things were happening fast; new things were piling up. I heard noises in the night, a man shouting, a single bang like a door in a draught, two sets of footsteps, light and heavy, crossing the yard. I heard the absence of a grating chain, and the nothingness that the wind leaves when it falls. But I didn't see him go.

The morning was still. Downstairs, Aunty Ena was sitting at the piano with her fingers held over the keys, as if she was waiting for someone to crank her up. Her gaze was fixed on the sheet music on the stand. She didn't move her head when she saw me, just her eyes.

Mr Stadnik had to leave, she said, He said to say goodbye.

What about Billy?

I shifted from one leg to the other. My boots weren't where I'd left them; the flags were burning cold.

He's taken him. This is no place for a pet. Go and put your boots on, she said, her voice under ice, Henry – Mr Stadnik – has left them for you in the scullery.

But my feet had got stuck to the floor. I didn't trust my legs. Aunty Ena bent her head, pulled a handkerchief from her sleeve.

We'll manage without them, she said, in a crooked voice, We'll just pretend they never existed. And if anyone asks, say nothing. It's nobody's business, after all.

~

Mr Stadnik had polished my boots and retied the knots with new laces made out of twine. He'd left them side by side, in the correct order, although as soon as I looked at them, I knew which one was the right and which was the wrong, without knowing how I knew. He would've been pleased at that. The boots had nothing inside them. I was hoping for a note, something from him, anything to tell me where he'd gone, and why. I pushed my fingers up into the dents made by my toes, all around, pulled out the tongue and held each boot up to the windowlight; still nothing.

His room was airless, dead quiet. Nothing there I could say was his. The wardrobe door was open, empty except for the stick of rosemary, crumbling to dust when I touched it. Nothing under the bed, his washbowl dry when I ran my finger round it; not a single hair, nothing. Nothing to say he lived. I looked in every other room. They were just as Aunty Ena said they were, empty, apart from the one above the parlour where the faint sound of music rose like vapour. I could picture her below, sitting at the piano, riddling her hands on the keys. Everywhere empty. At last, I tried the handle on the door of her bedroom. It turned but did not open.

All the colours smelled different in this new light. I walked into its sharpness; searched the field beyond the yard, the gullies on either side, and right up to the fence around the church plantation, where I wasn't allowed to go. I studied the trees inside it, looking for a sign; only dark in there, and the far-off, hollow cry of a bird. In the yard, Billy the dog's chain was snaked along the ground in a long length, as if he finally snapped it and went flying off into the sky. Mr Stadnik had given me a clue after all: he didn't like the corn, he said, what would Billy wish for, he said. Billy hated the chain and the outside; he would rather be back in Chapelfield. They would be keeping my grandfather company, Mr Stadnik sipping tea off his spoon and arguing, and Billy under the chair, his head poking out between Mr Stadnik's feet, just where he liked it best. Perhaps that's what he had wished for. They would have walked back together, starting at dawn. It was such a long way. Perhaps that's why they didn't take me; perhaps they thought I'd slow them down.

They would be at Chapelfield, is what I told myself, as if telling myself would make it real. But like a bird in panic, the fluttering inside me wouldn't rest. I searched the lane, the barn, calling for them, shouting their names, and then I searched the house again. I didn't want to believe that they'd gone without me. When there was nowhere else to look, I stopped looking.

sticks

What's in a name? I'll tell you. Everything, that's what: lies and truth alike. I've been called a hobo and a tramp and down-and-out; a dipso, a wino, even though I don't care for it. I only have it for medicinal purposes: to keep warm, to keep the ghosts away. Keep them at arm's length, if you understand me. I've been called a beachcomber too. I'm rather fond of that. I like the idea of me – the other me, the one who's living the life I haven't got – making scratches in the sand, the sun on her back, rake in hand. Once a woman at the food counter in Marks and Spencer's called me a derelict. Precisely, if I'm true, she *referred* to me as a derelict, which is not the same thing at all. She pointed her pink fingernail in my direction and asked the security guard if he couldn't 'do something about that derelict'. I almost turned round to see what on earth she might be talking about. Now I'm lying and that's *not* true. I knew what she meant, all right. Who she meant. I was used to it by then.

The security guard asked me if I intended to buy anything. It was after talking had stopped; I couldn't say what my intentions were. I couldn't say it was warm and dry inside. I couldn't say a single word that would have any meaning for him. I couldn't say I thought I was a ghost, how on earth could he see me. Or that I wasn't doing anybody any harm. I wasn't a thing unallowed, a symbol on a sign with a red line through it: a dog, or a cigarette with a smouldering tip. I simply couldn't say. And then it occurred to me that the woman was right. She had spectacles hanging from a gold chain, and wore the kind of hair they give old women these days, beige and woolly and puffed up like cotton wool. She was a lady with a purse in her hand and jewellery on her fingers and an orange mouth which let the words come out in the right order. And I was a ship at sea.

I went outside and had a shout. Don't ask me what the words were, it's letting them out that counts, not the order, not the meaning. Although if something does come out right, it helps. But it isn't essential. It's not a requirement of the shouting.

~

I have been Lillian and Patricia and Patsy. Mr Stadnik called me none of these. He called me Princess. I had nothing to remember him by. Scanning the room, wild with grief, my fingers trailing the edges, the creases, the folds; for a speck of dust, a single hair, anything to say he was here on the earth. I had been taught to believe in artefacts: to balance them, store the person in an object. The only thing he had ever given me – a toy made from an old glove – was stolen. Alice Dodd could never have known how much it would mean, once it was gone.

All my other bits, I kept in my case. And it was safe, it was safe for years. No one would want to steal an old cardboard thing. And besides, it had my name on it. No one would want that.

thirteen

Aunty Ena has put the maroon dress and the unlucky opal out of sight; she now wears no adornment of any kind. She doesn't play the piano any more, doesn't sing; and she never mentions Mr Stadnik. She won't talk about anything. She moves round me as if I am invisible, and soon I am, except if I make my way down the track towards the ditch, and then she takes me by the arm and turns me back inside, without a single word.

The windows grow dim with grime, making the inside soft as gauze against the prickly light. We don't look out; there is nothing to see we haven't seen before. The horizon stretches away as it always did, without needing us to remark on it.

One evening, a face appears at the glass, moonlit and grinning. I think it is a ghost, imagining that this is how it was for my mother at the end, and how soon my death would follow. But my Aunty Ena sees it too; she'll have no truck with ghosts. She goes out into the dark and speaks with it, comes back carrying two gargoyle masks that she throws straight into the pantry, fierce, walloping the back wall.

After that she buys tape at the post office, and has black cloth delivered for the windows. It's night all day then, except if I stand at the back door, where the daylight is harsh and full of tiny arrows. Aunty Ena turns the mirrors to the walls, for which I'm grateful, and covers the tap in the yard with a floor rag, binding it with string. The barn is locked. There is no need to use it. We bring her mattress from her room, dragging and pushing and sliding it down the stairs. It is the last thing we do. The upstairs is abandoned to itself; we sleep together on the floor in front of the fire. I like it; the nearness of her, the faint talcum smell and her thin arms golden in the firelight as she lets down her hair last thing. I listen to her breathing in the night. All this is to keep the ghosts away. Aunty Ena breaks her silence. She says No.

You are a very silly girl. There's no such thing as ghosts. We're having a war.

It was comforting to me to think that somewhere, my grandfather and father were still battling it out, still there, fighting over a name. Only later, the comfort leaves: it's not that sort of war at all. It's another thing completely.

~ ~ ~

At Chapelfield, the garden grows wild. Brambles curving over the path, the wall shaking itself down at the far corner, brick by brick, dropping onto the railway sidings below. With his hands in his lap, my grandfather sits under the elder tree. In the house, he sits under the stairs. Silence all around him, soft as a newborn. He thinks the quiet is outside, in the world. He thinks it has been growing steadily, creeping up, after all that noise. He doesn't understand, as people do who realize they are going deaf, that the world is pulling away from him. He doesn't think, after the screams and screaming bombs, that it's a bad thing, this silence. When he speaks, which he rarely does these days, he can still hear his own voice in his head. So he knows it's not that. It's not deafness, only quiet after bedlam, like the clear air after a storm. He thinks of me, and of Mr Stadnik, hoping we stay safe, hoping we are happy.

~

In another part of the city, a blue suit hangs in the window of the pawn shop. It jostles for space with other suits in more tasteful hues. They remain unclaimed.

~ ~ ~

We eat what there is, where we find it. Hunger is our companion. Scouring the earth for vegetables, we walk minute steps along the side of the verge where the beets and potatoes were bagged. Nearly all are gone; the few that are left behind are wormy and black. We eat standing up, wherever we happen to stop. Crumbs on the piano lid, the floor, the seat of the couch. Later when she finds them, Aunty Ena picks them off and puts them in her mouth, absently, without thought to what it is she might be chewing on. She won't sit at the kitchen table. I think she sees Mr Stadnik there, his napkin, big as a tablecloth, tucked neatly at his throat, his dainty fingers marking the air as he describes the progress of his day. She wears the memory of him in her face. At times during the day, I will find her lying on the mattress, her head beneath the piano. The world gives her a headache, she says, when she's tired of me asking. But it's a quiet world for us. It makes me long for Billy's hammering bark and the grating chain. Mr Stadnik goes very small in my mind, even smaller than real life: tiny, far away, vanishing over the edge of the horizon, until he is doll-sized and Billy at his heel is no bigger than a flea. He's barking, but I can't hear him.

We see no one except each other; we leave off speaking, not even to remark on the weather. Aunty Ena's words are few and carefully chosen:

God watches over us, she says, as if watching alone can make a difference to how hungry I am. Occasionally, when she senses that I've been out further than the bottom of the track, she'll look me in the eye.

God sees everything.

Inside, we see nothing. But from the back door, I can make

out people in the distance, horses in the field, and the scarecrow, hanging his head. But no one comes near, not even the vicar. After that one visit, he doesn't trouble us again. I stand at the back door, I walk the lane, circle the yard in a perfect round – anywhere, just to be out of the house. I see sky and land, sky and land, until the sky becomes the land and I can no longer tell where one begins and the other ends. I see birds in that first black summer, and then not a single one, as if they too had abandoned us.

fourteen

God sees everything, but he mustn't see me with Joseph Dodd. I'm down at the far end of the track, where I shouldn't be, looking for berries. It's the second summer without Mr Stadnik and Billy. They're not in my dreams any more. I've been here forever, with my aunt, with not a single other person: no one to talk to, no one to tell me that I've grown as tall as my mother was, or that my red hair is Telltale. No one to call me by name.

He saunters up the dusty path, hidden most of the way by the cow parsley, grown wild with the sunshine. He could have dropped from the sky. He is as tall as a tree. He's got no shoes on, his hair's all sticking out. I don't know what Aunty Ena will think if she sees him standing in the lane. He's got a big wide mouth. Eyes glittering like flint. He greets me.

'Bor.

I'm wearing one of Aunty Ena's summer dresses. It's too short at the knee, or the fabric is too thin: whatever it is, the dress feels wrong on me now, as if it isn't there at all. And I've got no hat; my hair's stuck to my head with sweat and grease. I don't recall the last time it was washed.

Found any? he says, eyeing the scratches on my hands.
I shake my head at him. He smiles, scuffing the dirt with his naked toe.

Want to find any?

I shake my head again, and at this first meeting, he just moves away, slow, like a cart horse, kicking up the dust on the road behind him.

The second time he comes, he stands and looks. Saying nothing, standing there, one hand on his hip, his shoulders shiny and conker-brown against the white of his vest. Making the day even hotter than it is; unbearably hot, so I have to take off my shawl to stop the heat of his look on me. He smiles as I do it. Next time, I tell myself, I'll do it again. And I'll wash my hair.

But next time, he's holding something. With the sun right above us, there's nowhere to hide. Aunty Ena is lying down in the darkness, her head under the piano, having a headache. God is in his heaven. The giant boy has his fist held in front of him, heavy as a maul.

Can I come down? he says, nodding at the house, Got something for you.

No, you can't.

My voice sounds faint in my ears. I'm not used to the sound. It can't be loud enough, anyway, because he doesn't stop. He walks steadily towards me, jumping the ditch, traipsing over the stones beneath his feet as if they're chaff. He's so near, I could tilt his chin, see Alice Dodd's birthmark underneath it. Closer still, and he's way tall, so I can see it anyway: a tea-stained clover.

My aunt doesn't like visitors, I say, turning away.

That's all right, he says, following close, I arn't visiting her. I'm visiting you, Beauty.

He goes ahead of me, sidelong around the corner of the barn.

It's locked, I say.

I know that.

Round the back, over the stile into the church plantation, and down through the thicket where I never go. The scarecrow can't see us, Aunty Ena can't see us; no one can. This is the beginning. I follow him. He sits down on a stretch of moss, leans back, grins. I take off my shawl. He smiles again, opening his fist. It's full of berries. This is the beginning of everything.

Have one, he says.

They are small and warm and sweet.

God can't see us here.

~ ~ ~

She's counting the years. Ena lying down, so close to the pedals that if she turns her head she can see herself reflected. She longed to press them when she first learned to play. Too small to reach, her feet dangling in mid-air, and the piano teacher saying in his soft brown voice, No need just now, learn the span now, his hand making a starfish on the keys. What was his name? Something foreign, something like Stadnik. No, she's getting confused. Small things betray her. She thought Henry was a romantic hero, because he spoke like a prince. Not a risk, not a threat. She couldn't protect him, and would not be allowed to keep him. The villagers had made it clear enough: any foreigner was unwelcome. She thought they could brave it out. But the vicar's words should have warned her.

You're putting everyone in danger to sate your lust, he said, enjoying his moment. Think of the poor child, he said, spinning her round and staring at her hair. The girl's hair. Extraordinary, platinum hair, like a starlet. And that wasn't real either, tarnishing like cheap metal, growing out red as rust.

~ ~ ~

What is it?

Joseph puts his finger to his lips,

Shhh, he goes.

He creeps up to the edge of the field, ducking low to avoid being seen. Puts his hand round the far side of the post, pulling at the thing, twisting it, until he's free again and running back breathless.

There you go, Beauty, he says, throwing the bundle of feathers at my feet.

What is it?

He cocks his head to one side,

Don't you know a bird when you see one? That's a crow. They nail 'em there, he says, pointing to the fence, Keep the pests off.

The smell was rotten: a green, retching stink.

What do I want that for? I say, through my fingers.

He frowns at me, turning the bird with his toe.

We're going to bury him, he says, lifting the bent wing in a pinch, That's no place for it. Birds ought to be flying, not nailed on a bit of wood. Not nailed up for everyone to see.

Where? I say, looking at the dry, cracked earth around us.

Over, he says, pointing to the high grass in the distance, It's easy, everything sink in that. Sink in a minute. Cows, horses, wagons.

Aeroplanes, I say, watching his face.

Birds, he says, Men.

~

We're fast, but the flies are faster. They thicken the air with the noise of heat, coming from nowhere to find the bird. Joseph runs to free himself from them; up ahead of me, the bird swings in his fist and the wings flap open like a wound. I can't keep up. Over, Joseph had said, but it's straight as an arrow, through the fields, into the reeds and tall grass bordering the edge of Middle Drain. Up close, the windmill stands massive on the skyline. Land turns to water under my feet, softening between my toes, sucking me in. I look up to find Joseph, and he's gone. He *can't* be gone; there's nowhere to hide under this sky. Standing still, all I can hear is the blood rushing in my head. Everything can sink in the fen, he said, sink in a minute. I call his name. I call his name and I call

God's name and I call until I'm hoarse; I'm calling, I'm roaring. He's all I have in the world. I make a wish, I promise, cross my heart and hope to die. I'm roaring in the stillness, turning around, listening for the haze of flies, anything, any sound: and then he comes out of the earth, hand over hand, sticky as the mud that nearly took him.

Careful, he says, backing me away. Close up, his face is ash, his skin shivering and dotted with black specks. The bird is gone.

Nearly buried us both, he says, trying to make a joke of it.

Don't, I say, Don't ever leave me again.

I make him promise that he won't.

~

Joseph knows all the birds; some by name and some by call. He says Father Peter gave him a book when he was in hospital, full of pictures. I ask him what he was there for.

Broke a wing, he says, Couldn't fly for a bit.

Mainly, he says, he learns by watching: from the tower, stalking the fen like a hunter, lying near the reed-beds, listening. I tell him about me, how I was called one thing, then another, and another.

A bird can have lots of names too, and with a knowing smile, And more than one colour. Doesn't alter what they are, doesn't stop 'em flying. They don't care what other people call 'em.

He shows me a feather, golden brown. When I ask him where it's from, he gives a slow cry, animal sounding, nearly pain.

That's from a boomer, he says, turning the feather in the sunlight, A bittern, too, it's called. They say the sound's bad luck.

I've never heard it, I say, superstitious now.

Maybe you won't, he says, They're like us, they keep away from the world – trailing the feather along my arm.

Getting hot now, he says, leaning back to stare up through the trees, Take that shawl off, won't you?

Joseph's stories are about priests and bells and babies at the font. He talks all the time, of towers and earthquakes, hiding and secrets. Undoing the laces on my dress.

Look, he says, catching a strand of my hair and holding it up to the light, Them above us would want it for the angels. I can tell him anything; talking comes easy now. I confess to Mr Stadnik's dye, now long grown out, about how my hair is Telltale. Joseph gives me a dark look.

My mother always say there's no mistaking a Dodd, he scratches at the birthmark under his chin, We got our stamp, and you, Beauty – tangling my hair between his fingers – You got yours.

The birthmark under his chin is perfectly smooth. Between the talking and the stories, is bliss.

We must have a plan, he says, laying me down into the moss; and we do plan, afterwards, telling each other that we'll run away. We'll run away, we'll do it tomorrow, to the end of the world.

Through the summer, and on through the year; into green, then russet, the brown stings of bracken, until the sky is ice blue through the naked trees above our heads. We lie down on the earth, and when it's too cold, we lie on sacking. The year turns itself over, another summer comes. We promise each other, every day, we'll run away tomorrow.

stones

Sometimes talking's like being behind glass, the words can be hard to fathom. I couldn't tell with Carol whether I was near or far in my talking. I took out my plastic bag with the face on it, and showed her the angel hair inside it. She pulled a face.

Ur. It looks very . . . musty, she said.

She didn't want to touch it, I could tell. I put the bag away again. It wasn't helping.

Why not make a list, she said, You know, of all the things you've lost.

Got stolen, I said, not liking her now.

All the things you've got stolen, she said, And then you could show it to the police.

She went away to get a piece of paper and a pen. I sat in the cubicle; I was thinking about the bag in my pocket when I heard them laughing, her and the other girl called Debs, and in the gap in the curtain Debs was waving her hand in front of her and bending double. Her face was still very pink.

A woman arrived with a heap of dresses to try on. Carol showed her into the other changing room and pulled the curtain on her. I could feel the heat of the woman as she squeezed herself into the clothes, zipping and breathing, her body smell leaking through the gaps, over the partition, filling my air. I'm glad I didn't smell like that.

When Carol came back, she didn't have any paper in her hand, or a pen; she had a hat. Two hats.

Here you are, she said, Can't have you going out in the weather without something on your head. Which do you prefer?

I looked at them for a bit. One was a peaked cap with a squiggle on the front and a navy trim. Not me, I know when a hat looks ridiculous. The other one was a beret. A *berrett*.

That one.

She put it on my head.

Come on, time to face your public, she said, suddenly very brisk. She sounded odd, as if she was sharing a joke – but not with me. I wanted to thank her for everything, but the shop was busy now, and Debs was spraying something in the air from a can, spraying behind me as I left, as if there was a trail to cover, as if I were a fly, a wasp, and the words I had formed to say to Carol were running like rain on a window. She had her hand on my shoulder, pushing me, nearly pushing me, out of the door.

The list, I said, finding words.

Tomorrow, Winnie, all right? Another time, Win.

Win

Winnie

Winifred.

I didn't know she knew my name.

part two: after

fifteen

I became Winifred Foy while I was standing on a chair. It comes back sharp as a knife; the chair with its wooden legs creaking under me, and Jean Foy moving round me in a circle, her mouth full of pins. She was altering one of her dresses to fit, so that I could go with her to the meeting on Wednesday evening. Why should I care what I'm called? I thought, after she'd told me what my new name would be. I'd had so many names already: Patsy, Lillian, Pikey, Princess, Beauty. I didn't care about losing my old name. Didn't care about the new one.

As far as I could tell, I'd been back in the city a week. I'd come on a train, in disgrace, with my green case tucked between my legs, wearing Aunty Ena's coat over Aunty Ena's dress. The dress was too short, and tight around my middle; the coat too long and too thick for the weather. It stank of mothballs. I didn't want to sit in a carriage where I might be noticed, so I stood at the window in the corridor and watched as the outside slipped away. Past the mud flats with the broken boats, the farms crouching low against the earth, and the glittering river, cut by a figure making strides along the embankment. She waved as the train went by, and for a second I yearned to be her, down by the river, in the early summer sunshine: no sickness, or shame, or Telltale hair. The train sped up and there were no more people I could wish to be, just fields and churches, more fields, more churches, all exactly like the ones I'd left. So many of them, skimming into a muzzy blur. It made me think of all the other girls, just like me, all the other Joseph Dodds, and a hundred Aunty Enas, shrivelling to nothing in the middle of the dead brown land. I stopped counting, looked the other way. I was going back to Chapelfield; there was nowhere else. My aunt had sent a telegram, she said, explaining the Matter. That's what she called it.

Your grandfather will have to deal with you now, she said, passing one long hand over the other as if she could wipe me away, It's no business of mine.

All through the journey, I thought about what he would say, what kind of rule he might have to invent to deal with this Matter, so shameful, such a disgrace. I was hoping Mr Stadnik would be there. He would know what to do.

It was a long walk from the station. The streets looked ordinary at first, just as I remembered them, and then I turned a corner, and there was a pile of smoking rubble, a spume of dust, as if the earth had split its belly. More ordinary streets, then sky where there used to be a factory; a hole in the ground for a church; a tumble of bricks, burnt wood, bent wire where a row of shops once stood. A cottage with its face peeled off and the furniture inside turned over and broken, like a ransacked doll's house. On and on through the city; the same and different at every turn.

Chapelfield was still standing. I knocked on the door and waited, thinking of a long time ago, a key and a watch hanging heavy on a chain round my neck. My grandfather worrying about me, always worrying. I couldn't understand what I found: I found nothing. I looked in through the letterbox, half expecting Billy the dog's wet muzzle on the other side. I saw the cupboard door under the stairs, slightly open, with an upturned bucket beside it in the hall. Of course, my grandfather would be in the garden on such a fine day. Around the back of the house, climbing the steps and standing on the bridge where I didn't want to be – where I first saw Joseph, all balances. But the garden below was overgrown, the wall crumbled down on the track, the glass panes in the greenhouse smashed and winking in the sunlight. My grandfather was gone and by the look of it, had been for a while. He wouldn't have known about the Matter, about me and my shame. I had no idea where my father might be. There was no one to ask, nowhere else to go.

There's a big park, a sort of heathland, on the edge of the city. The road cuts it into two. My father almost took me, once. He'd promised me a boating trip on a lake, but we never got there; The Flag was on the way, and that was where we always used to stop. It was still there, and open for business. I went into the snug round the back, wanting a drink of water. The man who brought it to me looked as if he'd rather put it in my face than in my hand. He had the same look Aunty Ena wore when she found out.

~ ~ ~

I'm in the yard, on my knees, holding my head under the tap. Aunty Ena's voice sounds very far away.

What's the matter with you?

I don't know. Sick like never before. I lift my head to look at her and the ground comes up like a slap. Aunty Ena takes me inside and lies me down on the mattress. The room jitters round my head.

Think I'm a fool, she says, pulling on her coat, Think I don't know what's going on – what you've been doing with that boy?

Only what *you* did, I say, You and Mr Stadnik. There's no shame in it. We're getting married.

She fetches her gloves, tucks them into her coat pockets as she bends close to my face. Her words are tart as bile,

Of course you are, she says.
She locks the door behind her.

~

I stood outside The Flag and drank the water. The heath on either side of me was a deep emerald green. Along the middle of the road, a man was dragging a cart. I moved over to the corner of the yard, away from his eyes, and sat on the wall I used to sit on with my father. Ginger beer. The thought made me retch. The man hadn't seen me. He laid down the handles and went inside. A skinny dog leaped from the cart to follow him.

~

Aunty Ena still doesn't speak, but it's a new kind of not-speaking. It says everything. We're expecting a visit from the vicar. She cleans the living room, dragging the mattress into the kitchen and leaning it against the stove where the vicar can't see it. I think he's coming to talk about the wedding we're going to have, Joseph and me. Aunty Ena doesn't say. She guards the house, she keeps close, so I haven't been able to get out and see him. But I don't want to. I don't want to do anything except put my head under the tap and feel the cold water rushing across my scalp. The vicar doesn't come. Not the first day or the second. Just when she starts to give up, cursing him under her breath, a boy knocks on the door with a message.

It's over, he says, again and again. It's over! It's over!
She locks the door, running behind him, and as soon as she's gone, I climb the stairs. From the high window, where Mr Stadnik could see the sky, I watch them as they race down the back lane. The church floating in the mist. Birds in a black frenzy round the tower. A boomer's wail from a far corner of the fen, sounding just like the boy on the step. It's over. It's over.

The hair on my head is standing straight as corn, but there

are no shooting stars this time, and it's too late, now, to make a wish. I know without being told that Joseph is gone.

No need to run, I tell her.

~

When I finished the water, I left the glass on the wall. I couldn't face the barman again. I made a choice – the heathland. It reminded me of Joseph and the church plantation. I picked up my case and walked into the trees.

sixteen

It was Jean's brother, Bernard Foy, who found me there. His stroll on the heath took an unvarying route, not too far in, but away from the road; it was his habit to walk alone before a meeting, to set himself up for the day ahead.

When you live a life as *extraordinary* as mine, he said, drolling out the long word, You want an ordinary start to the day.

His ordinary start began early on Friday morning. There was nothing in particular to attract his eye, nothing unusual to remark upon to Jean, he said, who didn't get out much and liked to hear of the world. Jean was not only Bernard's sister, she was his housekeeper and assistant. He would describe the mist rising off the lake, a bird arrowing the sky, the zag of a rook, calling in the distance. Bernard was thinking about the meeting that evening, about who would be in the congregation – and what he could find to say to them.

His flock are mostly women, with husbands recently dead, or Missing Presumed. They always think the worst, he said: his twice-weekly gatherings are packed. In the early days, when he still had the Gift, he could see the spirits, rattling along behind the crowd like a string of tin-cans on a honeymoon carriage. The living want to picture their loved-ones in heaven, he said, but they can't stop imagining other things: a husband lying face down in a ditch, or a son, hanging on a wire. They read reports, and fear something worse than the worst. Bernard, in his Gift, saw auras and haloes; the past rolled out in front of him like the Pathé Gazette. He was their conduit; conveying messages of utmost triviality. For him, he explained, there was only one real message: the fact of everlasting life on the other side. He enjoyed this proof and the skill he had of convincing others. So, when the gift left him, Bernard didn't stop. Instead, he described himself as their filter, happy to provide relief wherever he could. He assured me he wasn't a charlatan; he was merely Temporarily Blocked.

Looking over the water, Bernard prepared for the meeting: he considered names. Harry, Arthur, George.

Who is the George outside of life? he'd ask, putting his head a little on one side, squinting into the distance.

That's *my* Georgy!

Hmm. Yes, I think it *is* your Georgy. Be patient, my love . . . he's moving close. Rise please, sir. Yes. Georgy's here with you now.

If the name was not forthcoming, Bernard employed other methods; nothing too strange, no jewels secreted under a floorboard, no dark secrets, and certainly no pain. Flowers would often solve the problem.

Why do I see roses? he'd say, to a swoon of raincoats and hats. Or, staring blankly above their heads,

I can see the letters BB – or is it RR? Show again please, sir. Do show again.

Bernard used his gift wisely; it's just that, these days, nothing would come. So many dead, and no one moving across. He imagined a waiting room filled with men, patiently standing in line.

The threshold is treacherous at the best of times, he said, narrowing his hands into a small gap, as if I would see them there, in the space between. He lived with the hope that the backlog would clear.

And then Bernard had a vision. He saw an apparition

across the still water, floating on the mist. He told me how he saw me raised up from the ground. I tell you, I was standing there, on a patch of muddy grass, the water at my feet. He said I spoke unearthly sounds. I tell you, I was counting. To a hundred, and back down again from a hundred to one. Mr Stadnik taught me that: how a heart can be broken in many places. I was counting the places.

I would have carried on with my plan, if I hadn't spotted him, the fat man peering over a frond. I'd been living on the heath for a week. I had seen only one other person in that time, an old man collecting sticks. I avoided him.

Bernard found me before I had the chance to drop myself in. I was going to float like a girl in a painting, through the lilies and into the black; float away to the end of the world. He said he studied me from a distance. Standing there with Aunty Ena's coat on, and shoes with the toes cut out, and a little green case at my feet. We walked the path together; me dragging my case until Bernard took it, hooking it under his arm. His small talk was easy and soft. Bernard didn't tell me then about his work. He pointed out the ducks, the clock tower, the numbered pedalos moored up on the far side of the water. They dipped up and down of their own accord, as if an invisible man was stepping from boat to boat.

Someone has disturbed the water, he said, Would that be you?

The reeds were tranquil, the water would not tell.

Each boat was numbered.

Why don't they have names? I asked.

It's easier for the man in the tower to call them in, he said, cupping his hands and making a voice, 'Come in Number Seven, Your Time's Up!'

He was funny. In another time, not this one, it would have made me smile. I counted the boats. I was shy of him.

Thirteen, I said, for something to say, That's unlucky.

No, no, my dear, you'll find there are only twelve.

When we rounded the tower where the boats were moored, we counted again.

You see, he said, Only twelve.

Number Nine was here! I put my toe against the empty mooring to show him the space. The lake was still now, no boats out. Bernard smiled.

You are a Godsend, he said.

~

His hall was brown. There was a clock in a box, and a gilt mirror above an elephant's foot filled with umbrellas. The light was sucked into the flock wallpaper, the patterned runner, mahogany banister.

Wait here and I'll get Jean, he said, turning to the deep end of the hall. He cast no shadow; there was too much gloom. He came back with a woman in a patterned pinny. She had her hair cut short like a man, and carefully pencilled eyebrows, which she raised and kept there. She didn't say, Call me Jean, she said, What now? as if he had brought a dog home. From the sharp corner of her eye, she took me in. She showed me she was taking me in; beginning at my blistered toes with the dirt ingrained, my bare legs, the grass stains on my dress. She stopped at the third button down, as if she could already see a baby nuzzled. Not for nothing was she the Spiritualist's Assistant. Up and down again, her eyes in the corner of her head.

No bags? she said.

Bernard offered up my case. I understood that I was meant to be staying. Like my name, staying made no difference to me. It was just another place.

~

She let me know how she saw through me. Next morning in the kitchen, I sat at the table while Bernard went about his preparations. Jean Foy peeling potatoes, me with the carrots from the garden, claggy with earth; both of us unused to company.

Just pull the tops off for me, the green bits, give them a twist. What was the big attraction down there at the lake, then? Twist and pull, girl. They won't bite,
looking at me out of the corner of her eye, and me the same at her. She was framed in the window, so all I saw against the light was a sharp silhouette, like a cameo brooch. The back of her was closed, the ties of her pinny criss-crossed and knotted tight. A potato mooned in her hand,
He thinks you have something,
scrubbing the potato under the tap; and in the silence that came back,
He thinks he will make something out of you. He thinks you are a *find*.
She said it sharp, *find*, as if it were a knife. I smoothed the green fronds of the carrots, trying not to think of angel hair, or smell the earth, like a slow ache, rising off them. There were lilies on the water, and a face peering over a fern. I didn't know how long Bernard had been watching, what he had seen.
Jean filled a saucepan and carried it to the table. She set it down heavy in front of me, the water spilling over the sides, and went back to the sink to say the rest.
God knows what. Slip of a girl with not a pot to piss in. How old *are* you? Sixteen?
Nearly, I said.
But he thinks you can help him, you know.
A pause. I was supposed to ask a question so that she could tell me how. But she wouldn't look at me and I didn't care. She had to ask, because I didn't care at all about helping. I didn't care about anything. Joseph had flown, my grandfather had gone; my father could be anywhere. I was no one to anyone; that was all that mattered. Curiosity got the best of her.
What was it then, what you did?
The water in a pool on the table, like a lake. What did I

do? The water holding itself to the surface, shivering, then soaking away into the grain.

What impressed him, I mean.

As if reading my mind.

We counted boats, I said, rubbing green between my fingers.

And?

And there was one missing that I thought was there. Number Nine. I must have counted them wrong, I said.

Wrong, she said, You counted them *wrongly*. But Bernard counted them rightly? Right?

She turned at last from the window and smiled. It was a lit smile, to show me the joke. I nodded. She took the carrots from my lap, and began twisting the heads, pulling out their hair.

We'll find out then, shall we? Go into the parlour. Come back and tell me everything you see.

~

I knew only three rooms in Bernard's house: the kitchen where Jean gave me supper the night before, and where the next morning I watched and tried not to ruin the vegetables and was told not to touch anything and to make myself useful; the bedroom which was off her own bedroom, where her instructions to me to

Be quiet no tossing about

had me sleepless and desperate for the lavatory; and the bathroom, with its monstrous bath and giant basin ringed with black specks.

I couldn't find the parlour for doors. Jean made a funny face, then laughed.

My master's house has many rooms, she said, opening the furthest one and nodding me inside,

Everything you see, child, five minutes.

I came back and told her.

Marble fireplace, a photograph on top in a black frame, a settle under the window, a pair of fire dogs—

Tell me what you saw in the photograph, she said.

Mr Foy sitting in a chair with a beautiful woman behind him.

She looked at me steadily now.

A beautiful woman, that's what you see? With dark eyes and long dark hair?

Yes, I said, Very dark hair. Just like my mother's. Very beautiful.

Quite sure?

Yes.

Go and look again.

I was mistaken. There was no one behind Bernard Foy. I held it to the light. There was no one. Jean came to find me in the parlour, took the frame and placed it carefully back on the mantelpiece.

That was Bernard's wife. She's dead. And they don't have a Number Nine on the lake any more, she said, The boat sank. The boy drowned.

~

That night, she came into my room.

You don't need the Gift to see what's up with you, she said, When is it due?

I couldn't say. I didn't even know I was due anything until my aunt told me, and then I was on the train, and in disgrace. Jean spanned her hand across my stomach and stared at her fingers, as if they would give her the answer.

Not so far gone, she whispered, Not too late. That why you ran away?

I wanted to tell her then about being at the lake, stepping in to drown myself. How the water lapped my shoes. When it stilled, I saw inside it: the girl, looking back at me from underneath, like a premonition of what was to come. But Jean wasn't the kind of woman who understood about future ghosts; she knew only about the ones that were already dead. I told her I didn't run from anywhere; that I was sent away, in shame, for loving a boy, for wanting him to love me.

That's enough of that talk, she said, the hard edge back in her voice, Best keep it to yourself. And Bernard doesn't know, mind – pointing a warning finger – So don't go telling anyone. It'll be our secret.

you

Sometimes, over the years, you come back. It can be any-where. You like to take me by surprise, you like to lie in wait. I'm standing on the edge of the pavement, watching for the man to go green, or I'm listening to that woman in the doorway of the bingo singing a song, or I'm simply walking, as I do, thinking of nothing, and you'll appear. You come on the air. A branch of a tree making ribbons of the light. Early rain, washing you clean from the brick of a church wall. A particular bar of soap that people are keen on holds a residue of your scent. I follow them; I lose you. I can't tell what the smell is: something warm. Earth is in it. Sleep is in it. Love hides in the gap between finding and losing. I don't know why you keep coming back. It makes me broken.

seventeen

I am born standing on a chair! I am in a new life, with new people. I am new as a sapling, and like a new thing, I must put the pain behind me. No. I have no pain; that was someone else, some other person's life. Winifred Foy is their niece, just arrived from the country. Winifred Foy is who I am. I have a marvellous talent. I am their Godsend in a grey flannel dress. I'm going with them tonight, to the Meeting. I am learning a new set of rules. And a language.

You stay close by while we greet them, says Jean, pulling back my hair. She flattens it against my scalp, smoothing it down with her hand. I'm sitting on the chair now, in front of Bernard's desk, which is covered in what Jean calls her Beautifiers: a mottled tin with grease marks round the lip, a hairbrush and hand mirror made of horn, a comb with a pointed end, a grey rubber cap, a dish of dusting powder.

Keep still! she says, pulling again, She used to love it when I did it for her, she says, with a backward nod at the mantelpiece, She used to say she was in Heaven!
She means Bernard's dead wife, the one I saw in the photograph, with the long black hair. The one who wasn't there.

Mine's too red, isn't it? I say, remembering Mr Stadnik's remark to my grandfather, It's Telltale.

It's red all right. But that's the least of your worries. *That'll* be telltale in a couple of months, she says, prodding my lap with the end of the comb, And what'll you do then?

Do? About what? I say, trying not to think.

You can't pretend it's not there, she says, Girls get put away for less.

Like the girls in Bethel Street House all those years ago. Brown pinafores, grey-faced, wandering aimlessly round the rose bushes. Jean bends sideways, looks at me.

Don't worry. We'll get you sorted out, she says quietly, sliding the comb between her lips.

How?

She lifts the wig, places it like a crown on my head,

Be careful with this, now, she says, ignoring my question, It belonged to her, you know. There. Want to take a look?

Standing back to survey her work, Jean holds up the hand mirror for me to inspect myself. Inside the oval, Snow White looks back at me.

That's better, she says, Got rid of the pikey in you, that has. Look like any of us now.

What's a pikey? I ask.

The word is sharp in my mouth. I've never said it before, but I've heard it often enough.

Never you mind that, says Jean. Now remember to watch everything I do tonight – prodding me again – And I mean *everything*, she says.

Don't speak unless you're spoken to. Be polite. If anyone asks, you're my niece. You're Winifred Foy. And don't scratch!

~

In Jean Foy's dress and a cardigan smelling of parma violets, I'm shivering in the shade of St Giles' church. We're early, the caretaker has yet to bring the keys. When he comes, he jangles them in front of him, but says nothing. He doesn't even look at me.

It's a lovely evening, says Jean, to no reply. We follow the caretaker, not into the church itself but to a corrugated hut down the far end of the churchyard. There's no sign on the door; nothing to give away what happens. The man makes a show of unlocking the door, sighing and swearing under his breath. Disapproval comes off him like steam off a drayhorse. He speaks not one word.

The inside smells of mildew and stale smoke. Busying himself, the caretaker scrapes the benches across the floor, lining them up anyhow to face the front of the stage. He works like a man against his toil. I don't know why I expected a church. Jean crosses the floor and I follow her into a back room. It's very cold in here, even though outside it's mild still. On a hook on the wall is a cassock, with shoes hanging off a pair of trouser legs beneath it, as if a vicar has been hung up to dry.

Will Bernard be wearing that?

Tch, she says, hiding a laugh, Here, take these. And stop scratching!

She hands me two pewter jugs. I'm to rinse them under the tap and fill them with clean water. In the huge sink which she calls a trough, I rinse the glasses piled up on the draining board. We put the jugs and cups and glasses on the trestle table. Jean pours a thimbleful of cordial into each jug,

Makes it taste like barley water, she says, pulling a face. She opens a little bag of crackers and tumbles them onto a tin plate, centres it, and stands back.

Refreshments, she says, with nothing in her voice. We both stare at the spread; it looks mean.

That's all there is, she says, Nothing to be had in those bloody shops.

She takes an envelope from her handbag and waves it at me.

I'll give this to Happy out there, she says, And you – handing me a silver bowl – Put this on the table at the front door. And stay there with it. You never can tell with this lot.

What will Bernard say? I ask.

Bernard has yet to see me in his wife's wig. Jean pauses. She's about to say one thing – I can read it in her face – but she stops herself.

He'll say stop that bloody scratching! Now get to that door before they can sneak in.

The women, when they arrive – and it is *all* women, apart from a boy clutching the arm of his mother, and a very elderly man on his own – have to pay. I try not to show my surprise. I stand quite still in the doorway with my body in someone else's dress and my feet in someone else's boots, and an itching, heavy head of someone else's hair, watching the money fill the tray.

You fool, you fool, you fool. I say it in my head as they file through, watching the money mount up, until there's just me at the door, standing there with a tray full of coins. But then, as the evening begins, I think again: No, I am the fool.

Bernard steps up on the stage while they're still finding their seats. There's rummaging and coughing, and people fiddling with umbrellas. I can see them all. Row upon row of melancholy faces, waiting for the start of something extra-ordinary.

The usual, says Jean, from the corner of her mouth.
It doesn't feel usual to me. Underneath the wig, I'm getting more than an itch, more than a burn; a crawl of ants all over my head, and static heat, like an electric current, lifting me with a jump off the floor. Something pulling me up from the skin of my neck. I'm on tiptoe. Bernard, from the stage, looks at me. His arm held out straight to one side, introducing his new, special niece, showing me to the packed hall, *presenting* me to the gathering. I'm not ready.

It isn't like seeing a ghost, Bernard said, before we went on – as if that was a common enough thing to happen. He was looking a bit like he'd seen one himself, staring at me with his big, heavy eyes. He took my hands between his; they were ice.

You must be ready for whatever comes through. Don't be

alarmed if it happens. Be calm, and whatever else you might forget, remember: it's not the messages that are important, but the *message.*

That's what Bernard said to me. But I'm not prepared for this at all.

the gift

You can tell them that you think your life's a tragedy even though you're only fifteen and you've been stuck in the middle of a field for years on end because you were left there by a strange little man who could have been a circus act in another time, left there to live with a skinny old woman who looked like the woman on the clock in the city centre, and just like her, she only gets to go outdoors when it's Fair. Which is never if you've got blackout on the windows and no one comes to visit and you're afraid to put a foot through the door. And how if that doesn't drive you mad, then the first other person you see for years on end turns out to be the most lovely-looking creature you've ever set your eyes on, and what's more, he thinks *you're* lovely too. He calls you Beauty. And you'll both have a beautiful life together. Oh yes, you plan it and describe it and rehearse it, lying in each other's arms and breathing him in and breathing in the scent of the moss at his shoulder and not feeling the same kind of hunger any more, but a new one, sharper and more acid and more sweet. This hunger will boil your blood. Thinking, this is it for me, we'll have a place to stay but we won't have roses round the door because we live in the country and are sick to death of it; the stinging grass and the leaden sky and the animals and the insects, the flying things that drop in your ear in the middle of the night. What we want is a *car*. We want a car to take us to sea, where we can swim and lie naked in the soft dunes and see the birds fly over our heads and the waves coming in and out like a breath. We'll go really fast, all over, and further than that, *really* fast, *really* far, just me and you, down to the coast, to the end of the world. But the baggy old aunt discovers your secret, and if she can't have the little man then you sure as hell can't have that flint-eyed giant. Then he's gone, dropping from the sky like a hawk. You're sent back to your grandfather – because you're a child, really, just a child. That boy had no right to be meddling with you, even though he's not much more than that himself, because you're not right in the head, are you? You're not right in the head.

And then you're having a child yourself, and what do you do? You can't tell a soul. What do you do then, with no Joseph and everyone thinking you're not right in the head. And you can't hide, not with that hair, not in this city. Runs in the family. Pikey.

Seeing things. That runs in the family too. I never knew why my mother lay so still in her bed, afraid to open her eyes. Until I start to see them. Only I don't just *see* them: I feel them. The air vibrating in waves, and me looking from side to side, at Bernard, at Jean. Is this normal? Is this usual? So violent, the whole room shuddering, but the women on the benches are sitting still and expectant, not at all worried that the earth is crumbling beneath their feet. I couldn't have known: this was *my* earthquake.

The spirits don't rise quietly: they roar. Men and women and children. Too many children. Roaring in shades of blue. Turquoise and lapis and bluest blue. Blue like film-light, like twilight, like winter sky. One of them blue like my father's suit, gliding through me, making my body hum like a harp.

Pressing their way through the crowd, right down to the front, come the aircraft pilots. They are stinking from the fen;

they are shining like sapphires. Coming forward and politely removing their caps. Buzzing in my ear like flies. They would like to pay their respects to the young lady with the long black hair. They would like to say hello.

eighteen

The hair is shiny and thick.

Cut from the head of a Russian virgin, says Jean, as if it's a fact to be proud of. She says I must wear it to bed, so that we can get used to each other. At night, my hands are bandaged to stop me scratching while I sleep. In the mornings, my neck stiff and my forehead sweating, I'm allowed an hour without it. Then the wig is placed on a dummy head on the dressing table while Jean oils my real hair and slides the skullcap on.

Hair is a living thing, says Jean, Treat her as your friend. I would if I could, but the dummy wears it now, and she chooses to ignore me. Blank eyes, skin like chalk, a smile like a secret on her mouth. At first I was afraid of what Bernard might say, but he doesn't seem to mind at all. He says I remind him of good times, that I look like an exotic, a real Carmen Miranda. I try to talk to her, the Russian virgin dummy, but she never says a word, let alone sings a song. At night, her naked head shines like the moon. She has no name.

Every morning, Jean sits me in front of the dressing-table mirror. I get so used to the weight of hair on me that I feel too light without it. I'm clinging to the knobs of the drawers; if I let go, I might fly away. Today is important: we're going into the city for something special. The news has spread quickly; it's only been a month, and already I'm drawing a crowd. People are asking for private interviews; I'm known as the Girl with the Gift. Bernard and Jean talk about placing an advertisement in the paper, with a picture of me and writing underneath it. Perhaps that's what's so special about today.

Jean has combed the wig, and is fitting it to my head, teasing the hair back from my face and squirting lacquer to keep it in place. I am in the mirror's eye, but I'm not looking. I'm waiting for the heaviness that will pin me to the earth again.

Am I going to have my photograph taken? I ask, wondering why she's taking so much trouble.

Nope. Head still. Look up. Now, let's go over it again. This is our practice time. Jean coaches me in the Correct Methods.

The bit beforehand is crucial, she says, People want to hear from them that's passed over. It's all they come for. We encourage them to talk, prising their misery out of them: me handing round the cordial and the crackers, trying to look as if I'm not paying attention. Trying to find out who's died. Jean swears by it.

We never say die, says Jean, We say 'Passed Over'. What do we say?

Passed over, I say, eyeing the dummy.

Ears open, mouth shut, Jean says, Listen and Learn.

Listen and Learn, I say.

It's not enough that I can *feel* the spirits: I have to interpret them. The first few times, there were so many, I got in a muddle. I have to get the details right; I have to know who the message is *for*.

Bernard says it's not the messages, it's the *message*, I say.

Tch, she goes, He would! But if you get the wrong chap out there, we'll have a lynching. I don't want another do like last Friday.

Last Friday was Edward. He came blue as a baby's eye.

Edward, coming through for someone called Mary. So I asked, in the language I had learned,

Is there a Mary with us tonight? I have someone called Edward drawing near. Two hands shot up, one behind the other. One Mary, with a dead son – a son Passed Over, that would be – and the other with a husband Missing. I didn't know which was Edward's Mary, or Mary's Edward. And the spirits aren't helpful. They've got no manners. They shout all the time; they won't listen to reason. Bernard says I have to learn to control it, I have to be strict with them, like a schoolmistress with a naughty child. But the spirits can't be fooled: they know they can blow me down with a single breath.

Does he have a moustache? says Mary Number 1.

A limp? goes Mary Number 2.

I'm afraid I can't quite see him, I said, playing for time.

Ask him when's his birthday, then!

Ask him did he get my parcel!

On and on, trying to shout each other down in their desperation to claim Edward, who was all the while buffeting against me like the wind off the fen.

How should I know, I shouted back, fed up with all the noise. Jean put her arm round me and called an end to the meeting. In the back room, when everyone had gone, she slapped me on the face.

Never, ever lose patience, she said, her face hot and close, These people are *full* of grief.

As if I couldn't understand how that felt.

Afterwards, she declared that I needed Coaching, so that I would be able to tell which spirit was rising: this not only meant learning the language, but handing round the crackers and listening out for names, for any words of significance, for a clue.

It's not cheating, said Jean, when I complained, It's called *research.* It's called Learning Your Craft. And no back answers from you, lady.

~

Jean is sweet as a plum today. She's especially sweet. Slow to reveal this surprise, she smiles a little to herself; she hums.

Hewitt's an odd fellow, she says, her voice milky, But he's reliable. And one good turn deserves another.

What's a good turn?

It'll help your reputation, you know, if it goes well with Hewitt.

If *what* goes well? What must I do?

Just a reading, she says, casually, He wants to talk to his mother. Died last winter of the influenza. All you have to do is sit there and see what comes through.

What if she doesn't want to talk to *him*?

Well, that would be understandable, says Jean, with her familiar cackle. In which case, you'll make it up. Tell him she misses him. Tell him she says she's very sorry about Dora.

Who?

Dora, she says with an exasperated breath, Was his fiancée. Ran off with his brother. Look, I can tell you what to say, but I wouldn't worry – that woman's mouth went like the clappers when she was alive, and it'll be no different now she's dead. She'll come through, all right. Just be strict with her and nice to him. None of your larks. You be sweet to Hewitt, and Hewitt'll be sweet to us.

How? I say, How will he be sweet?

The hair on my head is warm as an animal skin. Jean smoothes it with the flat of her hand, as if she's stroking a cat. She answers me slowly, a soft burr.

He owns that lovely shoe shop, don't he? Get you a pair of nice new shoes. Something suitable for those little feet, she says, Something *divine*.

~

The man is eager to greet us; he stands on the step, half in, half out of the door. His top lip beads with anticipation. This is my first meeting with Hewitt.

Aha, Miss Foy! So nice to see you. Do come in,
his hand not quite touching the small of her back, gazing up at her with his pale eyes,

May I say how fetching you look in that coat. And your niece. I saw you last week at the meeting, my dear. Such a gift!

As he locks the door behind us, Jean flicks a look at him, one of her sidelong glances. I've seen that look before; she fires it at Bernard when he pretends he hasn't been in the drinks cupboard. What kind of fool do you take me for? it says. Hewitt passes behind us, edging towards the back of the shop. I can hear the air rushing through his nose. I'm taking it in, every detail: the overpowering smell of leather; the long counter with a ledger on it and a glass cabinet in front; the window with an arc of words, just an outline, unfinished, I'd say. A few dowdy shoes, left feet only, on display shelves. I'm also taking in Hewitt: small and ginger with a beak-like nose, lost, nearly, in his apple face; a thin, darting tongue; the watery eyes and the tiny voice, a pitch too high, trapped in his throat. And his old-fashioned air, slippery as Vaseline.

In here, he says, too gaily. With a flourish like a barker at a sideshow, he pulls a curtain aside. Beyond it is a darkened room. We're supposed to pass through, but Jean stops at the threshold,

I'll just wait here, she says, very solemn.

Hewitt gives a nod, and lifts the curtain again.

Shall we proceed?

He's found the correct tone now; he's whispering like a priest.

A stone-cold room with the blackout still on the window, and beyond it, a kitchen. A room with an acrid smell, full of murder. I have to concentrate on what there is, but my legs are jumping. In the corner is a velvet stool placed in front of a daybed. A cushion on the bed, with a quilt folded over the end. That smell is murder. I know in a second that his mother died in this room. Hewitt invites me to sit on the daybed, takes a matchbox from his waistcoat pocket and fiddles with the lamp on the table. As he waits for the flame to catch, his hands tremble. I've never done a private interview before – a reading, Jean calls it, as if I'm a fortune teller – but she was right. I don't need to worry: as soon as Bernard lights the wick, there's a chill against my eye, as if I'm peeping through a keyhole. His mother comes instantly, blue as the flame, hot as pig-fat, furious.

You. Sit – I find myself saying the words, pointing to the velvet stool at my feet. Trying to control her, I reinterpret:

Sorry, I say, Your mother would like you to sit here.
Hewitt takes his position. His face is ecstatic. The bald patch on the top of his head shines like a moonlit pond. I have a terrible urge to cuff him, knock him sideways onto the rug. It isn't me. I sit on my hands. I'm trying to do as I'm taught, I'm trying to interpret the waves of heat his mother sends out. I don't always understand the things the spirits say, and this was no exception. Sometimes I'm able to stop the worst of it before it comes out. Not this time.

Who bribed his medical? she says, glowing like coal.

I was unfit, he says to me, in an injured tone, but before he can finish she's laughing in my ear.

Unfit. That's you all right, she says, *Is that why she left you?* It comes out in a blurt. I put my hands over my mouth and clamp it shut. Why can't she say nice things, or tell him something useful. But they very often don't, Bernard says. The spirits are selective, he says. That's why we are interpreters. That's why we must take control.

Hewitt's mother moves behind me, butting against my back, heavy as a clog. Not another word, I say in my head. You just behave.

No, no – I say, putting my hand to my head, playing for time – She's telling me that *she's* unfit.

Perhaps she means her illness? he says, At the end, you know, she was very sick.

Sick of you, maybe. Not sick of life.

I can't say that.

She means Dora – I lie, watching Hewitt's amazed face – She says that Dora wasn't fit to clean your boots.

HaHaHa! Very good, girl. Considering that's all she ever did.

In the dim light, Hewitt's eyes shine like jelly.

She said that?

Yes. And how sorry she is for you – all the while his mother in a storm around me – Sorry that you're all alone. But it's for the best, she says. You'll find true love soon. Someone worthy of you.

Hewitt grabs my knee, clutching at the fabric of my skirt as if he's about to tear it off. He starts to sob, pulling me sideways towards him. His mother laughs again.

He'll have that off you in a second if you don't watch out, she says. *Serves you right for getting carried away.*

She says she likes what you're doing to the shop, I lie again, wrenching my skirt back.

Yes – he smiles tearily at this new thing – I'm reinvesting, tell her.

Reinvesting my arse. Spending my money! That's my money down the drain.

If she shouts any louder I'll go deaf. I've warned you, I tell her.

And I'm warning you. He'd murder his mother for a ha'penny. Why d'you think I'm here? Why d'you think you're there?

I'm very sorry but she's fading, Mr Hewitt, I say, bending low to avoid her buffeting my head.

Are you feeling faint? he asks, peering up at me, May I get you a glass of water? He goes into the kitchen and lights a lamp, turning up the wick so that I can see a wall stacked with small white boxes, a sink with a basin on the drainer. He brings me a drink.

It was very – brief, he says, resuming his position on the stool, Not really what I expected.

I'm sorry, Mr Hewitt. Sometimes they rise for only the shortest time. Sometimes, they . . . they don't wish to spend too long away from Heaven.

~

'Too long away from Heaven!' hoots Jean back at me, However did you think of that, child?

We're walking down St Giles Street towards the Catholic cathedral; I'm telling her about the reading. She's very pleased that it went so well, after all. When we first came out into the front of the shop and found her surrounded by the ring of shoes that she'd been trying on, she looked furious. But I did all right, she says. She says I'm learning fast.

Hewitt seems very satisfied. He says he'd like another reading. Says it makes him feel more at peace.

Can't think why, I say, which makes Jean stop still on the pavement.

What did you say?

Can't think why *he* should feel at peace.

I don't know whether to tell Jean what his mother said. I'm not so certain now. It wasn't really what she said; it was the smell. Murder in that room, the colour of iron. I could taste it. We walk on, under the trees and round the side of the cathedral. I've never been in; people say it's like the inside of a whale.

Was it interesting, then? says Jean, Did she tell you anything in particular?

Her voice is slight, casual, but her eyes are wide, fixed on the roof above us. In the late sunshine, a faint, greeny-blue light comes off it, nearly the colour of the sky itself. But it's a cold, dead sheen; to me, it's the colour of restless souls. I don't care what the inside looks like, I don't care if it's a palace; I don't want to find out, if that's what's waiting for me.

He's a murderer.

There. I said it. Jean stops again.

Murderer? Who? she says.

Hewitt. I could smell it. And – I could see it, even. And taste it.

That's just you, she says, You and your daft ways.

His mother said so too.

Jean let out another hoot.

Ha! And you believed her?

She's in spirit, I say, Why shouldn't I?

The light on the roof was dancing now. I wasn't going in there. It was full of them.

Why should the spirits tell the truth in the afterlife, Jean says, When they don't in this one? Bernard was right, Winnie. You're a real find you are; you're bloody priceless.

above rubies

Jean and Bernard were decent enough people. They gave me everything a body could want: food, shelter, new clothes, a new name. They took me in, and at that time no one wanted another mouth to feed, and all on a whim Bernard had one fine morning during a walk in the woods. But it was Jean who fashioned me. It was Jean who Took the Trouble, she said, To Do What Was Necessary. She invented a new me; a girl with an extraordinary gift, she said, who wasn't stupid at all, she said, but who just needed Tuning. Just needed to know a bit more about life. A new person in a new world. The trouble was, I couldn't forget the old person in the old world. I had family. The old person in the old world couldn't forget.

I tried, once, to tell her about Before. It had been snowing on and off all morning, not like real snow, but those bitter pips you get sometimes, freezing when it hit the ground into a knobbled crust of ice. We were in the parlour, doing our coaching, drinking Jean's herb tea, watching the light drain from the day. Something in the smell of the herb reminded me, so I tried to tell her, about my mother, my father, my grandfather – Mr Stadnik – all the people I'd lost.

Look around you! said Jean, Everyone has lost someone. And they don't moon about. They just get on with it. You should count yourself lucky: that's your living, the dead. Your bread and butter.

I don't know if they're dead – I said, thinking of my father's suit, humming through my body that first time in the hall – I mean Passed Over. No one has risen.

Don't think *you* choose who rises, snapped Jean, and then, in a cool voice, The door's open, if you want to go. Go on, go and find them, your little family. Show how grateful you are!

~

I didn't go: of course I didn't. I was only fifteen. Not like fifteen-year-olds now. I've met a few down at the Ark, and once, a desperate time just before I went back to Hewitt's, a couple of girls sleeping under the canopies in the open market took it into their heads to keep me company. They weren't shy girls; not homeless, they said, but Roofless. And they laughed together when they said it, as if it were all a joke. They were afraid of nothing and no one.

But at fifteen, I *was* afraid; I had no money, I was pregnant. All I had was a head full of buzzing sounds that I couldn't make sense of. No one wanted me; my father never came, Mr Stadnik slipped away in the night, Aunty Ena sent me back to town to a grandfather who had vanished. People said I was simple, but that would scare anyone, simple or not. But Bernard found me, and *he* said I was his Godsend. Bernard and Jean, they wanted me.

I'm reasoning now – it's easy to do, years later, when the fluttering doesn't frighten you so much; easy to bring up ideas which you claim make you do one thing or another. Really, if I'm true, I simply let it slide. I allowed Jean to do whatever she wanted. I was her project; and in the end, I was glad to be useful. Not glad. Just aware sometimes that I was afloat when I would've sunk. Today there'd be a pill for it, whatever I had, a treatment, or a place to help you with all the hard edges in the world. I was only fifteen. It's not easy to explain, how bendable I was. Soft as butter. Not all there, they said. In those times, they'd just lock you up. Yes they would. I'd end up as one of those women in Bethel Street, walking round the rose bushes and counting birds in the sky. And Jean made me see I wasn't soft at all. I was a real find, she said, I was learning fast. I was definitely all there, and if others couldn't see it, then they were the fools.

I didn't know any better. I did what I was told, whatever the price.

nineteen

I think we'd like a little look out here first, Jean says, surveying the shelves. She glances around for a second, catching my hand tight, as if I'm planning to run away. It's a week later, we're back in the shoe shop and today Jean has made no special effort with my hair; she avoids my eye.

Not much in, is there?

No need for quantity when you have quality, Hewitt says, in his sing-song voice.

That'll be it then, she replies.

High up, at the top of the display, snug between a lace-up boot and a clumpy shoe, is a fawn-coloured slipper.

What about that? she says.

Hewitt takes a breath in.

Ah, Miss Foy. Very lovely. Very expensive. Kid, you see. Rare materials.

Jean's voice is sharp,

We'll *pay* for them, then, she says, If you'll be kind enough to measure her up. Something for afterwards, to take her mind off it.

Ah, of course, he says, as if he understands her.

I don't like the look of them anyway; they remind me of my mother's wedding slippers. I turn to tell Jean, but her face is set hard, her fingers locked in mine, bone to bone.

Let's get on, she says, moving the curtain aside.

~

It's dim in the room, and colder than the first time. Hewitt invites me to sit on the daybed, while behind me, Jean rummages in her bag. She takes out a little bottle, sniffs it, holds it out.

Go on, she says, It'll do you good.

The smell is of long ago: a scent of my father, and another, sharper odour underneath; acrid, biting; reminding me of something else I can't quite place. Jean tells me to drink. The liquid tastes black, like dry earth.

And again, she says, Get it down you.

Hewitt is in the kitchen. He runs his hands under the tap, wipes them on a little square of cloth. The noise of his breath hums from an age away, like a wasp in a shutter. It's colder still, with a whiteness all around me now, as if it's snowing behind my eyes. A pleasant feeling; numb.

What's he going to do? I say, the words high in my ears.

Just a fitting, says Jean, Now be quiet. Try to relax.

Hewitt sets to work. His fingers on my stockinged feet are damp. He straddles the end of the bed, placing his palms against my calves.

Just relax, says Jean, her hand cupping my face.

Hewitt is speaking. He squats like a goblin, and the words float up like bubbles, quivering above his head. Latest Device, one says, Best Methods, says another. In the soft light, his ginger hair turns frosty. Snow falls in the room, coating the bed with glittering flakes. Hewitt lets out a long white breath of air, as if in pain.

Aah, the words say, Not so far. Not *too* far.

His hand on the bloom of my stomach, pressing down, ice cold. A sharp point of light in his hand, shiny, metal; a shooting star.

A fine new pair of shoes, I hear, and, That's it. Good girl. Perhaps the slippers. So soft. So dainty.

~

Don't, don't!

The words are very far away, then closer, then inside my ear. I think it's Hewitt but the sounds is me. I'm sweating in my bed. The Russian virgin is on the dresser, she's wearing my hair and a smug smile. The pain is thick as tar. Jean sits at my side. We're in the back of Hewitt's shop. Snow falling from the ceiling. His mother is laughing at me.

Have that off you in a second, she says, *Serves you right for getting carried away!*

It'll be over soon, love, says Jean, then a cry above my head, What's taking so long?
She's stitching me into her dress; the needle goes in and out, tacking the flannel to the soft skin on my stomach. The Russian dummy goads her on.

Nearly done, says Jean, Keep still.
Hewitt floats above me like a zeppelin, pink, shiny, hissing breath. My father's here too, standing in his blue suit and smiling; he has something caught in his fist. He opens it, and a beetle zigzags up into the light. The horses, impaled on their poles, gallop over my head. Their saddles are jewelled with sweat. I'm flying now, I'm falling. My mother's bare feet are dancing on glass. Over the fields to the scarecrow, to Joseph with his arms wide, balanced like a trapeze artist on the edge of the tower.

Watch me fly, Beauty!
He's flying and falling, just like me.

Look! A shooting star, Mr Stadnik says, marching smartly up and down the room.

Let's make a wish, I say, but I'm as tiny as a bead. No one can hear me. Mr Stadnik marches. In his cupped hands, he carries a glistening lump of flesh.

Who broke it? he shouts, I must know who broke it!

~

When I wake up, Jean's sitting in the chair next to my bed. The dummy head is on the dresser; they're watching me.

You'll be better now, Jean says.

She feeds me soup from a spoon, blowing on it before she holds it to my lips. The spoon goes tiny and huge and tiny again, in and out. Jean's puckered mouth close up is whiskery, like the muzzle of an animal. The soup tastes of salt. I hear the voice again, floating above my head. It sounds like my mother.

Pain, it says.

Pain is only an opinion, snaps Jean, The worst is over, believe me. Now, have some more of this.

Her words go strange and soft then, seeping like oil into my ear,

We'll just put it behind us, she whispers, It wasn't meant to be. And as soon as you're up and about again, we'll get you those lovely new shoes.

~ ~ ~

I had an hour before my next meeting with Hewitt. It had been two weeks of Jean's soup, Jean's cajoling, her bedside talk. I took the tram to the terminus, but when it passed by the cathedral, I got off. I didn't want to go back to the shoe shop, even though Jean said I must. I was being foolish, as usual, she said; I shouldn't trust my instincts. She said I had plenty of uncommon sense but not enough of the other kind.

Hewitt's not a bad sort. And he's good to have on our side.

Why is he? I complained, not seeing any good in him at all.

Well, for starters, people always need shoes, she said, And what does Hewitt provide?

Shoes? I asked, sensing one of Jean's trick questions.

Free advertising, she said, with a smack of triumph in her voice, You'll see, he'll be telling everyone about you. He might even let us put up a poster in the shop. And some would say he's quite a catch . . .

But she read the look on my face. The little, squeaky man with his Devices and his Methods. Not a chance, my look said.

I'll meet you, she said at last, Once I've finished in the post office. I'll be there before you. All right? You won't have to be alone with him.

But I got off the bus anyway, to be slightly late by the time I got to the shop. The cathedral roof was glowing. I stood and watched as it changed colour in the light: grey-blue in the rain, greenish-white when the sun broke through the clouds. No one else noticed, they were rushing about their business, hiding under umbrellas. They simply weren't looking up.

It hadn't occurred to me, before Bernard, that I might have a gift of any kind. I couldn't tie my shoelaces, didn't know what a clock said. He said that learning would see to that, simple enough stuff, and that I wasn't stupid, just unschooled. But a gift could not be learnt like an alphabet, he said. It can be brought on suddenly, by shock, by grief, by rage – even fear can do it.

I think when he found me, I had all of them. But since that time, I'd passed churches and graveyards and low houses – all kinds of places – and never seen a light like the one on the cathedral. There was a crowd of spirits up there; they must have pressed themselves right up to the rafters. They were clamouring to be let out.

I didn't go in. I walked down St Giles to Hewitt's shop, slowly, despite the rain, and stood outside. The lettering on the window was fresh gold: Hewitt's Shoe Repairs and Fittings, in an arc, with Bespoke underneath. I looked in, hoping to see Jean. A person looked back at me through the glass; it wore my mother's face.

Miss Foy! Winifred, my dear, do come in out of the weather! Hewitt stood at the door, beckoning with his small white hand. When I didn't move, he came towards me, following my eye to the glass with his name on it and my mother inside.

They've made a very nice job of it. Expensive, but then quality never comes cheap. Miss Foy?

He stood beside me, bending in. I put out my finger. His eyes followed, and he laughed. A small laughing man appeared in the space next to my mother.

Ah, Winifred. Do come out of the rain, your hair's getting wet. We have a mirror inside you could use, if you wish.

~

Hewitt's arm is round my shoulder.

Let's get these wet things off you, he says, motioning to the girl behind the counter. His face is smiling but his words to her are taut as wire.

Here you are. Take these.

The girl slides her hands along the surface of the glass. It's like watching her in slow motion: every move she makes is a grudge. She looks half asleep. She holds my coat between her finger and thumb, at arm's length.

Shall I go for my dinner? she asks, eyeing us both.

Half an hour, he says, glancing at his watch.

After she's gone, Hewitt flips over the sign on the door and pushes the bolt. He turns to me, and at once the beaming smile fails him. He looks as if he's about to cry.

And how are you? he says, his face in a crease.

I tell him I'm well. I don't tell him about the dreams, or the pain, or the blood, or the little boluses of – what did Jean call it? – *waste matter*. I tell him I am well.

Mustn't have you out in the rain, he says, You'll get a chill. Take a cab next time, my dear. At my expense.

I sit on the bench, and Hewitt sits by my side. His leg is almost touching mine. It's too warm now, inside the shop. He looks at me expectantly but I look at the fire.

Well well, he says, bending his head, catching my eye.

I tell him I've come to try on some shoes.

No, my dear, that's not how we do it – he says, smartly, with a professional air – I must measure you up.

Leaning sideways into me, he holds his hands palms out, making a shape with his fingers,

You see, the foot is the most delicate instrument, he whispers, Imagine how much work it does, every single day of its life.

He jumps off the bench and springs over to the cabinet. Scanning beyond the glass, he opens the clasp and puts his arm inside, reaching around as if he's hunting a ferret in a sack. He turns his head and grins at me, like a magician, waiting to see my expression of delight. He comes back with a long brown foot made of wood. Sits closer.

See, this here, it's called a last, he says, cupping the foot in his hand, It's an exact replica of a real foot. This one belonged to a very special person.

He turns it over, cups it between his knees, strokes it like a pet. I can hear his breathing: short, uneven. He gets down on his knees, just like he did the first time, in front of his mother's spirit, and the second, in front of me. But he isn't praying, he isn't wounding; he's crabbing around underneath the bench.

You're a very special person too, he says, reaching behind my legs, And you'll have your own little last, you'll see.

He hands me the wooden foot to hold as if it's a love token, his voice cloying, lollipop sweet, still reaching underneath me. He drags out a contraption, a shallow box with leather bands either side. To me, it looks like a tiny casket.

Boot off, he says, gesturing at the floor, Or – may I? – and begins to untie my laces. His fingers are quick, but it's still a struggle: Mr Stadnik's lesson has not been wasted. The urge to strike him is raging. I have to check – no vibration in the room, no blue gaslit mother-fury sweeping around the back of my neck – it's me, just me, wanting to bring the last straight down on his thick head while he crouches there, fumbling with my boot. He's muttering to himself, pulling on the heel until it slips off into his hand.

The foot must be treated with respect. Ah! Good shoes and a good bed, as my mother used to say—

A knock on the door stops him. Jean is peering through the glass, wiping the rain off with a gloved hand, as if she's waving at someone very far away. Hewitt springs up from the floor.

Your aunt, he says, in a dead voice, What a nice surprise. Jean isn't pleased, either. I can see it in her face. Perhaps I was meant to wait for her outside. She grimaces at my stockinged foot, raises her eyebrow when she sees the contraption with the leather straps.

Didn't you used to have a machine for that? she says, throwing her gloves down on the bench.

Ah, Miss Foy, I did. Certainly, I did. An amazing device. But it was declared dangerous, you know, he says, And my clients, they much prefer the personal touch.

While Jean gives him her look, I'm slipping my boot back on.

Well, I suggest you do your *personal touching* in the back, she says, We don't want anyone getting the wrong idea, do we?

Of course, he says, But not now, I think. My girl's due back in ten minutes. We'll measure you next time, my dear, he says, bowing to me, It'll be my pleasure.

all-day breakfast

There's not a lot of wisdom in age, despite what they say. Truth is, as you get older, things get further away. Objects, I mean, like telephone boxes and the shops and that. Places you have to imagine walking to, or in the case of traffic, getting out of the way of. And near up, everything's such a mist – you're practically blind. Well, I am. Can't see my hands up close: they're as blurred as a drunk. But I can feel them all right: my very own chicken claws, one in each pocket. Then there's the other stuff, memories for instance: now they really should be far away. But just one nudge and they're right under your nose. And it is *all* in the nose. That innocent scent wafting out of the chemist? That's my father's hands after he danced with my mother; and that particular, early morning winter air with a tang of spring in it? Joseph Dodd, waiting in the church plantation, twirling a feather between finger and thumb. It all means something. Like the rusty railing you've touched, which in a second is the iron chain of the swing you gripped so tight when you were five: fear and bliss, mixed. A pub with its door open to the world – any pub, anywhere, letting out the stink of beer and smoke – there's the pictures on a Saturday morning, with the close-up crush of my father's suit. Fat frying? Mr Stadnik's head, bent like a supplicant in front of Aunty Ena; and Aunty Ena herself can waft up at any time, in any corner of any room. As long as there's dust in it. My grandfather's particular smell is a rarity: pipe smoke, as dead to the air these days as he is. They come at random, they come in droves, reckless, unbiddable. Just like the spirits used to come. It's enough to drive you mad.

Why don't they warn you? Why don't they say that there's cruelty in the air? You go half blind, half deaf, your feet are so far away from you they might as well belong to another person: a lame one, at that. Eating's a burden. Sleep is a stranger. So many bits of your body stop working, you hardly care any more. It's a joy to think you'll soon be dead. But not the nose: it does its job too well, it hoards your whole life. I can't remember what I ate for supper, but fifty-odd years can be five minutes ago. Leather. Hewitt is, and always will be, leather. I couldn't pass a shoe shop without the dread of him ghosting up. My own shoes are pre-worn, Salvation Army. They were someone else's first, and that someone else wore plastic shoes. Synthetic won't trouble me.

I didn't want to get confused about what was stolen. It might only have been a day gone by, but I could tell it was leaving; so much else was filling up the space. That girl who stole from me, she'd left the door open; the outside was pouring in like rain down a gutter. Write a list, Carol had said.

I sat in the Korna Kaf at the bus station and thought about it. I normally enjoyed sitting at the very corner table of the Korna Kaf, right in front of the curved window, because the whole world goes by. You can watch but you don't have to take part. I wasn't enjoying it this time; I had a lot to think about. The lady in the pink check apron came over. She normally does.

Nice hat, she said, Here you are, love, putting a cup of tea in front of me. She always did that, and she didn't have to say what she said the first time she brought me a cup of tea, because me and her, we've got an understanding. When I've finished it, I have to leave. That's the understanding. I think she's kind enough, but when I don't dream of a room and fill it full of things, I dream about walking in and ordering the

All-Day Breakfast Only £1.99!

It's funny the way they think putting £1.99 will make you believe it's not really two pounds. I'd have the All-Day Break-fast Bonanza: Bacon Sausage (2) Kidneys stroke Black Pudding Egg Tomatoes stroke Beans Mushrooms Fried Bread stroke Toast.

I'd like my kidneys devilled, I'd say. No mushrooms.

You need money to do that. And to get money, you need a place. But if you have no money, it's not easy. You try finding a Fixed Abode, as they call it, without any means of fixing it. And if you have no fixed abode, you can't get any money, not off the assistance, anyway. I went there once. I didn't want help with a room; I had the notion of asking them for a car. It seems a ridiculous thing now, but then, I just wanted to take my car to the end of land, and live in it. I didn't even know you had to learn how to drive. You could say I'd been very sheltered; it wouldn't be a bad supposition. So I found the place where they're supposed to give you assistance, and I waited. There were lots of other people, waiting and smoking, and one man who wouldn't sit down and went off now and again to kick a wall. I waited until someone – a woman with her baby – said I had to pull a piece of paper from a box on the stand and they'd call my number. She went and got it for me, and I took the piece of paper and waited and twiddled my thumbs and waited and just before closing I spoke to a boy behind a glass.

Where do you live? he asked, holding his pen above the form he was filling in for me.

I could've said, I live in the present.

I couldn't have, because the words were failing. And besides, I didn't have it – the way to explain things – it had abandoned me. I've got it now, of course, now everything's coming back; the rats are piling on to this sinking ship. But at that time – the filling-in-a-form time – I was derelict. I was simple again. I was back before Before. So I told him the truth: I didn't live anywhere. I just wanted a car.

Where would we send the postal order? he said, placing his pen down on the form.

Why not put it in my hand?

It seemed a reasonable request. I wasn't getting angry like some of the people in the waiting room were when it came round to their turn. That woman with the baby, she'd been sitting there for hours. But he wrote my name on a piece of paper and pulled the shutter down, leaving me on the other side, staring at the slats.

It wasn't a completely wasted journey. Someone had left the frame of an old pram outside, in the gutter. I took it with me; my case was so heavy, and I didn't know how far I'd be going. It was ideal, really, as if it had been left there just for me. My case fitted it perfectly, and it was easy to pull along. I enjoyed the sound of the wheels behind me, the grip of the handle – white ridged plastic – feeling all the bumps coming up off the road. All that was good.

It wasn't abandoned, the pram. I stole it, if I'm true. It had a carry-case, and bedding and a small brown teddy. It had three coloured rings attached to the frame. Then there was someone behind me – a woman – calling out. I thought it must be the owner of the pram, so I raced away as fast as I could with my lucky find. It's not as if I stole a baby, just a bit of metal on wheels. It was such a long way to walk, such a heavy case.

That was an age ago: thirty-odd years. I haven't starved to death. Haven't been arrested. It used to feel bad, the hunger, but one good thing about getting old is that you're not so bothered about food. I never gave a second thought to the woman in the waiting room, sitting with her baby on her lap and her pram outside with the tied-up dogs and bicycles. Not until I got robbed: that's given me more ideas than I care for. The menu in the Korna Kaf with all the breakfasts on, well, that was just another idea I had – I wasn't the slightest bit hungry for food – it was the *thought* I hungered after, of being able to have the thing I wanted most in the world. Imagine an empty room, and fill it. Imagine a plate, cover it in food.

And then it came to me: it's a menu, and a menu is only a list. A list of food to order, pay for, and eat. I could make one of those. While I drank my tea, and watched the world running about under the rain, I did it, without any assistance at all.

twenty

Confound Expectation! See And Believe!
Winifred Foy Has a Gift – For You!

On page two of the newspaper, inside a thick black box, is a picture and some writing. The letters are bold and swirling and black. Winifred Foy is me, but I can't say I know her. Underneath the photograph, in dense script, it gives the time of the meetings and the new place, which Bernard calls a Venue. We had to move; the old church hall was too crowded, the caretaker said, a risk to life and limb.

Too bloody popular, more like, said Jean, and to me, You're too good for your own good.

It might have been one of Jean's back-handed compliments, like saying I was a fine one when I did the wrong thing, but there was no mistaking her tone. At first, she seemed happy enough that the benches were filled to bursting, people standing at the back, coming to see us from Fakenham, from Ipswich, even. It was when the clapping began that her mood changed. I don't know who started it; not a regular, not a face I knew. I'd just been bringing through a small boy for an elderly woman down at the front of the hall: her grandchild, who had died years back. He had a terrible, draining cough, and looking at the colour of him made my eyes water – blue as a starling's egg, the palest, translucent blue. There was nothing particular about the meeting, apart from the little boy. The grandmother and the women on either side of her had a cry, but they do anyway, sometimes; Bernard calls it an Occupational Hazard, he says I must get used to it. At the end of the session, when I'd sat down on the chair that Bernard said I should use these days – to give me An Air of Authority – someone at the back began to applaud. Then more people clapping, and more, until everyone was on their feet and the sound was raised to the ceiling. To me it was a noise full of joy.

No one wants a repeat of that, said Jean, when we'd got back home, We're not a circus act.

She looked to Bernard for agreement, but his face was closed, impossible to read.

They're simply showing their appreciation, he said, helping himself to his night-time brandy, Think of it as a sign of respect.

Of respect? she cried, Not respect for the dead, that's for sure – and pointing her finger at me – *She's* turning it into a pantomime.

She is doing no such thing, he said, relocking the cabinet in the sideboard and easing himself down into his seat. There was an ache of silence in the room. They often bickered, but this was an argument brewing. I'd never seen Bernard so stony. He held his glass up to the light and gazed through it, as if it held an answer.

What she is doing – he said, after taking a long, measured sip – Is bringing us good fortune. That's all there is to it.

Jean spoke no more about the clapping that time, but the way she did my hair before the next meeting, scraping it against my scalp and jamming the wig down on my head, I knew that despite the finality of Bernard's remarks, Jean definitely thought there *was* more to it.

Let's not have any hysterics tonight, she muttered, prodding my shoulder with a stiff finger, Let's not get things out of proportion. This isn't the music hall, you know.

But the applause had nothing to do with me. By the end of the following evening, not only was there clapping, there was a man standing on a chair, with his fingers in his mouth, whistling. People were out of their seats. Bernard was standing too.

The idea for the advertisement came after we were given notice on St Giles hall. Jean had mentioned a photograph once before, so when Bernard said we should place an advertisement in the paper, with a picture of me, Jean's reaction was a surprise.

Why not a photograph of you, Bernard? You're the attraction, after all. It's your life's work.

Not pretty though, am I? he said, with a sudden, mirthless grin, Not a crowd pleaser, like this one.

Jean went quiet. She looked over at me, back at him, back at me.

You call that pretty? she said, You need your eyes testing.

~

Bernard got his own way. We went, all three of us, to a studio he knew on Colegate. The photographer was a tall, bald man with a bent back. He leaned on the arm of the sofa, offered me a cigarette from a silver case.

She don't smoke, said Jean, And she don't take any clothes off.

She'd got the idea just by looking: the room was full of framed pictures of young women, smiling coquettishly over a bare shoulder, lying on a rug in a swimsuit, pouting, with their hands in their hair.

We don't want her looking like a tart, said Jean, frowning at a gallery of simpering faces, She's a clairvoyant, not a showgirl. Are you sure we're in the right place? she asked Bernard, who was trying not to notice the pictures. He gave the man an embarrassed smile.

We'd like her . . . enigmatic, a little mystical, he said, Nothing too . . . flamboyant.

The man said he would do his best.

~

According to the picture in the newspaper, I am half mystery, half wonder. All hair. There's a swirling vapour around my head that wasn't there in the studio, and two points of light, like tiny slivers of stars, in each eye. It looks exactly right.

He's certainly done some work on that, says Jean, holding the paper at arm's length in front of Bernard and his breakfast, I don't know about packing them in. Looks to me like she'll scare them off.

Bernard raises his head from his plate of porridge.

Well, I think she looks marvellous – it really captures the mood, doesn't it, Win?

It's just like it is, I say, wanting to take the picture from Jean and hide it in my room so I can look at it again later. I've never had a photograph of me. I didn't know my eyes had pieces of the sky in them.

No good asking her, says Jean. 'It's just like it is!' – What's *that* supposed to mean?

Bernard sighs, and pushes his plate away. Jean is peculiar these days, argumentative for no reason. This morning it's the photograph that's vexing her, but any little thing can set her off.

What she means, my dear, is that it is a very good likeness. It's beautiful, just beautiful.

Bernard tries his best, but that isn't what I mean at all.

It's different, I say, trying not to make Jean angry, It looks like the feeling – when they come through. Like my hair is doing that,

I say, pointing at the vortex of light in the picture. Bernard is nodding in agreement.

Yes, Jean, you see, that's how the Gift manifests itself to

her. The photographer has simply interpreted her aura. And, in my opinion, he's done very well.

My aura, yes, I say, wanting to sound like Bernard, That's exactly how it looks.

Thank you so much – says Jean, acid – For enlightening us. How silly of me not to notice your *aura.*

~

We rehearse every spare minute, to prepare for the opening night. Bernard has moved his chair into the bay window, trying to make the parlour look like a stage. He's been teaching me words. He calls it the Language of the Afterlife, although a lot of it is just being polite to the people in the audience, repeating the things they say. Jean calls it the gift of the gab. She says there's more to it than parroting. When I'm alone in my room, I practise my words on the Russian dummy. She never smiles, never weeps.

The vibration is with us now, I say, holding my hands outstretched, Bear with me, madam. Move closer, sir, if you will. A little closer. Would this be your husband, madam? I can see a church.

The dummy smirks on.

Or perhaps it is your son drawing near. Was he to be married? I have the letter M, you see.

Bernard says always read the face. The face will tell you everything. Look beyond the skin, he says. Because no matter what you think you can see, if you don't say the right words, people won't understand. And names are slippery; names are like grease, Bernard says. All you have to do is hit on the right letter, and the look on their faces will help you.

M or N, it isn't clear. I am but a lowly interpreter, madam. Please forgive me if the name is incorrect.

The dummy says nothing.

~

Bernard is singing. When he gets to the last line of the hymn, reaching for the note like a girl in a high, trembling voice, I have to come out and stand in the centre of the window, raise my arms, and say,

Good evening, ladies and gentlemen. We're honoured to have your company this evening. Please take your seats.

I'm no longer allowed to stand at the front door collecting money in the silver bowl. Bernard says it's undignified for the star to be seen 'consorting with hoi polloi', so he's formulated some new rules: I have to remain in the back room of our venue until the singing is finished and the light comes on above the stage. Then I must walk out with my arms raised, just like we do in the rehearsal. Bernard's had some handbills printed that we are supposed to give out to people in the street; it shows the photograph of me, with the words 'Winifred Foy, Clairvoyant Extraordinaire!' on one side, and on the back, a list of Testimonials from Satisfied Customers. Bernard made them up. A little embellishment, he said, and only what he'd heard spoken, anyway. He's given out fifty already; and he's instructed us to carry a few about our person, he said, should the appropriate occasion arise. I love it when Bernard speaks like that; he could give lessons to the King.

Jean is fizzing. She keeps to the kitchen, scrubbing the floor, the stove, scouring the tabletop, boiling vegetables until the room is full of steam and she is glowing with sweat. She mutters under her breath whenever I'm near.

Don't. Want. You. Out. Here – she says, rasping the brush across the tiles – Fraternizing with the hoi polloi. What will Bernard think?

~

I've finally managed to get it right, the words in the correct order with the correct tone, my arms raised in welcome, the slight smile on my lips.

Beautiful, says Bernard, Perfect!
Jean doesn't wait to hear more. With her headscarf in her hand, she marches into the parlour.

I'm supposed to run myself ragged with the refreshments and the setting out and the hoi bloody polloi –
snapping the scarf in front of her
 – *and* stand there like a skivvy at the door! And madam there –
snapping it at me
 – gets to sit round the back doing sweet fanny adams.

We can get a person to stand in on the door if you like, says Bernard, his voice meek as ever.

Like who?

Bernard doesn't answer directly. It's become his way, as if slowing down the conversation will ease the tension. It has the opposite effect on Jean, whose face goes purple in the waiting. He pulls the chair back away from the window, smooths the covers, carefully repositions the cushions. He doesn't look at her.

I'll make some enquiries for next week's meeting. And afterwards, we can advertise, find an assistant.

But she *is* the assistant, insists Jean, We can't afford to *pay* anyone.

Oh yes we can, says Bernard, Winifred's a great success. The whole city is talking. So I've decided: we'll be putting up our entrance fee.

~ ~ ~

Everything would have gone according to plan, it would indeed have been a great success, if it wasn't for that visit to Hewitt's shop. He'd called at Bernard's house the day before; Jean was in the kitchen and I was keeping out of her way, sitting in the parlour, doing one of Bernard's jigsaws. I saw Hewitt through the window, coming up to the gate. He rang the bell once. No sound from Jean, no footsteps in the hall. I held my breath, heard the flap of the letterbox as he lifted it, imagined him peering through the hole like a pig in a pen. Then he was gone, crossing the road at the end of the street.

I thought I wouldn't mention it to Jean. She wouldn't need to know. But Hewitt wasn't looking through the letterbox, he was dropping off a card. Jean brought it into the parlour, a smile of sly amusement on her face.

You have a suitor, was all she said.

She held the card up to the light, turned it this way, that way, enjoying the power of the words in her hand. Then slowly, carefully, she read out the message on the back:

'To my dear Winifred. Kindly do me the honour of visiting me at my premises tomorrow morning. I shall send a car. Yours, as always.'

He'll send a car, will he? Well, my dear Winifred, you must certainly *do him the honour*. Hark at old Hewitt – Mr Rochester more like!

~

To please Bernard, to not annoy Jean, I went. The car dropped me at the end of the road, and from there I walked, willing one foot to follow the other, right to the door of the shop. It was locked. The closed sign was up. Through the window, I could see he'd got a new serving girl, as sullen as the last one. She was leaning her elbows on the glass counter, cupping her face in her hands. When she saw me, she started, and rushed to open the door.

He told me to keep a lookout. He'd kill me if he missed you. He's in the back room, she said, nodding at the curtain, You can't go in, he's with a customer. Running late.

I waited on the bench near the fire, trying not to look at her. She was not making the same effort; she was staring at my head.

Is that a dye? she asked.

I couldn't tell her it was a wig. I said yes, it was a dye.

My mother does hers Venetian Blue, she said, To take away the smoke stain. It's called a rinse, you know, Venetian Blue. It doesn't end up blue, it rinses out. That's why it's called a rinse. You should try it.

I might. Thank you.

Black's a difficult colour to pull off, don't you think? she said, walking round the front of the counter, standing above me with her arms folded on her chest, Unless you're Scarlett O'Hara.

It was quiet for a minute, then she looked at me again, with mocking in her eyes.

You're not, are you? You're not *the* Scarlett O'Hara?

Spite in the air, an old, familiar scent. Looking up into her face, I saw the mark under her pink chin; fainter now, but unmistakable: the birthmark shaped like clover. This is Alice Dodd.

twenty-one

Alice Dodd shook her head when I said my name; she didn't
know me. Finally, I realized she might remember who I used
to be: I was Patricia Richards, but she would have known me
after that time, when I was Lillian.

Might as well be Scarlett O'Hara for all it means to me,
she said, Nope. Don't ring any bells.
She took up a duster from the counter, wiped it in a half-
hearted way across the glass, and sat down next to me.

Beats me why a person just can't be who they are, she
said, So why are you pretending you're that old bag's niece?
All the time she spoke, Alice kept her eye on the curtain, just
in case Hewitt appeared. I'd only been out of Jean's company
for half an hour, and already I'd made a mistake. I was too
eager; in my attempt to find out about Joseph, I'd said
too much.

We were sent away together, I said, trying to change the
subject, We were sent to the fens. In a wagon. You must
remember that.

I wasn't sent with no one, she said, I was on my own. On
a bloody farm with some stinking cows. Worked me like a
slave. I think I'd've remembered if *you* were there,
She took her eyes off the curtain and stared at me.

With that hair.

And your brother was sent away too, wasn't he? I asked,
trying to sound casual.

Her face froze.

It weren't his choosing, she said, after a beat, He hurt his shoulder in a fall. The army wouldn't have him. He was always falling, that one.

I remembered the first time I saw Joseph, balancing on the bridge. He told me how he watched me at Aunty Ena's house, how he climbed along the parapet of the church tower to do it, surveying the land below.

It's like being a bird, Beauty, he said, You can almost put your wings out and fly. Just like a bird in the sky.

And I remembered enough of Alice Dodd to know not to ask anything of her. I pulled out a handbill with my picture on it, and wafted it in front of my face.

If you're too hot I can douse that fire a bit, she said, Can't open the door when Hewitt's got someone in the back. God knows what he does in there.

Her voice lowered to a whisper,

Some say doctoring stuff, you know, for women. He's got a load of whatyamacallits – *devices*, that's what he calls them.

Rolling and unrolling the handbill, I sat, and said nothing. Devices and machines and gadgets. The fire was filling the room with a dry, parching heat; making my face burn and the hair beneath my wig itch with sweat. Then I understood: the story my father told me was true. He met my mother here, in this shop, before I was born. My hands rolling and unrolling the handbill are his hands, the heat is a crush of bodies, all eager to see the new device for measuring the feet. There's shouting and laughter and a small red-headed man asking his customers not to swear. Hewitt, demonstrating the marvellous power of his machine, has one eye on the men all in a line, the other on the pretty black-haired assistant with the beetle-shaped brooch in her hair. The fire was choking.

I'm here tonight, I said, pressing the leaflet into Alice's hand, Maybe you'll come. And your brother too.

Alice unfurled the sweaty piece of paper and read it. A bitter smile spread across her face.

I don't believe in the spirits, she said, Load of old squit. But my brother? Who knows, maybe he'll turn up.

~ ~ ~

The woman in the mirror was dressed in a high-necked white blouse and a brown skirt almost down to her ankles, a head of shiny black hair curling over her shoulders. Jean didn't bother much with me any more, so after she'd left to go and help Bernard get ready, I ignored the sneer of the Russian dummy on the dresser, and styled it myself. I never liked seeing through the mirror, but this time it was necessary. Tonight was going to be important; I wanted to look my best. The woman in the glass bent close, and with the tip of her little finger, rubbed a smear of Jean's beautifying Red across her lips. It smelled of blood but when she smiled, her teeth shone white as snow. She whispered a long-forgotten question.

Who is the fairest?

I could hear Bernard in the room below me, coughing and repeating a phrase, over and over. He was practising his speech for the opening. The words 'beautiful' and 'marvellous' brought another sound: Jean's familiar snort of derision. These were two of Bernard's favourite words. I could only guess that this time he was planning to use them to introduce me. That would explain Jean.

I never did get that fitting done with Hewitt, on account of what he called unforeseen circumstances to do with his customer in the back. I knew at first hand what they would be, even if Alice Dodd could only guess. Hewitt didn't get his opportunity to touch me that time, and my feet have got their old boots on still. Apart from that, I'm ready for tonight. I'm more than ready. I'm Beautiful. Marvellous. Perfect.

~ ~ ~

The venue is a gaunt church hall, chill enough to see your breath, with a pointed ceiling, a wooden stage along the whole of one end, and what would have been stained-glass windows on each side. They're clear glass now, turning silver-grey in the darkening light. The floor is speckled with chalky spats of white; above us, on a narrow ledge, doves are settling to roost. I'm waiting in the back room with Bernard, who is coughing and humming – tuning his voice – while the space around Jean is filled with a prickly silence. She says not one word to me, even though she's noticed my hair, and her lipstick colour on my mouth. She takes a slow, amused look at the length of my skirt. She speaks, sharp as a claw, to Bernard.

There's an old man outside telling me he's employed to help, she says, What shall I say to him?

Say he can help you set the chairs out, Bernard replies, just as brittle, Say he can stand at the door.

When she's gone, Bernard takes my hands in his, and sits with me on a little couch in the corner. His voice goes soft and sing-song again. He tells me that everything will be fine, that I must try to relax a little.

Every eye shall see you, he says, as if he's reciting a poem, And how marvellous you are.

When he leaves to begin the service, I sit alone in the back room, trying not to feel the fluttering in my ribs. The thought of every eye on me doesn't make me nervous; I'm used to being looked at now. It's the thought of one particular pair of eyes out there, smiling, dark. At these times, Jean would normally be at my side, peeping round the doorway, remarking on one woman's new hat, the awful state of another's coat. I miss her.

I can hear them moving about, settling into their seats; the way the brightness of the sounds become thicker and more clogged as every chair is taken and the hall is filled. When Bernard announces me, I take up my position on the stage with my arms raised, and ask them to please sit. I would take a seat myself, but Jean, out of ill will or forgetfulness, has not provided a chair for me. So I stand and look. A hundred heads, more than a hundred, with scarves and hats, bare and bald, removing gloves here, repositioning an umbrella there, all looking at me. Not one of them is Joseph. I can't see him. The faces are upturned, some smiling, a few familiar, but not one of them is Joseph's face. Alice and her spite. She wouldn't have let him know. High above the congregation are the doves, shuffling from side to side on a long ledge, now and then the last one in the line turning awkwardly around and resettling in the same space. Bernard has his eyes closed. His hands are carving a shape in the air: a balloon, a clock face – it's hard to tell what it may be until he opens his eyes again and fixes his stare upon a woman in the second row.

This is most peculiar, he says, smiling to show there's a joke coming, But I see a large red ball with a seal upon it. The audience is smiling too, now, but not the woman in the second row.

Did you go to the circus, madam? Were you taken there as a child?

She shakes her head. He's at a loss for a moment – the circus is a certainty, normally – so he pauses, puts his hand up as if he's listening to a message that must not be interrupted.

Then it's . . . he says, playing for time, That's it. A lady is rising, she wears a long coat. I see her holding your hand. Ah, thank you, madam, much obliged. You're watching the parade, she says.

At last, the woman in the second row nods her head.

We'd go see the elephants, she says, Come down from the station. My gran that'll be. She always took me.

The audience sighs, Bernard sighs. I know him well enough now to recognize it as the sound of relief. Sometimes, I can't tell whether he's making it up – Painting the Scene, as he calls it, or Bringing Comfort, if the woman is wearing black. But today, I know.

Then I have your grandmother with me. She's reminding you of the happy times you used to have. She's convinced there will be more to come. But you must let go of something first.

A flurry of wings on the ledge above.

Whoever you are looking for is at peace, he says, Would it be your sister?

Daughter, she says.

A flash of white at the back wall: a feather, spiralling down to earth.

Ah yes, your grandmother is what we call an enabler, my dear. She is bringing a message from your daughter. She is at peace, she is in your grandmother's arms. I would like to leave their love with you.

Silence in the room. The woman puts a handkerchief up to her face, presses it to her cheek. All eyes are on Bernard now, their conduit, their guide. The bird on the end of the ledge turns, flits open its wings and shows me its pearly breast; flies, in a swoop, across the space above their heads. Flying down towards me, sapphire blue, flying and falling; an arrow, a searchlight, a shooting star. And as I watch him, I am falling, too. Joseph has come.

shooting star

I try to think of it as beautiful. A clear sky, blue as a sugar bag. The colours below it are carved-out land. Green for the clutch of trees inside the plantation; butterscotch track between the tower and furthest farm. A flint church floats on a spray of corn. In the distance, a string of glitter marks the waterline. Birds in the field trail a farmer's cart, blowing like confetti in its wake. The stone of the parapet is warm and brown. Joseph is standing on the edge.

Just like a bird, he says, opening his arms wide, taking in a lungful of pure light.

Watch me fly, Beauty!

twenty-two

There's something familiar about the face, or not quite the face perhaps – the hair. The hair, that's it. Black as ebony, shiny as a door knocker. He's smiling; he's lost his teeth at the front. A pair of glasses, round and thick, sit on the tip of his nose. The eyes behind them are kindly. His smell is goose fat.

Princess, says Mr Stadnik, How wonderful to see you!

I'm in the back now, half lying, half sitting, on the couch in the corner. There's no one else in the room. I can hear Jean and Bernard in the hall outside. From the echo of Jean's shouting, I know everyone else must have left.

You fainted, child, he says, snapping his fingers, Clear out, pfff! That bird – it flew right at you.

He makes a diving motion with his hand, then stops suddenly, pulls himself back to look at my face.

Don't cry, he says, reaching in his pocket for his handkerchief, Don't cry! It's a wonder to find you. After so long. So long a time.

There's no blue about him; not the slightest hint. He's on this side of life.

You can go now, says Jean, appearing in the doorway, Mr Foy will pay you what we owe . . .

Her words drop away when she sees us together. It's like watching a silent film.

What's going on here? she says, finally recovering.

Mr Stadnik gets up from the couch, introducing himself with a smile and a bow.

That's all very well, Mr Stannick, says Jean, Now if you'll kindly leave my niece alone – she needs to rest.

But she is not your niece, states Mr Stadnik, with a wide, black grin – Is she?

They look at each other steadily. Without taking her eyes from Mr Stadnik's face, she calls out,

Bernard!

And again, almost a shriek,

Bernard! Come and see this!

~ ~ ~

For three days, I'm not allowed to leave the house. This isn't Jean's doing, it's Bernard. In a state of panic, he declares I am unfit to go anywhere alone. He doesn't quite put it this way, but I'm learning fast: I'm learning the language of lies.

You're very popular now, he says, And some unscrupulous types will take advantage. The man barely knows you – a lodger, you say, in your grandfather's house? I've seen him, he's no more than a tinker, a street sweeper, that's what he is. What kind of man is that to be associated with? A man who pushes a broom in the road! Don't you worry about him. We are here, Jean and I, to protect you. He won't bother you again.

This means: I'm very worried that Mr Stadnik will take you away from us. Our star turn. Our breadwinner.

I learn by listening. Jean is unable to speak quietly – or perhaps she doesn't care if I do hear; perhaps she thinks I'm too stupid to realize what I am to them. Perhaps she thinks I should show my gratitude by being their puppet. They have created Winifred, after all.

It's our teaching has brought her this far, she tells Bernard, who is sulking over his brandy, Not a pot to piss in when she turned up.

They're downstairs in the parlour, tight as a drum now, pooling their worries in the lamplight. Bernard's voice is dark and miserable.

She doesn't need us, Jean, he says.

She hasn't got the means to go it alone.

A long stretch of quiet, then one of Bernard's sighs.

She can leave whenever she chooses.

Jean's laugh cuts the air,

Then let her, she says, Ungrateful little madam.

Be kind, my dear, he says, after another pause, Be kind to the child.

She's no child, she says, and for a moment I think she's about to tell him about Hewitt, what he did. What we did. But there's only silence, and in it, and through it, I see a chance. In the morning I will ask if I can go to Hewitt's, to get my fitting done. I am their creation and their Godsend, after all. And a Godsend needs a decent pair of shoes.

~

It's a shock to see him. Jean is ahead, always ahead of me, and where better, she says, to get my feet measured, than in the comfort of my own home. Our little palace.

Normally, I don't do house calls, says Hewitt, but you, my dear, are a very special case.

He's wearing a mustard-coloured jacket and a cravat, like a country gentleman come into town for an outing. He has a large leather bag which squeaks when he opens it: tape measure, cream gloves, a sheaf of crisp white tissue paper, the little casket to put your foot in. Hewitt's Devices are spread across the floor. When she sees my face, Jean is triumphant. She excuses herself to the kitchen to make tea; really, she will stand and listen in the hall.

Any news from your mother? I say, willing Jean to march back in and stop me, Any *medical* troubles lately?

Hewitt breathes in his sing-song way, lalala.

She hasn't bothered me since, he says, No bad dreams,

no wakeful nights. You cured me, he says, and laughing to himself, Ex-or-cized the spirit.

I tell him straight away that I lied, that Jean told me what to say. Head down, very quietly, he says,

I know. I don't believe in all that rubbish. It's just entertainment, really, isn't it?

He looks up, serene, untroubled, almost smiling.

Then why did you ask for me?

I liked your face, he says, You remind me of someone I knew.

Fiddling with the leather straps, pulling on his gloves.

Why the gloves? Afraid you might catch something?

Hewitt reaches for my ankle.

My dear, allow me, he says, Medicated, new, from America. A massage first, you see, to relax the foot.

I could kick him now, that'd bring Jean running. But he takes my foot in his hand, brings it between his knees, and strokes it. I close my eyes, and think of his mother and her coarse words, and my own mother, and my own father. All gone. His hands on my feet are soft and warm.

~

He said they were the tiniest feet that ever had shoes made to fit. The most dainty and fragile, like alabaster, he said. Crouching with his head bowed, and me in the armchair with my leg raised and my petticoat glowing in the morning light. Taking the right foot and placing it in the box, pulling the strap across the bridge of my foot. Feeding the little lace through the hole, pulling it, measuring, marking, all the time stroking, sliding the wooden frame to toe and heel. His thumb caressing the arch, the skin below the ankle. A perfect fit.

Divine, he said.

twenty-three

Mr Stadnik turns his teacup round in a careful circle, examining the rim and then wiping it with the corner of his napkin. We're in the corner of Gurney's teashop, away from the window where people might see us. I'm not supposed to be here; I've run away. It was simple, in the end, not like running away in the stories my mother told me. Jean made me feel as if it was my choice, but really, it happened without me knowing. It would have been different if Bernard was there, but he was taking his walk – his constitutional. Jean was sitting in a chair in the window, sewing.

I'm going out for a bit, I said, pulling on my coat before she could stop me, To get some fresh air.

Fine, said Jean, tacking thread along the hem. She didn't make a move. But as I opened the door, she called me back.

Take that with you, she said, pointing to the corner of the room where she had put my case. She didn't look at me again.

Tell Bernard I'm sorry, I replied, not knowing what else to say.

You will be, was all she said.

~

Finding Mr Stadnik was difficult. When I asked people in the city, no one knew his name. A road sweeper, Bernard said, so I walked the roads, feeling the time stretch out in front of me, thinking of Bernard coming home, persuading Jean that there had been a mistake, Jean shouting at him. Then both of them would be bound to set out to look for me and bring me back.

On the corner near the pawn shop stood a cart, with a battered umbrella slung across the handles. I'd passed the shop many times since coming back from Aunty Ena's farm. Haunted by the memory of my father's suit hanging in the window, I would turn my head, look the other way. Today, I stopped. No suit. But the man coming through the door carrying two brown bags was Mr Stadnik. He gave me a broad, toothless smile, nonchalantly loaded his cart, tipped my own case into it, and pushed it ahead of him. As if we always met this way.

Princess, he said, Come and take tea with your old friend! The cake plate in the centre of the table has no cakes on it, just two dry-looking biscuits; a pot of tea the colour of straw, a small white jug of something like milk.

For what we are about to receive, says Mr Stadnik, lifting his cup and waggling his little finger in the air. He drains it in two gulps, takes off his glasses and breathes on them, rubbing them with the other corner of his napkin. He looks to be particular – fastidious, Bernard would say, if he could see Mr Stadnik now – but his coat is frayed at the cuffs and shiny at the elbows, his collar is grey, the skin on his neck is grained with creases of dirt. He's attempted a shave; in places his chin is scraped and raw, in others, dotted with white growth. There's a tie around his neck; the knot is small and tight and marked on either side from where his finger and thumb have been. He's older, dirtier, but to me he's just the same. I would just like to stay in this teashop forever, to be with him, with the steam running rivulets down the windows, and the soft rain, and the dull lead-grey of the sky outside. He's real and earthly and sitting only inches away from me, with his head a bit on one side, nosy as a jackdaw on a fence.

And they just come to you? he says, replacing his glasses

on his face and looking over them, They just . . . appear, that's it?

They rise up, I say, Mr Foy – that's Bernard – he knew straight off, when he found me. He said I was a gift from God.

He did, says Mr Stadnik, And you are. Indeed, you are.

I had already explained about Bernard and Jean Foy, how they looked after me, how Bernard found me when I was sent back from Stow Farm. How they taught me everything I know. Feeling ashamed, I don't tell Mr Stadnik that I've left them. He's preoccupied with knowing about the Gift; how it works, what happens when the spirits come.

I feel a vibration, I say.

Like an earthquake? he asks, raising his chin and staring at me through his glasses. Two tiny reflected windows hide his eyes.

Like a train when it's coming into the station. Sometimes like an engine.

He's keen on this idea. His finger traces a question on the cloth.

Ah – a motor car?

Bernard says words don't do justice to the Gift. Paint the scene, he said, In your mind's eye. So I try to paint one for Mr Stadnik.

Like the fairground, I say, When the horses turn. Their saddles all colours. The whooshing by your head as they roll past.

The *horses*? He raises one eyebrow.

The gallopers.

Mr Stadnik seems satisfied with this. He reaches for a biscuit and dips it up and down in his tea, until it breaks off and plops into the cup. Then he smiles.

And the colour, he says, fishing out the biscuit and sucking it off his spoon, Always blue?

Yes, different kinds of blue. The vibrations are blue.

Why not yellow? Or red? Or green? Why are these vibrations blue?

I have no answer. I want to please him, but I can tell that he doesn't believe in me, even though he stood in the hall that night and watched. Mr Stadnik was there because Bernard had given him a leaflet in the street, and asked if he might want an evening's work, putting out the chairs and clearing up at the end. Mr Stadnik didn't recognize me, he said, until I stood up and spoke. He hasn't mentioned my hair.

The spirits come to me in blue because that's how my aura interprets them – in the Afterlife, I said, pleased to find Bernard's words in my mouth.

Very good, says Mr Stadnik, Lovely colour, blue. But not because blue is important to you, in any way?

He looks at me for an answer, tries again.

And no one else can see these blue vibrating spirits?

No.

Eyes wider now,

Not even Mr Bernard?

No.

But he's a mystical? He sees this Afterlife?

It's called clairvoyant. Bernard sees them in other ways. He has visions of past events.

I understand, says Mr Stadnik, How nice it must be, to have visions.

He removes his glasses and rubs at them again. His breath wheezes as he smears the lenses. I have to correct him. This time, I know Mr Stadnik is not always right.

Sometimes it isn't nice, I say, Bernard says there are too many dead. Too many dead, too soon and too young.

Mr Stadnik nods sadly in agreement with this.

He is a philosopher, then, says Mr Stadnik, And this is what he tells people, your Mr Bernard?

No! He tells them – he gives them words of Comfort. He Ministers Comfort. He brings messages of Joy.

Bernard's words are the best way of describing what he does. Better than my own. Just when I think Mr Stadnik is truly beginning to understand, he leans close, conspiratorial, whispering across the table.

And glad tidings too, I think. So tell me, are there any dead people here, in this room? Those two over there perhaps, he says, jerking his head sideways.

The table he's nodding at has two elderly women in identical turquoise hats.

We don't say dead. We say 'passed over'.

Ah, now I've made you angry! he says, Forgive me. But why do you only see these passed-over people at certain times? How is it they only vibrate to you in a church hall? Why are they not crowding the streets, jumping off the buildings, out of windows, drowning in the blue rivers, falling out of the blue sky? Tell me, child. Why do they choose a particular time and place?

Mr Stadnik glances at the two turquoise women, gives them a grin, then turns back to me with a serious face.

Why *not* right here in this very room? he whispers, jabbing the table with his finger.

Bernard says we are conduits. The circumstances must be . . . amenable. But I have seen them outside, I say, thinking of all the spirits on the roof of the cathedral.

I see, says Mr Stadnik, eyeing the last biscuit, And you have never failed?

No one has said so.

Very good.

He goes quiet, head up, searching the room for the waitress. When he catches her eye, he waves.

And your grandfather, he asks, You've seen him, of course? I tell Mr Stadnik about going back to Chapelfield as soon as I got off the train. About how I looked, found nothing.

Then come with me, he says, pocketing the biscuit and replacing it with a coin, Let's see if we can't find him.

twenty-four

We walk from the teashop, tight under Mr Stadnik's umbrella, around the back of the market and up the steps, past a crater of mud and broken brick, and finally into Chapelfield. Bethel Street House is untouched, the bars on the tiny windows freshly painted. Little Ketts School, opposite, is still standing. Singing comes in waves from the building. It could be me in there, wearing my beret and worrying about the small things, like a name, Telltale hair, a bully with a birthmark on her throat. Almost, it could be yesterday. But Chapelfield Gardens is trampled into muddy scars, the railings have gone, and in the middle, where I first saw the gallopers, is the pagoda, dripping rain: bomb-wrecked and broken-boned. I know where we're going. We're going to my grandfather's house.

He's not there, I say again, I came back, to find him. There's no one there.

Mr Stadnik upends his cart against the wall, loosens the tie around his neck and draws out a long silver chain from under his shirt. It has a watch on it, and a key. He opens the door and waits for me to pass.

A smell of mildew and ash, and another smell underneath, of something rotting. The hall is filled, floor to ceiling, with papers, books, rags, boxes spilling their insides, bits of wood, broken pieces of furniture, all heaped up on each other. He leads me through it, squeezing a narrow path into the living room where we all used to sit, with my grandfather reading to us, poking the fire, tamping his pipe. It is dark and chill and choked with yet more papers, clothes and boxes. A few ragged shirts and suits hang from the picture rail, freckled with spots of mould. I try not to look for a blue one. Mr Stadnik passes through the door to the kitchen, where he surveys the room for a minute before placing his two latest bags high up, on top of a stack of others. The kitchen is stuffed with more of the same, crowding all the surfaces, filling every space. The fire in the living room is out; above the mantelpiece, a medley of clocks tick against each other. Each one shows a different time. Under the window, where a heap of blankets marks Mr Stadnik's bed, a dog is sleeping. Mr Stadnik nudges him with his toe.

Come and say hello to Princess, he says.
The dog crawls out of its nest, slinking towards me with its tail hooped under its body: a small grey dog with a pointed mouth.

What happened to Billy?
This *is* Billy, says Mr Stadnik, and then, correcting himself, Of course. This is Billy the Third, he says, A good hunter! We have uninvited guests here, Princess; but Billy is fast. He can catch them.

He edges past me, shifts an armful of clothes off a chair, balancing them on the edge of the table.

Forgive me, he says, Please sit down.
I know it will offend him if I don't, so I sit, on the edge of the cushion, feeling the damp seep into me. He takes the biscuit from his pocket, offers it to me, and when I refuse, he breaks it up and feeds it, piece by piece, to the dog.

You have so many things, Mr Stadnik, Where do they all come from?
He looks pleased for a second, as if he's about to have a good idea, then troubled by the thought.

They're not mine. People sell them to the man, he says,

And I get them back . . . for the people. Some of this – waving his arm around the room – is from the houses too, you see? People will come back and find nothing, not a brick or window. But I have their things here. I have them. I will keep them safe.

I daren't ask him how the people will know where to look. I daren't ask him who he thinks might want a dead man's clothes, a blackened chair, a collection of shattered gramophone records.

Mr Stadnik paces the narrow floor space, eyeing me over his glasses. Perhaps I have offended him after all.

Billy the Second – your Billy – he's gone, he says.

Another space of silence, and then in a soft voice,

Do they allow animals into the Afterlife, Princess?

bending down to stroke the dog, who slips like an eel under his hand and creeps back to his bed. Mr Stadnik smiles but when he speaks his voice is low, unfriendly.

So. You would like to see your grandfather again? he asks.

Of course! I say, Where is he?

You tell me, he says, snapping his fingers, Call him. Make him appear. He must be in your Afterlife!

Mr Stadnik is letting me know that my grandfather is dead.

It's not nice, I say, To tell me like this.

I couldn't admit the truth, even to myself. I had hoped he had simply gone away. I had hoped he would come back. Behind his glasses, Mr Stadnik's eyes are wide.

But surely you knew? You are famous in this city. You are a . . . wait! he says, hand in the air. He looks about the room, and from behind a clock, pulls out a leaflet with my picture on it.

Yes. You see, it says so here, Clairvoyant Extraordinaire. This is you?

Thrusting the paper at me. I would like to deny it, but his anger is brittle as a splint.

Why would he not come to *you*, Princess? Please, bring

him now. I have many friends passed over, you see, and none here, on this earthly earth. I would like to talk with him again. Sit by the fire, eh? he says, gesturing to the slump of ash in the grate, Have a good old *chat*.

I *can't* just call him, I say, The circumstances must be – amenable.

Mr Stadnik sinks down onto the blanket. Above him, spikes of rain on the window. His face is grey with grief.

Amenable, he says, Well, this was his home; that must be amenable. And here, I found him. I did not want to leave the farm, Princess, or you, alone in that world. I was sent away, you know, in the night, by men who didn't like a stranger. Men who would shoot a stranger as easily as they shoot his dog. Your grandfather was a brave man, to take me in.

Mr Stadnik gets up, passes by me into the hall, heaves open the cellar door.

This is where a brave man hides, he says, pointing down the stone steps, When he is old and cannot understand. This is where he dies.

Darker still in the hallway, with only a glimmer of light between us.

I do not doubt you see wonderful things in your head, he whispers evenly, Pretty children in bonnets, buried treasure, starlit skies. Go on, make money from fools. It's easy, in this time. Speak your fine words, with your fine clothes and your fine hair and your *gift*. But do not imagine that you bring comfort. There is no comfort in this world, and there is nothing in the next. The dead, Princess, are the dead.

the dead are the dead

It's hard to keep a friend who won't believe. No point telling him that the spirits decide for themselves when to come. They can be bloody-minded, spiteful as a child. The state of the house after Mr Stadnik got his hands on it – I should think my grandfather would have had a few choice words, if he ever turned up. But he never did. I could give reasons, quote Bernard's gospel. But Mr Stadnik had cast a doubt over everything. I thought I knew it all, until then. I was taught to believe – not just in the spirits, but in the gift they said I had. They'd turned my head, Bernard and Jean. I wouldn't sit on Mr Stadnik's dirty chair for fear of catching something. Fine clothes, fine words. Mr Stadnik was right about that. It makes me laugh now; these days my words are not so fine, and the only kind of seat I get to enjoy is a bench, marking time, looking at adverts for furniture I can never buy, in a freesheet I took from a rubbish bin.

I tried to keep Mr Stadnik, that was my mistake. I could have gone back to Bernard and Jean and made my apologies. But my insides were hollow. I had seen the ghost of Joseph. I *had* seen him, I was sure of that. It cleans you out like a dose of meths. If I think of that time now, it's white as a page. There was nothing left of me, after the hall, and the bird, after I saw Joseph fall. And it wasn't beautiful, try as I might to imagine it. He was young and afraid. He fell from that tower on a flat grey morning, like a stone into mud. No bells ringing out a wedding song; just crows, screaming in a ring above his head. That's all there was to mark his flight. No one told me, not Aunty Ena, not Alice, but it doesn't matter. Doesn't alter the fact. Fell like a stone.

Just when I thought there was no one else left, Mr Stadnik appeared, bringing a feeling I could hardly remember: safety. I thought he would look after me. I wouldn't have to stand in front of the faces and hope that I could make the right words come out. But then we went to Chapelfield, and I understood him for what he had become: a mad old man, buying back the pawn shop with his wages, picking over the rubble, hoarding the debris. As if these people would ever come back, turn up at his house, sort through all the boxes, hoping to find that silk blouse her mother wore when she got married, the father's sheet music, or his watch, or the silver-ware handed down, the tangled baby clothes. As if a single item could bring a person back to life.

When the rain stopped, we crossed into Chapelfield gardens. It was good to be in the air, that smell of light after a downpour. We wandered around the gardens, now and then Mr Stadnik bending to pull up a weed, or examine a fallen leaf. The wrecked pagoda stood in the middle of a patch of scrubby grass. We climbed the steps and leaned on the rail, side by side in our new, awkward silence, looking out across the trees. Hunched over, Mr Stadnik was even smaller than I remembered, almost grotesque, with his shiny black hair and his thick glasses and the film of grime on his skin. His cuffs hung loose about his wrists; on the right one, he wore a gold bracelet with what looked like a heavy charm attached.

What's that? I asked, A keepsake?

No, he said, touching his finger to the chain, Over there – pointing to a bank of shattered houses – I found this chain.

You're just keeping it safe, then, I said, Until someone comes to claim it.

Correct.

Bernard had a name for it, what Mr Stadnik did: Bernard called them the Vultures. We saw men like him all the time, sifting through the bombsites, trying to find something worth selling.

And this, he said, holding the charm up to the light for me to inspect, you will recognize.

It wasn't a charm: it was a small round brooch. The stone was lost. Aunty Ena's opal. He hadn't even mentioned her, yet he wore her only piece of jewellery.

She always said opals were unlucky, I said, Did she give it to you, then?

Of course, he said, his voice bitter, How can I be so stupid! You think I stole it. No. She gave this to me. As a token of love.

He jerked his other arm into the air, revealing the cuff I remembered he wore, its laces frayed with wear. Unfastened it. Held his wrist up to the light, showing me two livid lines where the leather bit into the skin, framing a series of coarse white scars.

And here is another token, he said.

I could read nothing in the marks.

What does it mean?

This lover was called hope, he said, A foolish name, don't you think? I carved it myself, after a different war.

My father's words came back in a whisper on his lips.

Cross my heart and hope to die.

He ran his finger along the scars, then carefully replaced the leather cuff.

They say hope is the worst of all evils, because it prolongs the torment of man. Believe me, there are far worse evils in this world. Never give up hope, Princess. Promise me.

~

The roof of the cathedral glinted through the trees. We walked to a clearing to get a better view. I wanted to keep him, still.

I was ashamed that I could think of him as a thief, when he was simply collecting bits of hope; keeping them safe for others to claim back. I thought by showing him the cathedral roof, he would forgive me. Perhaps he would recognize that we were both attempting the same thing; I was trying to give hope too, in a way. I wanted it to be like old times again. I was wrong to want.

Look, I said, Look at the roof, Mr Stadnik.

The sun was low in the sky, a bank of rose-coloured cloud above it. The cathedral stood proud in the dusk.

It's a roof, he said, shrugging, A fine example.

See? I said, pointing to where the blue light shone, soft as melt, See the spirits there?

A fine example of a zinc roof, he continued, Beautiful, how it takes on the colour of the sky. Like a pool of water. Watch, it will change in a minute.

We looked on as sunlight caught it, the blue dissolving into pink, pink into purple as the last rays sank away, then a simple, dull grey.

Your spirits have gone home, Princess, and so must I, he said, breaking from my side.

He looked baffled, bitten by a thought.

You are welcome to stay with me, of course. It is your home too, he said.

I told him I had to go back. They would be worrying about me. I lied for both of us.

Then take care of yourself, he said, and as he turned, Oh, beautiful hair, by the way, and the colour – just like mine. We two, we could be the exact same age!

He bowed, took my hand and placed the brooch in my palm.

A token of love for a Princess, he said, waving me away.

twenty-five

The woman eyes me suspiciously from round the edge of the door; the rain has been blown away by a bitter wind, leaving a sky black as jet. When the dark came down and the city shrank into itself, I thought again about Mr Stadnik's offer. I even went up to the door. He had taken his handcart inside. The memory of the clothes piled high in there, like so many discarded pelts – it was enough to stop me. I asked at The Steam Packet if anyone knew of lodgings. The man looked me up and down, considered a while, before finally directing me to Mrs Philips.

Mrs Philips does not look pleased at being disturbed so late. She won't let me in, despite the cold. A gulp of air whistles past her down the hall, banging a door deep inside the house.

I charge by the week, she says, In advance. I've got one room left if you're interested. It's a bit on the small side, mind.

She shuts the door on me, disappears down the hall, reappearing a minute later with her scarf on her head and a coat draped over her shoulders. We cross the road to the boarding house, where she lets me in.

Here's the key, she says, If you want to take a look, motioning me up the stairs.

When I get to the first landing, I realize she's not coming up.

The very top, she shouts, Private, it says on the door. Toilet's on the floor below.

The room is furnished with a single bed, a chair and a wardrobe. The sloping roof on either side of the bed gives it the appearance of a crib; the windows above it show the clear night sky. In one corner is an ancient stove, propped up on a pile of books; in the other are two filthy dusters, a broom and an empty tin of floor wax.

Private, it says on the door.

Perfect, I say, looking up into my two black squares of the night.

~

On the first morning, in the kitchen, I meet the other residents: an old woman who kept me awake all night with her cough; a younger one who sits shivering in an armchair next to the fire, her trembling hands reaching out, over and over, to steady her legs; one who stands by the window, not looking or speaking to anyone; and a fourth woman, freckle-faced, with a tinkling, nervous laugh, who makes up for the awkwardness by talking all the time.

Pleased to meet you, she says, ducking her head like a chicken, My name's Noreen. This here's Sissy – gesturing to the coughing woman – And over there by the fire, that's Emily. Hogging the hot seat as usual! Say hello to our new friend, Em – she won't stand up, my lover, it'd take her all day. Just on release, she is, from Bethel Street. And Georgie too, she said, pointing at the woman near the window, We call her Garbo. It's our little joke, on account of her not saying much. It's in the eyes, you know.

I won't be able to remember all the names at once, I say.

Don't you worry about that, says Noreen, You just tell us who *you* are. Not often we have such a lady in our midst. We'll have to mind our manners now, girls!

The other women look away. I can't tell whether they're embarrassed by her or by me.

Go on then, she says, in the silence, What's *your* name?

Winnie, I say.

Winnie what?

Just Winnie.

Her smile takes in the whole room.

First-name terms is fine by us, she says, We're all on first names here, aren't we, girls?

The others completely ignore her.

Anything you want, Winnie, just you ask. You're welcome to pool your points with us. That's what we do, and it suits us just fine.

I don't have coupons, I say, But I've got a bit of money. She gives me a roguish look.

No last name, no book, you're a mystery girl. Never mind. I know where you can get stuff. That's right, isn't it? Noreen says, to no reply. She leans in close.

But don't tell Mrs Philips. Stickler, she is. Doesn't like us to break the rules.

~

All the residents here are women, and more than the four I've met – six at least. Most of them have come from Bethel Street House. There's one who seems to spend all her time in the washroom, crying, and another one I've only ever heard behind her door; Mrs Philips and another lady take her meals in on a tray. She keeps to her room, and I keep to mine. Everything I need, I take up the stairs, hidden in my case.

Noreen is hardest to avoid. While the other women circle me like a pack, or stare blankly through me, Noreen goes out of her way to make an excuse to stop me on the stairs, just as I'm going out.

Business, is it? she asked, the first time. I thought it best to just agree, but she wasn't letting me go so easily. She gave me a narrow look.

I thought I recognized you from somewhere, she said, Maybe I've seen you about in the city. I work too, in a manner of speaking. Mrs Philips doesn't know, mind, so don't say. Careless talk and all that!

I said nothing; she wouldn't get any kind of talk from me. But Noreen was persistent, closing in with her sweet scent and her knowing little eyes.

Get you anything you care for, I can. I've got contacts. Give us a shout if you're wanting anything.

I said I'd remember for next time, and left it at that.

~

What I do, when I go out, is walk. There's no one I want to meet, so I avoid the main roads. I learn the passageways and cuttings and paths that lead onto open land. Each day, I walk a bit further. I just walk. It requires no gift and no thought. I walk until my legs ache and my feet are sore. It's a long way, I tell myself, a long way to the end of the world, and I must plan for it. I walk in a straight line, as far as I'm able. It's twenty-five miles to the sea. I have never seen it. I have no ambition, but if there's a wish inside me, it's to walk there.

~

When I run out of money, I go back to the pawn shop and I sell my coat. It's valuable, made of wool. All those things Mr Stadnik collected, the old suit jackets and the shirts and bits of baby clothes too tiny to bear, they're worth something. He said he was buying them back from the pawnbroker – to store them for the people. I'm thinking he lied. Perhaps he was really taking them in to sell them. I never saw what he had in those two paper bags. I can think anything now, of anyone.

Jean taught me many things, apart from the coaching and the hymns. I get by on very little, I can fashion a new coat from the blanket on my bed. It's no disgrace to wear it. When the cold creeps in at night, I lay my new coat across the bed, and it becomes what it used to be.

It's my boots that fail me. The walking has ruined them. I think of Hewitt, the soft slippers, and how easy it would be for me to just drop by, be polite. Then I remember his hands on my feet. I take the two dusters from the corner of the room, and tie them round the soles. It serves its purpose, until Noreen notices.

My God! she says, staring at my feet, Don't tell me you're going to work in them things? That'll never do. Us girls, we've got to stick together.

The following day, Noreen corners me on the stairwell, insists I follow her into the kitchen. Emily is sitting, head down, in front of the fire.

These are just beauty, Noreen says, pulling a bag out from under her arm, Got them from a chap I know on the market. Owed me a favour.

Not much of a favour, was it? You don't need coupons for those, says Emily, pointedly. Noreen ignores her.

That's right, she says, Just you try them on, see if they do the job.

She's brought me a pair of clogs. Wooden, with a scarlet trim.

They're lovely, I say, How much are they?

On me, she says, Think of it as a *gift*. Only don't tell Mrs Philips. I won't say anything, if you won't.

She gives me a bright-eyed, knowing look. Nothing is ever free, not even a stranger's kindness. Her face tells me everything. Noreen knows who I am – the person I used to be. I accept the clogs. I thank her. I pack my case, and when the two square windows go black, I begin to walk.

twenty-six

I'm eating the sky, eating it up. Walking straight, in through day and out through night, light falling on my shoulder, sinking low behind. My shadow grows long and thin. Best is when it's clear, with the moon cutting over my head like a scythe. On the ground, everything turns to silver. Stars sharp as pins. Often the sky is like that; going into it is like meeting your lover. I tell myself he could be any one of those points of light up there: that one, hanging like a sapphire on invisible thread. The walking is always best in the dark, when no one else is about. In the daytime, the distance is too near: a man a mile away can see you clearly. I rest when it comes light, spending the hours against the fencepost of a farmer's field, or the warming stone of a bridge. I get heat from the sun, a windless corner of a barn. I'm heading for the sea.

The spirits have left me now. I can no longer see them. But I see ordinary things, and wonder at Bernard, for whom the ordinary wasn't enough. A heron lifting off a lake, a cloud of golden midges hanging in the half-light, frost spangling the grass; these things are so much better than wearing fancy clothes, learning the language. Better than a blue spirit and a widow's tears. I see other blues now: trapped in a web on a windless morning, still as glass on flooded field, and all around me, the simple, open blue of the sky.

I think I can walk a straight line, but then the road will

turn to water under my feet. There's nothing to be done but to go back, join another road, and hope that it will last. The wind becomes unexpectedly brisk, metallic on the tongue. I imagine it blowing off the sea, mineral blue. I follow the scent, turning round on myself, breathing the air through my mouth, as if taste alone will find it. It feels like I won't ever get there, so when I come up over a field, find a road, see the tower of St Giles in the distance, I have to bite the tears away: it's then I know I never will.

part three: rise

menu

Feather
Locket
Brooch (opal missing)
Wooden foot
Hair

There was plenty of other stuff in my case. You don't last as long as I have and not accumulate. There was a woollen scarf I found outside Tesco's, yellow and green striped, very long; and lots of gloves. I'm partial to gloves – pity they never come as a pair. Usually, they're stuck on a railing, waving at the world. It's more often the right glove that's left behind. I know my right from left, Mr Stadnik taught me. My first glove came from him; I think that's why I adore them. My favourite is a pair of tiny mittens. Pure white, knitted, with little cartoon faces on them. I like plastic bags, too. They're everywhere, blowing down the road with nothing but the wind inside them, caught on the bushes, hanging from the trees like witches' knickers. I like the ones that have my grandfather's face on – they say KFC, the chicken place. He never wore a tie like that, and his beard needs trimming, but it's him.

I had Joseph's golden feather, the heart-shaped locket from my father, the brooch from Mr Stadnik and the hair from

Bernard's dead wife (not strictly inside my case, but stolen all the same). The divine wooden foot – well, that was a late addition. I never did get my shoes from Hewitt, despite his promises.

I left the teashop and walked out into the street. Hope is an affliction, all right, and I had it bad: of finding the girl who stole from me, of getting back everything that I'd lost. I should have known; the moment I made that decision – the first proper decision for years – trouble leapt up and bit me in the face.

twenty-seven

There's a paved area above the market, directly in front of the city hall. Everyone knows it. All sorts of people go to sit outside and have their lunch: council workers in their neat shirts and ties, mums out with their pushchairs, girls and boys, pretending not to notice each other. Then there's the rest of us, sitting where it's free, killing the day. I know some of them by sight: the Roofless girls, baiting a middle-aged man in a suit; the woman who keeps a dog in a pram, lifting the lid off a leftover burger; that lad that sings all the time. You can sit, eat, pass the day, use the public toilets when the attendant's got her back turned and get a wash if that's what you want, but mostly it's like a market *over* the market. People come to buy all sorts: drugs mostly, and knock-off, as they call it. You can get anything really, depending on who you ask. The benches are always full, but there's a long low wall to sit on. You have to eat your chips with the pigeons purring round your feet; their droppings spack the ground like stars. I sat for a while and watched them, waited for the words to come back. It was part of my plan to ask around, and I needed the language to do it. Thinking of Mr Stadnik put the idea in my head: perhaps the girl was trying to sell my stuff on. She would come here. I was just working out how to go about it, feeling the breeze pick up, skying the chip papers, when I heard a shout from the steps. It was Robin. He'd grown a little beard since he'd left Hewitt's place, had his hair in knots and a wide grin on his face.

Hey, Win! Cool hat, very chic, my dear! How've you been? he asked, sitting himself down beside me. I turned to face him.

Christ! he went, screwing his eyes up at the sight of my cheek, You've been in the wars, haven't you?

Have I? I said, not giving anything away.

What have you gone and done?

Dog bit me, I said.

Bugger. Let's hope she don't want a photograph, he said.

A photograph of what? I asked. I wasn't really paying attention. Robin was often on what he called a 'mystery tour'; and he had the opposite problem to me when it came to words. He had busloads of them.

Of you, he grinned, The big celebrity.

The big *what*?

He pursed his lips, drew hard on the roll-up between his fingers.

There's a lady been asking about you, he said, blowing out a ring of smoke, Asking all over.

What sort of lady?

He grinned again,

A pretty sort of lady, now you ask. Quite professional-looking, I'd say. Maybe you've come into money, Win! Someone might've left you a fortune.

That even made me smile, for a second. The lads used to like to talk about that, while they burned everything in sight, what they'd do if they came into money. The wind was circling our feet, swirling around us; in my chest, the tight feeling was creeping back. Like a bird's wings, fluttering.

What did she want? I asked.

Wouldn't say. Something about a long time ago. Trying to trace you. I tell you, Win, it's money! She'll be a private detective, wanting to reunite you with your great granny's fortune.

What 'something a long time ago'? I asked, Did she say? The bird's wings inside my ribcage, beating harder now.

Only that it was personal. I've seen her again this morning. No joy, she said, so I told her she might catch you at that place on The Parade.

I was never there.

You were there last time I saw you, he said, giving me a funny look.

I put my hand to my head, afraid the wind would take my beret.

I don't know what you're talking about.

The cobbler's — you know, your old boyfriend's place — what was he called? Hewson?

I wouldn't say his name, but Robin wasn't giving up: clicking his fingers, tapping his tongue against his teeth. Grit in the wind, stinging my eyes.

It was painted on the window, he was saying, Big gold letters, come on, Win. Howlett?

I was willing him not to say it.

He was never my boyfriend, I said, And I was never there. Robin put his hands up, laughing, clapped them in the blurt air.

Hewitt, that was it! I see it now: big gold letters. Hewitt's Shoe Repairs and Fittings!

bespoke

Hewitt sits in the room above his shop, working at what he describes as his Design Table. It's a just a bench, the sort they have in church, with a long wooden table in front and drawers underneath. There's a box at the end, full of tools, and a whetstone for sharpening them. His Patterning Device is simply a sewing machine, the exact same model as Jean's. He likes the language of his trade – his Art, he calls it – but I like the objects. While he works, I sit and look at his tools, the awl blades different sizes and the handles worn; the wooden feet of his customers, each in their own compartment, going all the way up the wall. Some of them are shiny and new, others are covered with leather pieces, stuck here and there about the shape of the foot.

Amendments, Hewitt says, when I ask him what the pieces are for, Never tell the customer that their foot has got bigger, and never mention bunions – just say that some small adjustment must be made.

I'm in hiding. Hewitt is hiding me. I came to the shop on a Sunday; I knew he wouldn't be going to any church. I was desperate. The clogs Noreen gave me had made my feet bleed, and despite wrapping them in paper, my toes were so sore and bloody and swollen, I couldn't walk without crying. If he was delighted to see me, which is what he said when he finally opened the door, he didn't let on; just took me upstairs to his workroom, sat me on the bench, and told me to remove my stockings. He left me alone while I pretended to do it. In truth, my legs were bare. He returned with an enamel basin of milky water, a towel slung over his shoulder.

Feet in here, he said, Soak them.

The blisters had broken, and the skin had rolled back in strips, sticky with blood and black with dirt from the road. They didn't look as if they belonged to me. He was calm until he picked up my clogs.

Cheap rubbish! Vile! he shouted, throwing them into the wastebasket under the bench, Never wear cheap shoes, Winifred!

Beggars can't be Choosers, I said.

You are no beggar. You could have come to me.

I started to tell him about leaving Jean and Bernard, but he flapped his fingers at me.

I know all that. Do you think I care? Do you think I — of all people — would believe what they're saying about you?

My mouth was dry. I could barely get the words out.

What are they saying?

Hewitt smiled, a small ducking of his head.

That you are a thief, of course, he said, as if that would be a natural assumption. I could tell from the enjoyment on his face that being accused of theft wasn't the worst of it.

And that you made . . . improper, shall we say, yes, that would be a good word for it, improper suggestions to Bernard.

I'm no thief.

I would have denied the other part, too, but Hewitt was in full song.

I know Mr Foy very well. He was in love with you. And Jean is a jealous woman.

But she's his sister!

His smile was growing.

And you're their niece, that's right, isn't it? You're their niece from the country, with a marvellous gift.

Hewitt gave a little shake of the towel and laid it at my feet.

Jean is Bernard's Companion, he continued, His Spiritual Assistant. Bernard doesn't need to say what else she is – people make assumptions, my dear. As they will about you. Not everything is as it seems in this world, Winifred.
He went over to the bench, opened a drawer underneath the work table, pulled out a length of linen and wrapped it slowly round his hand.

Life is full of assumptions. Take me, for instance, he said, narrowing the gap, whispering,

I *assumed* that you despised me. And yet, where do you turn for help? You come here. Any port in a storm, isn't that how it goes? Well, you're safe enough with me. And you're welcome to stay for as long as you like.
He looked hard at me in the silence that followed. I wouldn't answer him. I wouldn't tell him that I wasn't planning to stay. He knelt down, smoothing the towel out as if it were a prayer mat.

I won't take advantage, if that's your concern, he said, And I won't tell them. I won't tell anyone. It'll be our secret. Cupping his hand round my ankle, raising my foot in the air.

It'll have to be, he continued, Don't want anyone finding out. It all counts against you. All of it.
Looking up at me, blissful,

Now. Let's see if we can't do something about these poor little creatures.

~ ~ ~

I do stay; I have nowhere else, and Noreen's gift has hobbled me. I hide away upstairs, sleep in the workroom on a low couch Hewitt has made up, with a bolster at one end to keep my legs raised. He's left the blackout on the windows; he says that sunshine is bad for leather. The air is breathless. I have a few things to do: make tea, toast, sometimes sew a little by hand – pieces for him, a frayed cuff, a patch on a shirt where the elbow has worn. He doesn't trust me with the machine, and never lets me work on the leather. Mostly, he just likes me to lie in the corner, while he cuts and stitches and hammers in nails. Occasionally he'll tell me who owns the shoe, who needs something special for their wedding day, who has inherited a lovely pair of boots that need new soles, but often he hums tunelessly under his breath, the lamp above him turning his hair into a glowing frizz of copper wire. He works late into the night. I fall asleep, and when I wake again, it's morning, and he's still there, working at the bench, the blade against the whetstone buzzing like a wasp.

At first, Hewitt doesn't touch me. But every day he creeps closer. Edging up to the couch, his tongue curling over his lip, his hands fondling the air around me. The nights are the worst, with the darkness so thick, the airless heat, the dead animal odour of leather. Even if I can't see him, I can tell when he's near. Like a hound disguising his scent, Hewitt covers himself in the smell of his trade: a leather tape hanging round his neck, a leather jerkin with laces at the front, a pouch slung low at his belly where he keeps his darning hooks, a chamois cloth, a sharp crescent blade. The creaking, stinking scent of him in the blackness.

I know it's not your first time, he whispers, every time. In the mornings, he pretends nothing has happened, bringing me tea, or a piece of gossip from downstairs. I never show my face down there: Alice still serves in the front of the shop. Alice would betray me. Hewitt brings me gifts from his mother's room: trinkets, old gazetteers showing distant places where there are purple mountains, violent sunsets, the aching space of a shoreline. Then he talks freely, about business, the beauty of his art. But mainly, about love.

See these here, he says, pulling open his box of tools, Guess what we call them?

He knows not to wait for a reply.

We call them St Hugh's Bones, he says, with a look of mock astonishment, Fancy that!

I don't want to see. When I think of bones, I picture a comb like the one my mother had, a thin hair hanging from it. But there are no bones inside his box, just tools – blades, little wheels, wooden handles.

Who was St Hugh? I say, sensing a catch.

Ah. Funny you should ask that. He was a shoemaker, too, says Hewitt, warming to his story, Who fell in love with a beautiful girl! And guess what her name was?

I'm no good at this game; the look in his eye gives me a tight feeling in my stomach. Hewitt goes on, oblivious,

Her name was Winifred! he says, triumphant, Now, what do you think of that?

I could tell him that Winifred is not my name; I could tell him that I'm no one, not a beautiful girl, certainly not the sweetheart of a shoemaker. I speak very little, but I make noises, to try to seem impressed. It's easier not to provoke a reaction. It's easier to move out of reach, inch back to the window where there's a little more daylight and a little less of him. He can suck the air away in a second. In equal measure, he oozes charm and rage; promise and threat come in one breath.

I'll make those shoes for you one day, he says, stroking a long strip of hide, When I'm sure you're not going to run away in them!

~ ~ ~

It was a close evening, summer on the way. I was in the workroom on my own, with nothing to do except look at the book Hewitt had given me; he said it once belonged to his mother. Inside were poems on glossy paper, and printed colour plates of wide skies, mounds of silver sand, wildlife. I didn't care much for the poems, but I liked the pictures of the birds, their colours and their strange names. Avocet, bearded tit, shelduck, plover. I recited the words under my breath, as if I could cast a spell to take me away from the thoughts in my head, the smell of skinned beasts: oystercatcher, garganey, tern. Pinpricks of light through the blackout, falling like sparks on the floor; not a breath of air in the room. Shingle bank, sand sedge, grey-hair grass. Everything remained as it was.

Sometimes I could put myself right inside the photographs, move through the salt air, hear gulls cry. Picture a room full of dead hide, and empty it. Fill it with a clear shorelight. I wished for a life that wasn't mine. No Hewitt. No stink. Walk all day, with nowhere to get to and no one to think about. Turn round, walk back, as the night sank down at my feet. No hot, darkened room. No other time. No me.

But the spell wasn't working. I couldn't stop the people in my head: Bernard and Jean; my mother and my father; my grandfather, bent like a scarecrow under the stairs. Mr Stadnik was worst, catching me when I least expected it, his bare arm in the rainlight and his eyes full of grief. And Joseph, always Joseph, winging his way across the fen sky, soaring like a plane above me.

I rolled up the blackout, opened the sash, just a crack, to let the breeze in. The smell of leather was making me choke; it lingered on my skin last thing at night, it steamed off the tea Hewitt brought me in the mornings. The air outside was so sweet. I could hear people passing on the street below, a child laughing, one man talking to another.

Hewitt was in his office, doing his accounts. I'd never been allowed in there, so it took me by surprise, him poking his head round the door and calling me inside. I thought he was going to be angry with me for opening the blackout.

I think it's about time, he said, his arm trailing in my wake, That we gave you something to occupy yourself. You seem quite rested, much better now.

Inside, the room was cool. A chair and a leather-topped desk, a lamp, a blotter with tiny figures scribbled all over, and his pen, lying on the accounts book. A square of open window on the far side of the room with the sun angled across it.

I'm a busy man, he said, Busier all the time, now that things are picking up again. Only the dead and the dead poor have no need for shoes.

He laughed, as if this fact was funny.

I've been thinking of getting in help, anyway, but why look any further, he said, his eyes twinkling and his head on one side, When we've grown so fond of each other?

Dark green flock paper, and all around the walls, gilt-framed pictures of people in various poses, crammed side by side, above and below. Faces everywhere, smiling, grim, staring out at me; a gallery of watchers.

The Hewitts go back a long way, he said, following my gaze, This here is my grandfather, he set the business up. As you can see, the outside looked very much the same.

He pointed to a fat man wearing a chain.

And here he is as Lord Mayor.

A band of light from the window cut the picture in two. Below was a long photograph, a line of people on the pavement in front of the shop.

I'm thinking, Winifred, about a partnership. You and me, if you understand what I'm proposing.

The long photograph was hard to make out, I had to bend, shield the glass from the sun.

It's been very difficult for me – to trust a girl again, he said, leaning in, trying to get my attention, But you're very special. We'd make a good pair – he took a snort of air at this joke – And you would be accepted here, as my wife.

The people in the photograph were standing in a row, one of them with his hand up, shielding his eyes from the glare. I could feel Hewitt waiting for my answer.

That's me, he said, stroking the line of hair across his head, Much younger then, of course. We're going back – oh, must be eighteen years! So I understand that you might find me a little . . . mature.

Next to him, a woman with her arms folded across her chest. Hewitt pointed his thumb at her.

That's my mother, he said, God rest her.

At the end of the line, there was one more woman, almost edged out of the picture. She wore an intense look on her face, a high-necked blouse with a frill, and her crowning glory, a nest of thick black hair.

And that, I said, putting my finger on the glass, Is *my* mother.

~

Hewitt was quiet after that. He hummed a little to himself, as if there were a tally in his head he couldn't quite make add up. He puffed his cheeks out. His face went pink, pale, pink again. We studied the photograph for a few more seconds, his eyes sidelong, looking at me in a new way.

Of course, that's not your real hair, he said, matter-of-fact, You don't have your mother's colouring.

I told him it belonged to Bernard's wife.

And what is so awful about your real hair?

My grandfather said it was Telltale.

Albert Price. I remember him. Scary old devil. So – you stole the hair from a dead woman? he asked, getting close to his meaning.

They gave it to me, Jean and Bernard. They said it made me look exotic.

No, no. You stole it, he cried, triumphant, as if solving the puzzle, So, Jean Foy was right after all! You're nothing but a thief. You must understand, Winifred – whatever you call yourself – this alters *everything*.

~ ~ ~

He said no more about a proposal, nothing about the picture in the office with my mother squeezed into the corner of

the frame, nothing about my telltale hair; nothing about anything. He took me by the elbow and levered me out, finger
and thumb, through the door of the office, as if I might infect
him. Back to the workroom and the high stink of leather.

He had me down as a thief: it suited Hewitt, all of a
sudden, to leave me entirely alone. So stealing the bread,
ripping out the colour plates of the birds; these were easy
things. I stole the useful and useless, all thrown in my case: a
pair of shoes a size too small, a square of muslin, a polished
silver buckle, a cube of chalk. A handful of nails. A toothbrush.
His mother's beaded gown, loosed free from its sheath and
smelling of stale perfume. I stole the small money Hewitt kept
in a pot on the mantelpiece. I stole one of his bladed tools,
and put it in my pocket. I stole his back-door key, threading
it on a shoelace tied round my neck. If I laid a hand on a
thing, I stole it: I was nothing but a thief, after all. When I
had filled my case, I hid it under the couch and waited for a
pause in his evening routine, calculating enough time to slip
away without another confrontation. Hewitt spent an age on
the telephone in the hallway. I couldn't hear what he was
taking so long to say, but I could feel his look, burning through
the wood of the door.

He had summoned Jean: she was always there before me.
Both of them, thick with it, loaded me and my case into a
cab and sat close on either side of me, in silence, in sunset,
until we reached Chapelfield. I thought they were taking me
back to my grandfather's house. I thought Hewitt simply
wanted rid of me. I was a fool. We were going to Bethel
Street House.

She needs to understand the value of property, said Hewitt,
To respect other people's possessions.
He smiled sadly, trying to charm the Sisters,
She has no family, you see. We tried our best, both of
us. But her stories – very damaging, he added, in a knowing

whisper, Damaging to a man of my position, who only wished to help. You do understand?
Jean gave him a sly, knowing look; she understood well enough, but she wasn't about to take my side.

For a short while, just until she gets herself right, she said, showing the Sisters the mark on her hand where I'd bit her, She's normally very placid.

~

A short while, she had said, handing my case to the Sisters. A short while, which would not be short at all: not a week, or a month, or a year, but forever.

It remains this way forever. This is how it is.

twenty-eight

Robin had summoned a devil, but still I followed him. He led me down the steps and through a run of stalls selling watches and gold chains, secondhand records, drawings of cartoon dogs in pink frames, until we were at the far end of the market, near the food stalls. It was packed with people, all of them eating: mushy peas out of plastic bowls, chips, hot pork sandwiches. Robin was moving too quickly for me, I had to grab him by the coat.

I'm not a thief, I said, through the steam and stink of fat, She's the thief.
He ducked under an awning, pulling me with him out of the way of the crowd.

What are you on about? he said. He looked impatient, glancing over the heads towards the Guildhall and the trees.

She's the thief, not me.
The pain in my chest was mighty now, but I had to tell him. I was pushing the words out, noise by noise.

They put you away for it, I said.
I thought at last he would understand me, but he just stared.

She only wants to talk to you, he said.
She stole my stuff.
He folded my hand into his, and led me on.

Just a friendly chat, he said, pulling me behind him.
On a wall under the tree, a brace of old men were sitting side

by side, getting themselves a suntan. There was burning, down my throat, in my chest, as if I had taken lye. I couldn't see past a gang of boys, blocking the pavement. I couldn't tell anything for the burning, and the words, spinning from my mouth. Robin pointed to where the two old men sat, someone bending over in front of them. It was her, not as young as I'd remembered her, but the same girl – a woman, if I'm true – crouching now at one of the old men's feet, pulling something from a folder. A piece of paper. Crouching down. It was her, but older, much older than I'd thought.

I was just wondering, she was saying.

The first man was wearing a red neckerchief. I'd seen him around. He was shaking his head, and the one next to him just kept giggling to himself, as if he really *did* know but wasn't about to say. Robin stood in front of me, coughed and bowed, as if he were a magician and I was the trick.

Ta-ra! he went, This is the lady you're wanting, I think.

He put his arm round my shoulder, just like she had, that first time.

You remember, he said to her, We spoke the other day. Told you I'd find her.

She looked as if she'd seen a ghost. Still staring at me, she nodded.

Can we go somewhere, she said, ignoring him, For a chat? I wasn't having no preamble.

Give me back my stuff, I said, Give it back.

She looked at Robin.

What did she say? she asked.

Give it back!

I can't . . . can you ask her to calm down?

I told her I was calm. I told her to give me my stuff back. The laughing man's mouth was black and wide, the neckerchief man was clapping. Pigeons doing their dance all around us. The words spinning like a top. I told her, and I told her again. Robin pulled me tighter into him.

Steady on, Win, he said, You're not making any sense. He turned to the girl.

She thinks you've stolen her stuff, he said.

Is there somewhere we could go? the woman repeated, as if I were deaf, and looking at Robin – Perhaps if you came too?

She moved away from the men, inched slowly towards me. They were on either side of me now, Robin and the woman, trapping me between them. The neckerchief man clapped his hands in the air, scattering the pigeons in a whip of feathers and dust, scattering the sounds in my head.

A thief! Nothing but a thief.

I couldn't tell if it came from her mouth, or from mine.

RULES

is written in a fine, sloping script. Unlike the ones my grandfather pinned on the back of my door, these are stuck up on all the walls of Bethel Street House, in bold letters, so that everywhere you look, you're reminded, and every time you break a rule, the Sister can point to the notice and ask you what it is you've forgotten to do. I forget to wash. I don't know how they can tell, but they always catch me out. 'Cleanliness is Next to Godliness' they say, pointing to the first rule on the list. We all have to wash in time for prayers, which happen in the chapel, before breakfast. Miss a wash, miss prayers, and you'll get no breakfast. I discover from reading the rules that we are not patients but Objects, who through prayer and guidance may be Restored. Most of us are ordinary girls, except the older ones, who were ordinary once, perhaps, but really are objects now: pieces of furniture that you walk around, try not to break. I am an object too: I am a thief. Denying the fact has also made me a liar. Others are depraved, which means they go with men, and some are here because they're poor. It's all the reason that's needed.

There are no clocks, no calendar, nothing to tell you where you are in the world, because really, you are out of the world now. But in the day room at the front of Bethel Street House there's a row of high windows, facing out onto the street. They're too far up to look out of, but the sky is visible, showing the tops of the trees in Chapelfield. You can tell the seasons from them. The day room has a wireless which doesn't work, too many chairs, and nothing else, unless you count the old woman, slumped like a sack of sticks in front of the fire.

The opposite to the day room is the night room. Mine is window-barred and barren. I'm not allowed to have my case in there with me; it's kept in the bootstore in the cellar for the time when I may be Restored: although I know by look-ing at the women that some of us never will be. Worse, I can't tell who might have to stay here for life, or why. It could be me.

Restoring involves cleaning, working in the garden, making things for outside people to buy from a stall in the market. The senior Objects, the ones the Sisters think they can trust, look after the rest of us. They earn privileges which are written in a ledger, just like the one Hewitt used to keep. It all counts, we are told, it all counts for us. We know there is another tally, and that this one counts against us: the owing and debt carefully registered in black ink.

On Mondays we have Meeting, which is held in the day room from two until four in the afternoon. We have Conver-sation, which means we're supposed to talk to each other. There's nothing to say, but that doesn't stop Noreen, who ended up here after Mrs Philips in the boarding house found out about her night-time jaunts into King Street.

Well. A girl's got to earn a bit of money, she says, not in the least bit on the way to being Restored. She tells me there are others here too: the one with Greta Garbo eyes who spent all her time looking out of the window, and Emily, who is here because of her nerves. I don't ever see them. When I ask one of the Sisters where I might find Emily, she tells me she is in a closed wing. I'm jealous of this; I imagine her nestled beneath the feathers of a bittern, near the warm, beating heart of the bird.

Noreen pretends to have access to the papers. Every week, she tells us the latest news of the world, as she puts it. A Princess gets wooed by a Prince from a foreign land. A Princess gets married and a King dies and she gets to be crowned and more Princes and Princesses are born. It's not news to me; my mother used to read me these stories when I was little. One time Noreen tells us that a man has been sent into space; after that, we know not to believe a word she says.

The Sister – it could be any of the women who work here, they all wear the same clothes, the big crucifix, the chain of keys swinging from their belts, and they are all called by the same name – has to keep telling Noreen to let the others have a chance to speak. But when I ask who the wicked Stepmother is, who is the haughty Queen in this tale, Sister tells me to be quiet too, and that I should stop saying such ridiculous things and think of something that might be interesting. But there is nothing interesting, because nothing happens. We would go back, if we were allowed, but back is confused; back is just a story, and sometimes it causes pain. Sister discourages us from going back. Memories are not Approved subjects; there must be no Before. I give up on Conversation; I learn a different language here. It's one we all understand: pauses and sighs, the wind blowing rain on the high windows, the rustling of long skirts, a jangle of keys. Sometimes there is screaming too, which is a language all of its own.

Saturdays are special. Depending on a Rule kept or an Improvement made, some of us are taken out into the city, where we are made to follow each other in a long crocodile, one brown-pinafored shape after another, like a row of cut-out dolls. People stare, children trail behind us with limping walks, calling out names. I choose not to go on these excursions – I have enough people in my head to mock me, without seeking them out. No one forces me to go into town, but I can't avoid Sundays. That's when the Outside people come here. If it's fair, they're allowed in the garden where those of us who do not have visitors tend the roses, or bring the Outsiders tea on a tray. Because I have no visitors, I tend the roses. No one remembers me.

twenty-nine

The place is called Mezzo, which is Italian for Expensive Cafe. Robin told me that, while we were waiting for the girl to get served. The windows are sheet glass and the tables are metal and bobbly on top. It felt very cold inside. Normally, we're not allowed in, not even for a cup of tea, but this time the boy at the counter was all smiles.

What would you like, Win? Robin asked, sitting me down, Anything you like – holding out a long white plastic card – It's on the lady.

The lady, as he called her, was standing at the bar. Now and then she looked across at us, an anxious face on her, as if Robin really might do some magic and make me disappear. She wasn't a girl, I'd give him that: close up, you could see the lines round her mouth, and that dropped flesh under the jaw that living gives you. But she was no lady, and I told him.

Slow down, Winnie, it's a free lunch, Robin said, She only wants to ask you some questions. Just tell *me* the answers, and I'll tell her.

He lowered his voice,

But no shouting, okay? Don't go showing me up.

The boy brought over three cups, and put a plate in front of me with a rolled-up pancake on it, even though I didn't ask for anything. Robin called it a cheese wrap, but it didn't taste

like any cheese I knew. It had a smell of dirty socks; the filling
burnt my mouth.

I want tea, I said, when I saw the froth in my cup, but no
one seemed to hear me.

The girl – the woman – was talking to Robin.

I've been down at the night shelter, she was saying, Trying
to trace a Miss Winifred Foy.

Robin pointed his thumb at me.

You've found her, he grinned.

It's a personal matter, she said, eyeing me but still only
talking to him, And I wonder if she'll . . .

She stopped, stared straight at me.

I'd like to ask you some questions – it's to do with that
place on The Parade. A long time ago.

Where you robbed me, I said, sharp as a whistle, Not so
long ago.

She ignored me. I glanced at Robin: he can't have heard,
because he was still looking at her, looking and nodding.

This would be 1970, she continued, Can you remember?
May 1970. You lived at The Parade, didn't you?

The bird was in my chest again, fluttering, fluttering.

I lived nowhere, I said, but it sounded wrong. My words
were blurring. I repeated them, tried to say them differently,
but they were coming out wrong, the wrong sounds, or no
sounds at all. The woman and Robin were both looking at
me, his smile fading and his hand on my arm, and she was
saying,

Maybe if I show you a picture,

but try as I might, the words had left me. There was only the
bird, scrabbling to get out.

I lived at Bethel Street, I said to Robin, Bethel Street
House.

His eyes went wide, but he seemed to understand because he
nodded at me.

The new apartments, he said, Used to be a nuthouse. Sorry, Win. An institution. She says she was there.

The woman shook her head,

No, according to this – pulling out a pile of clippings from a cardboard folder – She was released.

Her voice was high up, gliding over the top of my head, over the counter and up to the ceiling,

You were, weren't you? she said, fanning the papers at me, You'd been let out by then?

Something was trapped in the back of my throat, jamming my words.

That was not my life, I wanted to say, Don't think you can own me just because you know my name. A few scraps of paper won't own me. A name won't own me.

I had to shout to do it – to make them listen, just like that time in the supermarket when the woman called me a derelict. I should have shouted all those years ago. When people don't listen and the words get stuck, you must shout. Like the spirits, scrabbling to be heard. You must roar. Otherwise you are nothing. I told her, I told him, I told everyone in the cafe. I wanted everyone to hear how it is.

You're never let out! No one comes to set you free. Not for a hundred years. Not ever.

release

It wasn't just that I was in Bethel Street House: it was in *me*.
The feeling is just like being underwater: sounds distorted,
movement slow – everything beautifully clear, in vivid colour,
but just out of reach. The girl in the lake all those years ago,
when Bernard found me, she was a warning. I was looking
at my future. The Sisters might as well have killed me as set
me free. They don't tell you that this feeling will come back
in your life, like a sweat of malaria, a night terror from
childhood; that you will never entirely shake it off. They don't
tell you that the world doesn't work on Bethel Street rules.
They tell you only that you are free to go, now.

It wasn't a hundred years. It was twenty-four, if I'm true,
twenty-four years and I was out in the air again with my case
full of stolen goods and a pair of shoes a size too small. I had
finally Reformed, which meant that I admitted to everything
– that the spirits were only in my head, that I would never
steal another thing, not so much as a daisy from the park, that
if I needed help, I would go straight to the Assistance and
present the card they gave me to whoever was behind the
counter. My progress in Bethel Street House – learning to be
clean, to look after the others, to sew a straight hem on a
skirt using their Singer – meant that I would be able to find
work. I had someone to turn to, they said, writing a name
on the back of the card. I told Noreen I would put in a word

for her, knowing that not only would I never find the word that was needed, but that it would make no difference. Noreen remained unreformed, refusing food and prayer and hissing like a snake whenever she felt like it. She was past going anywhere.

I didn't want to go, either. Twenty-four years: buildings grow, and fall, and grow again, money gets smaller, colours get bigger, sounds are louder, people are faster – everything has changed. But not you: same clothes, same skin underneath them, same bones.

The Sisters gave me my case and directions to the halfway house and let me out by the side gate. I went straight back round the corner to my grandfather's house with an idea of seeing Mr Stadnik. In Bethel Street, his words would rise up like vapour, catch me unawares: a young girl in the scullery with her bandaged wrists, carefully stacking the plates; the day room full of empty faces; the washroom, with its arc of blood on the ceiling. I wanted to tell him that I'd learned about the torments of hope, about the many places of a broken heart. The door to Chapelfield was open, beige blinds on the window and a pot plant with its leafy edges crisping in the sunlight. A brass plate on the wall read Underwell's Solicitors. I didn't go in. I could tell from the umbrella stand in the hall, the creamy swirls on the carpet, the smell of office, that this wasn't anybody's home.

I walked on. The morning was so bright, so sharp a light, it hurt my eyes. All around me the smell of dust. Noise came off the road and out of buildings, and people were everywhere; all going fast, not at all like being underwater. I thought I might be stared at, but no one took the slightest notice. I walked the streets just like anyone, behind a girl in a short skirt, her eyes painted black, then a woman with a pram and two babies in it. As soon as I'd noticed one baby, I couldn't stop seeing them: asleep in the arms of their mothers, lurching forward on the end of a pair of reins, standing over a dropped lolly, wailing. They were everywhere – in photographs in a wool-shop window, wearing a crochet top or a hat with flaps; a plaster boy with a calliper and a hand out at the corner of Woolworth's; painted on the side of a house, looming down at me, pink-cheeked and kiss-curled and massive. I saw what the world had become while I was away from it: a place full of children.

Gurney's teashop was still there. I wanted a cup of tea more than anything, from a little pot with a jug of milk, just like I'd had with Mr Stadnik. The women serving looked just the same, with their frilled aprons and their worn-out sighs, but they couldn't be. I was forty years old; it didn't take me long to understand that nearly everyone I knew would be dead. The Sisters had given me an address on a card. There was my case at my feet, with everything I owned inside it. I was just anybody, nobody. I thought, then, it would be possible to go on, order the tea and drink it and pay for it. I sat in Gurney's and tried to have a plan; it was important to have one, Joseph had taught me that.

I would go and find the birds in the pictures, have a life by the sea. That was it. I would go to the Assistance and explain to them that I didn't need the room in that halfway house on the Dereham Road, because I was going to the end of the world, just like we had planned, Joseph and me. All I needed was a car. They could find me one of those, I saw plenty enough of them on the streets. I didn't want a house or a garden – no tamping bulbs, no twining flowerheads, and definitely no roses – I'd had my share of them in Bethel Street garden, with their cloying stench, their cunning thorns, the sudden, unexpected bulb of blood on the thumb. I wanted a place where nothing would happen, where no one would call me by a name. I could lie down in the dunes, watch the birds crossing my sky. I would never see another spirit, never steal another thing. All I needed was a car. This is what I would say. I walked towards the Assistance with the words rolling over on my tongue, repeating them under my breath, afraid that the language would leave me.

I couldn't have known, could I? As if simply saying the words could make a difference, as if I could ignore the beating in my chest, the thoughts in my head, simply by saying some words. But the words were just noises. They didn't mean anything. I couldn't admit what I really wanted, not even to myself. I still can't, if I'm true: I can lie to myself as easily as lying to others; as easily as they can lie to me. Denial trails me like a dog.

thirty

Robin was telling some tale about me to the boy at the bar. He was tugging at his beard, pointing over his shoulder and shaking his head in a sad way. He brought a bottle of beer back to our table, followed by the boy, carrying a tray. On it were two tall glasses of water with ice in them, and slivers of lemon.

If I could ask you to just keep the noise down, the boy whispered, carefully putting the glasses in front of us, Only it disturbs the other customers.

Robin winked at him, angling himself sideways, close to my chair. He put his hand over mine and pressed it flat.

She'll be fine now, won't you, Gran?

His look was serious but I could tell he was having a good time. I saw it in his face: almost a grin shining out of it.

All right now, Win? he whispered, when the boy had gone, Get some of that inside you. Make you feel better.

I drank it straight off. It wasn't water, it was gin. It was cold and hot all at once. In my chest, the bird turned, fluttered, folded its wings. The woman was waiting. As soon as I put my glass down, she started up again.

I just want to ask some questions.

Robin smiled at her, took a swig of his beer.

Go on, he said, We're all ears.

She gave him a sidelong look, drew a breath and fixed on me.

I'm called Janice Barrett. Does that mean anything to you?
I couldn't say it did. So I said nothing.

You don't remember? Perhaps if I showed you a picture – she said, fumbling again with her bits of paper – Of me back then.
She had reams of them, old newspaper cuttings with photographs, dates on the top in a ring of black ink. I didn't want to see.

I know your face well enough, I said, And your name. Thief. That's your name.
They both looked so amazed, I thought I'd have to repeat myself. The words were back, but I couldn't be sure of the order.

Everything I owned, I said, You stole.
She glanced at Robin.

Did I hear that right?
He nodded, eyebrows up, draining the last of his beer.

I stole from *you*?

Everything I owned, I said.
Her face fell. I'd caught her out. There was no denying it now. But she was cunning; she changed tack.

It was you, Winifred, who stole, she said, sounding just like one of the Bethel Street Sisters, Doesn't the name Barrett mean anything at all to you?
I didn't need to think to give her an answer.

Your name means nothing, I said, smart with my new words, But I know your face. A face is my prisoner for life.
She took another breath, bent her head towards me. Her voice was hard as flint.

You took *me*, she said, It was May 1970, and I was five months old. You stole me. From my mother.

finder's keepers

The Assistance building was what used to be the old labour exchange. As soon as I was in it, I needed to be out. The corridors were painted a shiny tobacco green, the colour they used in Bethel Street, and the only light inside the hall came from two sunken squares in the ceiling. The air was blue with smoke. The feeling came back straight away: I was swimming through the haze of spirits, underwater again. I took no no notice of the people at first; some of them standing in line at the counters, waiting their turn, others leaning against the walls, smoking. I wanted not to notice that man over there in the blue suit, smiling at me, that sunken-eyed pensioner holding a length of twine. I tried to ignore the sound of a bird, cooing on a ledge above me. There was a line to wait in, and wanting to be anybody, I joined it. But after a while my legs ached and my feet inside my too-small shoes were hot as coals. I had been twenty-four years in the company of women, and now I was surrounded by men. I gave up on the queue, followed an arrow that I thought would lead me out into the fresh air again. It took me to a room with more men, standing around the walls in ones and twos, and a row of wooden seats in the centre of the floor. I sat next to a woman with a baby. It was the comfort of seeing her that made me sit there; that, and my aching feet. I swear to you, I had no intent.

You have to take a ticket, she said, pointing at a contraption on the wall. When I didn't move, she got up, lifted the baby onto her shoulder and went to wind one out for me. She wore a headscarf with zigzags all over it. Her face wasn't that young; she could have been my age; could have been me. The baby had the reddest hair.

I've got red hair too, I said, when the woman gave me the ticket with the number on it. She glanced at my head, but didn't argue.

Supposed to be lucky, she said, with a laugh like a sob, Takes after her dad. He'll be lucky, if I don't catch him.
The child stared at me with those eyes all babies seem to have: perfectly round, helpless blue.

What she called? I asked.

A mistake, the woman said, with another bitter laugh, That's what she's called.
I'd done years of Conversation at Bethel Street, but without the help of the Sister, I couldn't think of anything to say to that, so we were quiet, sitting side by side, her with her baby in her lap. The machine on the wall was clicking over numbers. I knew it couldn't be a clock: there's no such time as ninety-seven.

When your number comes up, you go over there, she explained, pointing at the row of counters, And they give you a slip – waving hers at me – Then you wait some more, until they call your name.

The machine clicked again, a man kicked a wall, an old man leaned out over his chair and spat between his feet, the machine clicked, clicked, the air got thick with smoke and hot with breath, and we waited, the woman and the baby and me, side by side, like friends. The thought did not occur to me. Even when the man came and stood at the door of the office and called out Mrs Barrett, it did not occur to me to offer. The baby was in her arms, she could have just carried her in. But she didn't do that. She bent down, scrabbling for her shopping bag beneath her seat, her headscarf slipping off her thinning brown hair and gliding to the floor, all in slow motion, all underwater. When the boy called again,

No Mrs Barrett? like a question, turning over the sheet in his hand, she shouted,

Hang on, will you! – handing me the baby, just for a second, until she got her bag over her arm and picked up her headscarf. And then the words came out:

She'll be fine here with me, love, you go on, I said, Get yourself sorted out. I'll mind the little one.
She looked back at us from the door, and smiled. I couldn't have been thinking of it, could I? I had promised not to steal another thing, not so much as a daisy from the park. And I wouldn't, seeing her smile like that, I wouldn't steal her child. But she was gone such a long time. The machine clicked over, the man kicked the wall, the old one spat between his feet. They didn't look at us. The baby asleep in my arms, straggles of her unlucky red hair stuck to her brow. She was too hot. It was no place for a child, all that smoke and him over there spitting: catch TB, she could. I slipped off my shoes, not to make it easier to run away – even then, to be true, I hadn't got a thought in my head – but because the baby was so restful, snuggled against me.

I think I even dozed myself, for a while, because when I woke up, I put the baby on my shoulder, just like her mother did. Only I was her mother now, and she was our child, mine and Joseph's. She was no mistake. I lifted my case with my free hand, and swam, under blue water, to the door. Past the arrow pointing the way back, past the corridor with the long queues of dead men, faster now, looking for the double doors, faster, out into the sunshine, pouring from the sky in a blessing. Just like the day she was created. There was a pram with a teddy in it and three coloured hoops clipped to the frame. I dropped my baby in. Put my case on the rack underneath. I was away. We were away.

thirty-one

They would have seen me, Robin and Janice. I'd excused myself, told them I needed the toilet. I slipped out easy, they were huddled over the table, looking at the newspaper pieces. Her with her hair hanging all over her face like a camp follower, pointing at the pictures, and Robin shaking his head again in that sympathetic way he had. I left them to it. But that cafe is all glass: they would have noticed.

I always go back. It's easy to say run away, go far, but it's just not possible. A man can see you a mile away. Land turns to water under your feet. I went back to The Parade. In the yard at the back, the dog was still barking, jumping up at the fence, so I made my way round to the front. The door had been busted open, hanging off its hinges. My legs wouldn't get me up the stairs. I sat down on the floor in the front room, down with the pieces of burnt wood, crushed cartons, empty cans and broken glass. I just sat and waited. I didn't have a plan.

Of course, they knew where to find me. They were on my heels. Robin came in first and crouched at my side, so Janice had to kneel down as well, making a face as she pulled her coat round her. Robin put my case on the floor in front of me.

It was only under the stairs, he said, Shall we have a look? He went into the street and caught a corner of the board on the window, tore at it. It gave slightly, and he jumped again, holding the edge this time, pulling it away in a glitter of sudden, streaming light. I could see Janice clearly now, one hand combing at her fringe, the other shading her eyes; Hewitt's Shoe Repairs and Fittings in shadow at her feet. Robin tripped back in, shaking the dust from his hair.

Let there be light, he said, Go on, Win, see if it's all there. Janice spoke for me.

It's all there, she said.

He turned on her, wide-eyed.

How do you know? he asked.

She was lost for words. I knew what that felt like well enough, so I enjoyed watching her search, taking in the room while the language did its dance in her head.

I thought you were dead, she said, at last, But we came back this morning, and you'd gone.

Robin was prowling the room.

We? Who's 'we'?

The police, she said, twisting her head to follow him, You can't just leave a dead body, you know. It's against the law.

And stealing isn't, he said.

I didn't *steal* her stuff. I was just . . . going through it, she said, facing me again.

Robin gave a little snigger.

Tell it to the judge, he said, under his breath, Fuck me. Win was right about you.

He walked a circle round us, one hand trailing the wall, muttering about how you should never shop your mates. He could have been talking to himself for all the notice we took; we weren't listening. Janice's eyes were ice-blue in the window-light, fixed on my face.

You brought me here, she said.

I did.

My mother never liked to talk about it. But before she

died, she told me. She wanted me to know. She said that you'd done something.

Staring hard, as if she'd given me a clue.

She said you'd *taken* something that was mine. I had to make sure. But there was nothing in there – gesturing to my case – That had any meaning to me.

I opened the case and fumbled about inside. The white baby mittens were easy to find. I held them out to her.

These belonged to you, I said, You can have them back now.

Janice took the mittens, turning them over and looking hard at the cartoons embroidered on the front. She held them to her face, breathed them in.

What were you thinking of? To steal a child?

I could have told her I was thinking of a soft spring evening in the church plantation, where she was made, the sun spark-ling red through the trees and the scent of the forest beneath me. About Joseph and me planning our escape, in a car, to the end of the world, me and him – and her too, nestled deep inside. Or I could have told her how he jumped off the tower rather than face the shame of it, and how I went to the water to drown myself until a fat man looked over a frond and turned me into his gift from God. How the shoemaker, here, in this very place, took her out of me, piece by piece, with a bone-handled contraption used for scoring leather, not knowing, with every cut, how much of his own flesh he tore, his own blood spilled. How for years I was afraid to think and unable to speak, because all my thoughts were of her, and all my words about her. She would be *my* gift, bringing Joseph back to me – to us – and we could all live happily ever after. But I couldn't tell her any of that, because she would think it was just a story, and everyone knows that stories aren't real. So I told her what she wanted to hear; trying not to shout, trying not to roar. It was only what all the rest of them said.

I was thinking of stealing you, I said, offering each word

up to the air, Because I am a thief. I don't know any better.
I'm not right in the head, you see.
Her lip curled with disgust.

That's what my mother said,
holding the mittens between finger and thumb, turning them,
inspecting them,

That you were a thief – and a liar.
She looked at me directly, a familiar, jutting chin.

You knew that woman in the welfare office, didn't you?
Alice Barrett was her married name. Alice Dodd to you. She
said you were always weird, even as a kid. But she thought
you were harmless. She told you Joseph was still around.
Married as well. You knew better, all right, Winnie.

Janice raised her chin. On the skin underneath, I expected
a birthmark, a tea-stained clover. There was nothing.

You didn't steal me because you couldn't help it. You stole
me out of spite.
The roaring was close again now, bubbling on my tongue.

Your mother was so spiteful, I said, And a liar. And a thief.
She said Joseph knew about me, locked up all that time. She
stole everything from me.

What? Like a baby, for instance? she said, her eyes full of
loathing, What could she possibly want to take from *you*?
I couldn't say what. A bedraggled glove with the eyes sewn
on crooked? A chance to meet my lover again? It was a
lifetime ago. Janice wouldn't understand what was important
then. A length of twine, a rotting beet tilled over in a field, a
pair of slippers in cornflower blue. Mr Stadnik understood,
though. All the small things, he saved; to keep away despair.

My hope, I said, She wanted that.

So you stole hers.

For just one day, you were mine. One day, and then she
got you back.
Janice looked round the room, glanced at Robin, perched like
a cat in the window. She gave a little jink of the head.

Eventually. But not as I was, apparently. So, if you don't mind, she said, and opened her hand.

I nodded at the mittens in her lap.

You can't stop, can you? Even now. These, she said, throwing them down on the floor between us, Aren't anything to do with me.

Robin bent over and picked them up, held them to the light. He let out a snort.

Bart Simpson!

Exactly, she said, not taking her eyes off me, But *she* wouldn't know that. Now, if you don't mind, I'll take what's mine.

Holding her hand out flat in the space between us.

There's nothing else, I lied, I have nothing that's yours.

some lies

The local paper described me as a monster. Well, it would, wouldn't it? Makes a good front page. They said I was a butcher's daughter too, practised with a knife. That was just false. He might've lived upstairs, but he was no father of mine. *My* father told stories, and lies, even, and might have pawned my mother's slippers and brushes, but he never cut up an animal. The *Telegraph* said I'd done it before, stole a baby, but the mother got to me in time and never reported it. Then they'd had reports of other sightings. I'd been everywhere: Lincoln, Newmarket, Colchester, trying to steal a baby. All lies. The *Times* even ran a feature called Babysnatch Women, about kids that go missing from hospitals, warning mothers not to leave their children alone in their pushchairs when they're out shopping. The first time, the day I left Bethel Street House, I saw two babies side by side in a pram. Neither of them was mine. All the articles missed the point: I wasn't stealing Alice's child, I wasn't stealing anybody's child. I was taking back my own.

The pictures were the worst. Some of the earlier papers had used the studio portrait, twenty-odd years before, but once they got hold of that one of me outside the court, it was that and only that, time and again. I'm in black and white and looking blank, I'm like the Russian dummy; I wasn't thinking of anything. There was no hope, no burning pain of hope, only the reality of going back to Bethel Street, and the cool closed wing waiting to cover me. Evil, was how they described it. The face of Evil.

There was only one picture of Alice: Reunited, said the headline, in big letters above it. She's holding the baby in her arms, smiling but haggard, starved of that spite at last. The baby was wearing a little hat.

There was no mention, in any of them, about the Telltale hair. It wasn't even reported at the hearing. Alice wouldn't want to draw attention to it. But two and two, that's what she said, that day in the Assistance. I recognized her straight away.

The old fella's put two and two together, she said, nodding down at the child, He's upped and left me with this little lot, and now Hewitt's done a flit. Good riddance, to both of them.

She never changed her sly ways, looking at me from the corner of her eye.

You're out, then? she said, leaning into me through the fog of smoke, a little grin playing on her mouth,

How long for?

For good, I said, trying the words.

Must be over it by now.

Over what, I said back.

Our Joseph. They say it sent you round the bend, him jilting you like that.

So nonchalant, as if I would know all of this, as if I were just another person to gossip with; tell the story of some poor woman, some poor fool. She shifted her baby from one knee to the other, grinned wider.

Of course, *he's* got a different story. Said in those days, you were anybody's. Trying to trick him into marriage. But that's men for you, isn't it, love? she said, eyeing the baby on her lap,

They're all the same. Say anything to get out of trouble.

thirty-two

The time for words had come.

I called you Daisy. That's what we'd planned, Joseph and me, a little boy and a little girl: Daisy after his mother, and Albert after my grandfather. I brought you back here; there was nowhere else. Hewitt was gone – done a flit, Alice had said, and the key to the back door went sweet into the lock. Just me and you. I took you upstairs, through the workroom, to his office. I wanted to show you your grandmother, but all the pictures were gone.

Once I'd settled you into the pram, I went to change. We were off to meet Joseph in half an hour, on the bridge. He was taking us to the Regent to see the *Ziegfeld Follies*, then to the fair for the dancing. As I washed myself, it came to me that somewhere, I'd lost my shoes. The gown in my case had a smell of Hewitt's dead mother, but it was long, down to my ankles: it would cover my feet nicely. My mother used to say she would dance barefoot. Well, I would do the same.

We waited all night, on the bridge, watching the sky sink over Chapelfield, the houses going yellow, grey, stone black. No lights in the windows, no grandfather in the garden below. It wasn't a garden any more. It was a concrete square, with a pair of gates on the far side and yellow boxes painted on the ground. Joseph would have seen us. Once I'd had the thought, it wouldn't go away. He would have seen us waiting there, he would've seen your hair. It was Telltale. A child should have the father's stamp, I knew that. That's what he used to say – we've all got our stamp. It's not like a name; you can't just change it when the fancy takes you.

The skin on a baby's head is so soft, isn't it? Loose-fitting, as if the bone underneath is too small for it. It feels like a little skullcap all its own, the skin, moving like velvet under your fingers. Cut the scalp, and it bleeds forever.

I was careful, mind. In the workroom, the whetstone was hard to turn, but I hadn't forgotten. Many long hours I'd spent, watching Hewitt sharpening his blades, listening to the buzz of steel on stone. Hold the edge here, and watch the sparks fly off in a shower, red and white, like the light through the trees when you were made. An edge so fine, Hewitt used to say, travelling the blade along the down on my arm, it could split a hair.

You were very still. I was careful with you, really, supremely careful. And I took it all off, every single last hair on your head. You didn't make a sound.

It was Telltale, you see. I had been a long time in hiding at Hewitt's; I recognized his stamp. It had to be removed.

~

Janice was staring at me. It was hard to know, with that look on her face, whether it made sense to her.

He didn't show up, I said, trying to get her to understand, We waited on the bridge, oh for hours. You could've caught pneumonia. And me. No shoes! What was I doing?

You panicked, didn't you? she said, in a small voice, All that blood.

I took you to the hospital.

You *left me* outside the police station. Waited until someone came along and claimed you found me on the steps. It's all here, she said, tossing over the file with the newspaper cuttings, In black and white.

It was just a scratch, I said, feeling Robin's eyes on me, It was nothing much.

She put her hands up, scraping her fringe back off her face, the skin pale and freckled in the light. To show me the long white scar, running like a frown along her hairline.

What did you do with the hair? she asked.

It had sat against my breast like a second skin. For over thirty years, I'd hidden it away. A memento of a lost child, hope in a spool of copper red, proof of life.

It's never left me, I said, handing it over. Janice stared at the bag with the softness inside it, drew out the ringlets and feathery wisps, stuck together, flattened by time into a solid red mat.

She looked like she might cry, but she didn't. She laughed, high-pitched, mocking.

Is this it? she cried, Is this what it's all about? A dirty bag of dirty stinking hair?

Telltale, I said, They were all ashamed.

Robin shifted from the window.

I've had enough of this, he said, Are you coming?

He bent over, put his hand out, just like Prince Charming, and she took it, pulling herself off the floor. She whispered in my ear.

My mother always taught me to feel sorry for people like you. But I don't. I really don't. Here, she said, tossing the bag into my lap, Keep your telltale hair, if it means so much to you. I hope you rot in Hell.

I will, I said, to the empty room, Thank you.

rise

I took my things out of the case and settled them on the floor, item by item. It was hard to see in the dimness. I'd been without my case for just two days: it felt like a lifetime. The heart-shaped locket, Joseph's feather, the opal brooch that Aunty Ena wore, all still there. A greasy black wig, like a dead bird, which I wouldn't be wearing again. The divine wooden foot lay in my lap, its brass plate blackened from the touching. I could feel the imprint of the words engraved: Lillian Price. My mother's name first, and then my own. Hewitt once held her foot as he had mine, in a darkened room behind this one. All my things over the floor, where men had scuffed their feet in a long line, eager to be measured by an amazing machine; where the man who wanted to be my father had met the woman who was my mother. They looked so small, my things, and desolate: a brooch with the opal missing, a feather, a little bag of angel hair.

Cold coming down, and a soft light. I'm waiting for the blue. They'll all be here soon, all except Hewitt. He's not invited to this party.

Here she is now, standing in the doorway with her arms folded and her hair all piled up on her head, her crowning glory. My mother, looking down on me.

Who is the fairest, she says, and before I can say, You are, my Queen, my father bows and takes her by the waist, turning her round the floor. He's wearing his blue suit, she's barefoot, with just her nightgown on. They don't seem to care. He lifts a candle high in the air; their shadows fall away like silk.

Over at the window, Mr Stadnik is surrounded by a ring of dogs, with Aunty Ena at his side, tranquil as the Virgin in a peacock-coloured frock. He holds her hand. My grandfather is tamping his pipe, saying,

I don't know what to think of this, Henry, it's all a bit sudden.

Ena twists her long neck to face me.

We're waiting for a shooting star, she says, We're going to make a wish!

The night slides into the room, fading the colours: we are gentian, now. Outside, a last flurry of birdsong, like falling silver. Through it strolls Joseph, nonchalant, grinning. He's come on the air. A branch of a tree making ribbons of the light; a sudden rain, a residue of scent. I can't tell what the smell is; something warm. Earth is in it. Sleep is in it. Love, hiding in the gap.

Hello, Beauty, he whispers, sitting close beside me, And what do you wish for?

I wish for nothing. The bird in my chest has flown; the words are no longer needed, and I have no more accounting to do. I can be anyone I choose, now: a woman on a riverbank walking in the sunshine, an ordinary person sitting in a tearoom. Anybody, or nobody. I have all I could possibly want, here with me, at the end of this world.

I collect the bundle of scarves, the lost gloves, the wooden foot, everything, pile it all in a heap, and put the candle to it. The flames when they catch are as boundless as the sea. We gather round them, peering through the smoke at each other, like children at a bonfire. Across the thickening room, Mr Stadnik smiles at me and shrugs,

We live in hope, he says, turning back to look at the stars.